NEW YORK REVIEW BOOKS
CLASSICS

THE WORD OF THE SPEECHLESS

JULIO RAMÓN RIBEYRO (1929–1994) wrote novels, plays, journals, and essays, but he is best known and admired as a short-story writer. Born, raised, and educated in Peru, he spent much of his adult life in Paris, where he was a journalist with Agence France-Presse and later a cultural adviser and ambassador to UNESCO. His work has been translated into scores of languages, and he was the recipient of the Peruvian National Literature Prize (1983) and Peruvian National Cultural Prize (1993), as well as the Juan Rulfo Prize (1994).

KATHERINE SILVER is an award-winning literary translator and the former director of the Banff International Literary Translation Centre. Her translations include works by María Sonia Cristoff, Daniel Sada, César Aira, Julio Cortázar, and Juan Carlos Onetti. She is the author of *Echo Under Story* and volunteers as an interpreter for asylum seekers.

ALEJANDRO ZAMBRA is a Chilean writer, poet, and critic, now based in Mexico City. Among his books are *The Private Lives of Trees*, *Ways of Going Home*, *My Documents*, and *Multiple Choice*.

THE WORD OF THE
SPEECHLESS

Selected Stories of Julio Ramón Ribeyro

JULIO RAMÓN RIBEYRO

Edited and translated from the Spanish by
KATHERINE SILVER

Introduction by
ALEJANDRO ZAMBRA

NEW YORK REVIEW BOOKS

New York

THIS IS A NEW YORK REVIEW BOOK
PUBLISHED BY THE NEW YORK REVIEW OF BOOKS
435 Hudson Street, New York, NY 10014
www.nyrb.com

Library of Congress Cataloging-in-Publication Data
Names: Ribeyro, Julio Ramon, 1929–1994, author. | Silver, Katherine, editor, translator.
Title: The word of the speechless : selected stories / by Julio Ramon Ribeyro ; edited and translated by Katherine Silver.
Description: New York : New York Review Books, [2019] | Series: New York Review Books classics.
Identifiers: LCCN 2018052624 (print) | LCCN 2018059347 (ebook) | ISBN 9781681373249 (epub) | ISBN 9781681373232 (alk. paper)
Subjects: LCSH: Short stories, Peruvian—Translations into English.
Classification: LCC PQ8497.R47 (ebook) | LCC PQ8497.R47 A2 2019 (print) | DDC 863/.64—dc23
LC record available at https://lccn.loc.gov/2018052624

ISBN 978-1-68137-323-2
Available as an electronic book; ISBN 978-1-68137-324-9

Printed in the United States of America on acid-free paper.
10 9 8 7 6 5 4 3 2 1

CONTENTS

INTRODUCTION

Ribeyro in His Web

IT'S NOT easy to get a fix on Ribeyro's own face, since his appearance changed a lot from one photo to another: his hair long or short or half grown-out, with or without a cigarette, with or without a moustache, wearing a serious expression or a slight smile or in the middle of a surprising peal of laughter. It's as if he were choosing to put curious people off with rudimentary disguises.

Ribeyro's face is that of a law student who had contempt for the legal profession, or a Lima native who wanted to live in Madrid, who in Madrid dreamed of Paris, in Paris longed for Madrid, and so on, chasing grants and lovers, and especially in search of time to waste writing, in the solitude of Munich, or Berlin, or Paris, again, for a long stay.

Ribeyro's face is that of a solitary man who let the dirty dishes pile up and flicked ashes off the balcony. Ribeyro's face is the face of an eternal convalescent who was born in 1929 and died in 1994, two years after starting to publish *La tentación del fracaso* (The Temptation of Failure), the astonishing diary he kept for more than four decades.

"He was, perhaps, the shyest person I've ever met," said Mario Vargas Llosa, who is surely Peru's least shy writer. Enrique Vila-Matas, on the other hand, went mute when he met Ribeyro, and not only from admiration but simply "because of the panic provoked by my shyness and his." Ribeyro was a shy man who thought Peruvians were shy: "We have an unhealthy fear of ridicule; our taste for perfection drives us to inaction, forces us to take refuge in solitude and satire," he writes in his diary.

*

"My life is not original, much less exemplary. It's just one of many lives of middle-class writers born in a Latin American country in the twentieth century," he says in an autobiographical essay.

Even in the most confessional pages of his diary, an impersonal mood persists that keeps him safe from exhibitionism or anecdotalism. Ribeyro writes to live, not to demonstrate that he has lived. A fragment from 1977 is, in this sense, revealing: "A true work must start from the oblivion or destruction (transformation) of the writer's very self. The great writer is not one who truthfully, in detail and intensely, describes his existence, but one who becomes the filter, the weave, through which reality passes and is transfigured."

Was Ribeyro a great writer?

Although a large part of his diary remained unpublished (Seix Barral's last publication goes through 1978), *La tentación del fracaso* reveals Ribeyro as one of the greatest diarists of Latin American literature. His stories, meanwhile, quickly earned him the title of "best short-story writer in Peru" (although there was always the joker who would define him, very unfairly, as "the best Peruvian writer of the nineteenth century"). In an entry from 1976, he evaluates his literary destiny with disenchantment: "discreet writer, timid, hardworking, honest, exemplary, marginal, private, meticulous, lucid: here are some of the adjectives applied to me by critics. No one has ever called me a great writer. Because I am surely not a great writer."

He liked to present himself as a third-string player who had scored one magnificent goal. But it must be said that during the final years of his life he played to a full stadium, responding courteously to his pestering fans.

Ribeyro's stories lend themselves to piecemeal reading, inviting us to leaf through them to the rhythm of Metro rides and secretive workday parentheses. But it's difficult to go back to work after taking in the brushstrokes Ribeyro prepared patiently, searching for that "sober emotion" Bryce Echenique talked about.

In the seventies and eighties, Ribeyro's stories made the rounds under the title *La palabra del mudo* (The Word of the Speechless— a different selection from the present volume), an allusion to the marginalized people represented therein. That is, Ribeyran characters par excellence: weak people, cornered by the present, victims of modernity. As Bryce Echenique, again, has observed, Ribeyro appears in his stories to be a compassionate Vallejo, stuck at ground level.

The drive to depict that sad and unequal Lima coexists from the start with a veiled autobiographical projection, which takes on greater clarity not only in his stories but throughout his work. Ribeyro wrote novels, plays, and "proverbials," as he called his historical digressions, in addition to valuable essays of literary criticism, and two strange, intense books, *Prosas apátridas* (Stateless Prose) and *Dichos de Luder* (Luder's Sayings), in which he laid the groundwork for *The Temptation of Failure*.

While his colleagues were writing the great novels about Latin America, Ribeyro, second-class citizen of the boom, gave life to dozens of simply magisterial stories, which, however, did not live up to the expectations of European readers. And he knew it well: "The Peru I present is not the Peru that they imagine or depict: there are no Indians, or very few, miraculous or unusual things don't happen, local color is absent, the baroque or the verbal delirium is missing," he says, with calculated irony.

In *Dichos de Luder*, Ribeyro slides in an elegant reply to the question of why he no longer writes novels: "Because I am a short-distance runner. If I run a marathon I risk reaching the stadium after the audience has already left."

*

Alonso Cueto said in a recent article that Ribeyro's novels tend to lose tension and interest. He was surely thinking of the forced lightness of *Los geniecillos dominicales* (The Little Sunday Geniuses), or of the slightly watered-down skepticism of *Cambio de guardia* (Changing of the Guard). *Crónica de San Gabriel* (Chronicle of Saint Gabriel), on the other hand—his first novel—is, with utter certainty, a great work.

Of that novel Ribeyro says, "above all it is the story of an imaginary adolescence, of a strange family, of a land both generous and hostile; it is the chronicle of a lost kingdom." Ribeyro chooses the mask of Lucho, a Lima teenager who, in the course of a year of slow-moving life, is the target of his cousin Leticia's whims, and witness to the injustices of a world in labored decomposition. The novel feels its way forward, searching for a precise and closed language: "When I looked at her from up close I found, astonished, that her pupils were of such singular opacity that the light from the windows lit them without penetrating." The lost kingdom of San Gabriel, he says in his diary when he finishes the novel, "is the writer's time, the countless days of beauty that I sacrificed to imagine these stories."

The 1964 diary features this admirable definition of the novel, though it could also work to describe the creative process behind a story or poem: "A novel is not like a flower that grows, but rather like a cypress that is carved. It does not acquire its form by starting from a nucleus, a seed, and growing through addition or flowering, but rather by starting with an herbaceous mass, and cutting and subtracting."

The writer who prunes runs the risk of ending up without a garden—a necessary risk, in any case. "Silvio in El Rosedal" or "At the Foot of the Cliff," perhaps Ribeyro's best stories, evoke a novelistic effect, so to speak, the same way that Ribeyro's sentences tend to brush up against the intensity of good poetry.

*

Though I know it's too late, let me apologize now for the number of Ribeyro quotes that this essay contains. I've tried to quote as little as possible. I've failed. And in what remains of this text, I will continue to fail.

A fragment from *La tentación del fracaso*: "When I was twelve years old, I said to myself: One day I'll be big, I'll smoke, and I'll spend my nights at a desk, writing. Now I am a man, I'm smoking, sitting at my desk, writing, and I say to myself: When I was twelve years old I was a perfect idiot."

Another: "I have a great distrust for men who do not smoke or touch alcohol. They must be terribly depraved."

"At a certain point my story and the story of my cigarettes blend into one," says Ribeyro, in "For Smokers Only," his indispensable "self-portrait as a smoker."

He looks back on his first Derbys, his Chesterfields as a university student ("whose sweetish aroma I still remember"), the "black and Peruvian" Incas, the perfect pack of Lucky Strikes ("It is through that red circle I must necessarily venture in order to evoke those long nights of study, when I would greet the dawn in the company of my friends on the day of an exam"), and the Gauloises and Gitanes that decorated his Parisian adventures. Then Ribeyro evokes the saddest moment of his life as a smoker, when he realized that in order to smoke he will have to give up some of his books: so he exchanges Balzac for several packs of Luckys, and the surrealist poets for a pack of Players, and Flaubert for a few dozen Gauloises, and he even gives up ten copies of *Los gallinazos sin plumas* (Featherless Vultures), his first book of short stories, which he ended up selling by the pound to turn them into a miserable pack of Gitanes.

The story abounds in passages that a nonsmoker will judge unrealistic but that smokers know are utterly accurate. For example, the night when Ribeyro throws himself from a height of eight meters in order to retrieve a pack of Camels, or, years later, when he overcomes the strict injunction against smoking by hiding some packs of Dunhills in the sand that he runs to dig up every morning.

Ribeyro deserves a primary place in the liberating library for smokers that consists of, among other necessary books, *Zeno's Conscience* by Italo Svevo, *Cigarettes Are Sublime* by Richard Klein, *Puro humo* (Pure Smoke) by Guillermo Cabrera Infante, and *Cuando fumar era un placer* (When Smoking Was a Pleasure), the self-help essay by Cristina Peri Rossi that includes this heartfelt poem (which nonsmokers—once again—will wrongly think exaggerated, but for us is a declaration of the utmost amorous intensity): "It has been just as hard / just as painful / to quit smoking / as to quit loving you." I repeat: these images possess an inarguable beauty for those of us who believe, as Rocco Alesina thought, that "smoke doesn't kill, it keeps you company until you die." It's certainly inconvenient to read that story of Ribeyro's if one is in treatment with varenicline, the drug capable of taking smokers and turning them into depressed citizens of the global world. (It is worth remembering, in this regard, the testimonials of people who, after successful treatment with Champix, confessed an enormous existential anxiety. "Now that I don't smoke, everything is infinitely lamer," said my friend Andrés Braithwaite, who was famous for decades for his enthusiastic puffing.)

Instead of the semi-wakefulness Breton and company advised, Ribeyro preferred to write in a state of semi-drunkenness. Again, my apologies, but I can't resist citing in its entirety a section of *Stateless Prose* that could well be understood as an alcoholized version of "Borges and I":

> The only way I can communicate with the writer inside me is through solitary libation. After a few drinks, he emerges. And I listen to his voice, a voice that is a bit monotone, but that continues, at times imperious. I record it and try to retain it, until it grows blurrier and blurrier, more jumbled, and it ends

up disappearing when I myself drown in a sea of nausea, tobacco, and fog. Poor double of mine, to what terrible pit have I relegated you, that I can glimpse you only sporadically, and at such cost! Sunk within me like a dead seed, perhaps he remembers the happy times when we coexisted, or even more, when we were the same and there was no distance to overcome or wine to drink in order for him to be constantly present.

"Kafka is my brother, I've always felt it, but he is my Eskimo brother; we communicate through signs and gestures, but we understand each other," writes Ribeyro.

Beyond the perceptible nearness in some of his stories of the fantastic, the similarity—the family tie—between Ribeyro and Kafka appears, fully, in moments of veiled humour like this one: "I am a relatively precious and fragile thing; I mean, an object that has been hard and costly to make—studies, travel, readings, jobs, illnesses and so I regret that this object has no possibility of yielding its full potential. To acquire something and throw it away is senseless."

Or the following fragment, which recalls the Kafka of "Eleven Sons": "I'm afraid that my son has inherited nearly all of my defects, along with those of my wife, which is just too much. Mine alone would have been enough to make an intelligent wretch of him."

In concert with the author's skepticism, Ribeyro's characters have a problematic relationship with history. It's difficult to decide if his political acquiescence corresponded to a moral imperative or if he just assembled, along the way, a suit that was tailored to fit him. The seed of Ribeyro's lack of political—though not social—commitment is in this entry from 1961, written after composing a manifesto on the role that writers should play in Peru: "More important than a thousand intellectuals signing a virulent manifesto is a worker with a gun. Ours is a sad part to play. Moreover, what sense does it have, what decency can there be in drafting this declaration in Paris, listening to Armstrong and drinking a glass of Saint-Emilion?"

In 1970, after leaving the position he occupied for a decade at the Agence France-Presse, Ribeyro took a post at the embassy and then at UNESCO, waiting out, through 1990, the rotating democracies and dictatorships. Guillermo Niño de Guzmán, his editor and friend, has this pertinent memory: "His eagerness to maintain his diplomatic position can be understood because it was his modus vivendi (his literary income was insufficient), but it entailed an excessive cost: the loss of his political independence."

Ribeyro makes room in his diaries for some guilty reflections on loyalty. But unbelief prevails, or maybe it's the conviction that great historical gestures are mere lapses, after which mediocrity and misery are exacerbated. The news that reaches him from Latin America affects him, but he is much more affected—and he is the first to recognize it—by his long hospital stays and his hand-to-hand battles with the blank page.

At the news of the coup in Chile, Ribeyro, naturally, signs the usual manifestos, but he insists on distancing himself, on separating the waters: "During these times Tyrians and Trojans unite, forget their quarrels, and row in the same direction, although, it must be said, not with the same goals." The imperative to act is at odds with his pessimistic view of history: "The two French sweepers at the Metro station, wearing their blue overalls, speaking in argot, grumbling about their work—how has the French Revolution helped them?"

So, who was Ribeyro? Ribeyro was, as Tabucchi says of Pessoa, a trunk full of people: "It's as if there existed in me not one but several writers who were fighting to show themselves, who all want to appear at the same time, but in the end can't manage to manifest anything more than an arm, a leg, a nose or an ear, oscillating, messy, jumbled and a little grotesque."

The crisis of the novel is, for Ribeyro, the result of artifice: "For some time now, French novels have been written by professors for professors. The French novelist today is a gentleman who has nothing to say about the world, but very much to say about the novel," he writes.

He goes on, then, pointing to "modern" literature (an adjective that in Ribeyro tends to be contemptuous): "Each new writer cross-checks his work with that of the writers who came before, not with the world. In this way we reach a rarification in the novel's material, which could be confused with esotericism." New writers, he concludes, "try to make of their work not the personal reflection of reality, but rather the personal reflection of other reflections."

Of Salinger's novel *Franny and Zooey* he says: "The characters move like graduates of the Actors Studio."

This judgement about Carpentier is decisive, written after reading the first seventy pages of *El recurso del método* (*Reasons of State*): "The novel is a bazaar of proper names and erudite references. This defect is accentuated because of another character trait that I believe I see in Carpentier: the fear that for being Latin American and a Communist he will be reproached for ignorance of Western culture. And so he flaunts it, but with a tropical exuberance." Ribeyro can be ruthless: "It's as if a newly rich man shows up to the party wearing his most elegant suit and all his jewels. Carpentier's style, more than beautiful, is bejeweled."

"Need to construct my life again, my spider web," writes Ribeyro in the mid-fifties, with full awareness that to live is to continually remake a tabula rasa. He is not that hero of Borges's who only at the last second just before feeling "the intimate knife on his throat"—understands his destiny. Ribeyro is not a hero but rather a man who every morning, now far away from his Lima neighborhood, looks at himself in the shards of the familiar mirror. More than a life ordered in stages and partial defeats, Ribeyro invokes a dubious destiny every day. From there arises the predilection of readers like Bryce or Julio Ortega for "Silvio in El Rosedal," a beautiful story about the slippery art of reading the world.

"His lack of confidence in the future obliged him to limit his aspirations almost to the everyday sphere," says the author in *Para un autor-retrato al estilo del siglo XVII* (Self-portrait in the Style of the Seventeenth Century.) Anyone who has made it this far with me will be able to imagine how much fun Ribeyro had writing it. The end is beautiful and perhaps true: "He could remain alone and in fact had a certain inclination toward solitude, and he only accepted the company of people who did not threaten his tranquillity or bully him with their quackery."

—ALEJANDRO ZAMBRA
August 2006
Translated by Megan McDowell

THE WORD OF THE
SPEECHLESS

WHY *THE WORD OF THE SPEECHLESS*?

Because in most of my stories, those who are deprived of words in life find expression—the marginalized, the forgotten, those condemned to an existence without harmony and without voice. I have restored to them the breath they've been denied, and I've allowed them to modulate their own longings, outbursts, and distress.

—from a letter from the author to an editor,
February 15, 1973

from
FORGOTTEN STORIES

TRACKS

HE STOPPED abruptly in front of a black stain on the ground, as if he'd been struck hard and at close range. He tried but failed to continue on his way. The stain spread out in front of his shoes: shapeless, dense, and provocative under the noonday light. He bent down slowly and examined it carefully. From close up, its edges, though apparently smooth, had fluted contours, its eager pseudopods shooting out in all directions. It was blood. It was dry. There was, however, something alive about it that both sucked it in and held it with an uncanny force. He stood up to look ahead and saw other similar stains randomly scattered about, like an archipelago viewed from the sky. A few steps farther on, all traces of blood had disappeared, and, unable to explain why, he found comfort in a sense of deliverance. He and those stains shared something, and he would even swear they had flowed from his own body. But a little farther ahead there appeared more spatters, and then more, in irregular and brutal profusion, which took on hallucinatory shapes and dimensions, as if the hemorrhage had suddenly become unstoppable. And anxiety again overwhelmed him, making him dizzy and requiring enormous effort to keep under control. Farther on, however, the bloodletting returned to normal and, with geometric regularity, identical drops, evenly spaced and diametrically precise, began appearing as if they had been stamped into the pavement. His curiosity then rendered his fear tolerable, and he began to pursue it with a zeal that contained something both suicidal and enlightened. For many blocks he was riveted by the splashes, and the distribution of the drops revealed to him a human drama, which, without any discernible reason, appeared to be related to his own existence. Sometimes the drops agglomerated, only to take off again in an improbable direction, then stop once again only to change direction. His pursuit was becoming more interesting and more painful—like watching someone die—but also increasingly difficult. The drops appeared farther apart and became smaller until, once again, they disappeared without a trace. In vain he searched nearby for a door, a house, into which they had led. Then he despaired, as if the loss of these tracks meant the loss of his own life. He took off quickly down the sidewalk, his eyes glued to the pavement. It was then that he found a crumpled red object. It was a handkerchief. He was tempted to pick it up, but he settled for reading the monogram, and the entwined letters seemed to be part of a name close to his own. Then, a short distance farther on, new stains began to appear but now with a heretofore unseen abundance.

The track, instead of continuing in a straight line, zigzagged more and more, as if the man from which the blood flowed was staggering and about to collapse. The trees along the verge and the walls of the houses were also spattered. The stains, moreover, were fresher and hurt his eyes, like cuts from a sharp blade. Hence, his pursuit became more frantic. Now running, he saw that he was approaching his own neighborhood. Soon he was near his house. A bit later, on his own corner, and the blood kept increasing, mercilessly, pulling him onward like the coaxing of a Siren. Finally, he stopped in front of the door of his house. It was open, and the stairs bid him enter. When he looked up the stairs, he saw that the stains rose with them, like an undaunted reptile. He began to climb. Which room did they lead to? They continued down the hallway, past his parents' bedroom, hesitated in front of the bathroom, then continued on to his bedroom, ever more alive, as if they had just been spilled. They exuded a warm scent, and after enormous bursts, they stopped in front of the door to his room, which was ajar. He wanted to take hold of the handle, but he saw that it was full of blood, at the same time as he felt that something was falling heavily on the bed, making the box springs creak. There he remained, motionless. He remembered that the monogram on the handkerchief were his initials, and he no longer had any doubt that inside his room the spectacle of his own death had just taken place.

Lima, 1952

from
FEATHERLESS VULTURES

OUT AT SEA

SINCE they launched the boat, Janampa had spoken only two or three cryptic words, laden with reserve, as if he were determined to create an air of mystery. He sat facing Dionisio and rowed tirelessly for an hour. The campfires on shore had already disappeared, and the boats of the other fishermen, dimly lit by their oil lamps, could barely be seen in the distance. In vain Dionisio tried to read his companion's features. As Dionisio bailed out the boat with the small can, he stole glances at the other's face; the raw light of the lamp hitting him directly on his neck showed only a black and impenetrable silhouette. Sometimes, when he tilted his face slightly, the light crept up his sweaty cheeks or along his bare neck, and Dionisio could just barely make out a surly, determined face cruelly possessed by a strange resolution.

"Not long before dawn."

Janampa grunted, as if he cared little about such an eventuality, and he kept furiously stabbing the oars into the black sea.

Dionisio crossed his arms and started to shiver. He'd already asked for a turn at the oars, but the other had refused, and cursed. Moreover, he still didn't understand why he'd chosen him, precisely him, to accompany him this morning. It's true, the Kid was drunk, but other fishermen were available, fishermen who were better friends of Janampa. On top of that, his tone had been imperious. He'd grabbed him by the arm and said, "We're going out together this morning," and it had been impossible to say no. He had barely had time to grab his woman by the waist and plant a kiss between her breasts.

"Don't be long!" she shouted from the door of the shack, waving the fish pan in the air.

They were the last to launch, but they quickly caught up with the others, and in a quarter of an hour had passed them.

"You're a good rower," Dionisio said.

"When I put my mind to it," Janampa said, muffling a guffaw.

Some time later, he spoke again: "I've got a shoal of herring here," he said, spitting into the water. "But I'm not interested, not now," and he kept rowing out to sea.

That was when Dionisio began to get suspicious. Also, the sea was a little rough. The waves were high, and every time they hit the boat, the prow pointed straight to the sky, where Dionisio could see Janampa and the lamp hanging in midair against the Southern Cross.

"I think it's good here," he said, daring an opinion.

"What do you know!" Janampa said, almost angrily.

After that, he didn't open his mouth, either. All he did was bail when necessary, always keeping a wary eye on the fisherman. Sometimes he scrutinized the sky, keenly eager to see it brighten, or he cast furtive glances behind him, hoping to see the outline of a nearby boat.

"There's a bottle of pisco under that plank," Janampa said out of the blue. "Take a swig and give it to me."

Dionisio looked for the bottle. It was half full, and almost with relief he poured two big gulps down his salty throat.

Janampa let go of the oars for the first time, sighed loudly, and took the bottle. After finishing it off, he threw it into the sea. Dionisio hoped that a conversation would finally get started, but Janampa merely crossed his arms and remained silent. The boat, its oars abandoned, floundered in the waves. It turned slightly toward the coast, then the undercurrent pointed it out to sea. At one point a white-capped wave hit its flank and nearly capsized it, but Janampa didn't move a finger or say a word. Nervously, Dionisio looked through his pants pockets for a cigarette, and as he lit it, he glanced at Janampa. That second of light showed a face with pursed features, tightness around the mouth, and two slanting caverns feverish with the fire inside him.

He picked up the can and continued to bail, but now his hands were shaking. With his head sunk between his arms, he sensed that Janampa was laughing scornfully. Then he heard the smack of the oars, and the boat started to move farther out to sea.

Soon Dionisio felt certain that Janampa's intentions were not, precisely, to fish. He tried to reconstruct their friendship. They had met two years earlier on a construction site, where they were both working as bricklayers. Janampa was a cheerful guy who worked enthusiastically because his great physical strength allowed him to enjoy tasks that were difficult for the others. He'd spend the day singing, cracking jokes, and hanging off the scaffolding to flirt with the domestics, who saw him as some kind of Tarzan, or beast, or devil, or stud. On Saturdays, after picking up their pay, the workers climbed onto the roof and played dice until they'd gambled their earnings away.

Now I remember, Dionisio thought. *One afternoon I won his whole paycheck in a game of poker.*

He shuddered, and the cigarette fell from his mouth. Did Janampa remember? Though that didn't really matter. He, too, sometimes lost. Anyway, a lot of time had passed. But just to make sure, he hazarded a question.

"Do you still play dice?"

Janampa spit into the sea, as he did every time he had to answer.

"No," he said, and sunk back into silence. But then he added, "They always beat me."

Dionisio took a deep breath of ocean air. His companion's answer somewhat reassured him, though it also opened up a whole new vein of fear. Along the coastline he now saw a pink reflection. There was no doubt about it, day was finally dawning.

"Good!" Janampa said suddenly. "We're good here," and he pushed the oars into the boat. Then he turned off the lamp and moved around in his seat as if he were looking for something. Finally, he leaned against the prow and began to whistle.

"I'll cast the net," Dionisio said, trying to stand up.

"No," Janampa said, "I'm not going to fish. Now I want to rest. I also want to whistle…" and his whistles wafted toward the coast, behind the ducks who began to parade past them, quacking. "Do you remember this?" he asked, interrupting himself.

Dionisio hummed the melody his companion was hinting at. He tried to associate it with something. Janampa, as if wanting to help him, continued whistling, transmitting bizarre tones, his whole being vibrating with the music like a guitar string. Dionisio saw, at that moment, a barn filled with bottles and waltzes. It was a ring ceremony. He'd never forget it because that was when he met his woman. The party lasted till dawn. After drinking the traditional morning broth, they made their way to the bluff, his arm around her waist. That was more than a year ago. That melody, like the flavor of the hard cider, always reminded him of that night.

"Did you leave?" he asked, as if thinking out loud.

"I was there the whole night," Janampa answered.

Dionisio tried to picture him. There were so many people! Anyway, what possible reason would he have for remembering him?

"Then I walked to the bluff," Janampa added, and laughed inwardly, as if he'd swallowed some hot spicy words and was reveling in their secret. Dionisio looked from side to side. No, there was no other boat nearby. He was suddenly inundated with a renewed sense of unease and assaulted by another suspicion. That night of the party, Janampa had also met her. He clearly saw the fisherman squeeze her hand under the cordon of billowing sheets.

"My name is Janampa," he had said (already a little tipsy), "but in the neighborhood they call me Janampa, the handsome *zambo*. I work as a fisherman and I'm single."

Minutes earlier he had also said to her, "I like you. Is this your first time here? I've never seen you before."

The swarthy woman wasn't born yesterday, she was sharp and could spot a roughneck from a mile away. Janampa's act didn't fool her; she could see through him, see the vain and violent local Don Juan that he was.

"Single?" she said. "Word around here says you've got three women!"

and, pulling on Dionisio's arm, they swung around and started dancing a polka.

"Now you remember, don't you?" Janampa said. "That night I got drunk. I got as drunk as a horse. Too drunk to drink the morning broth ... but at dawn I walked to the bluff."

Dionisio wiped cold sweat off his face with his forearm. He would have liked to clear things up, ask him why he'd followed him that time and what he thought he was doing now. But his head was twisted in knots. He remembered other things helter-skelter. He remembered, for instance, that when he was living on the beach to work on Pascual's boat, again he came across Janampa, who'd been working as a fisherman for several months.

"We'll meet again!" the fisherman had said and, looking at his woman with his slanting eyes, added, "Maybe we'll play again like we used to at the building site. Then I can win back what I lost."

At the time Dionisio didn't understand. He thought he was talking about poker. Only now did he seem to grasp the full meaning of the sentence that rose from the distant past and fell on him like a ton of bricks.

"What did you mean when you mentioned poker?" he asked, suddenly in possession of a bit of courage. "Did you mean her?"

"I don't know what you're talking about," Janampa answered; seeing that Dionisio was shaking with impatience, he asked, "Are you nervous?"

Dionisio felt a tightening in his throat. Maybe it was the cold or hunger. Morning had opened up like a fan. His woman had asked him one night, after they'd laid down for the night on the beach, "Do you know Janampa? Keep an eye on him. Sometimes he scares me. He gives me strange looks."

"You're nervous, eh?" Janampa repeated. "Can't see why. I just wanted to go for a ride. I wanted a little exercise. Sometimes it does a man good. Fresh air ..."

The coast was still far away, too far to reach swimming. Dionisio knew it wasn't worth it to jump in the water. Anyway, what for?

Janampa—drops of morning dew were falling on his face—didn't move, his hands still gripping the motionless oars.

"Have you seen him?" his woman had asked him again one night. "He's always hanging around here when we go to bed."

"You and your ideas!" he'd said, still blind. "I've known him a long time. He's a huckster but doesn't cause any trouble."

"You'd go to bed early…" Janampa started, "and you wouldn't turn off your lamp till midnight."

"When you sleep with a woman like her…" Dionisio answered, then realized that he was approaching dangerous terrain and that it was useless to keep pussyfooting around.

"Sometimes appearances can be deceiving," Janampa continued, "and some coins are fake."

"I promise you, mine are genuine."

"Genuine!" Janampa said and let out a laugh. Then he picked up the net on one end and out of the corner of his eye observed Dionisio, who was looking behind him.

"Don't keep looking for other boats," he said. "There aren't any around. Janampa left them far behind!" he said, took out a knife, and started to cut some strings that were hanging from the net.

"Is he still hanging around?" he had asked her a while later.

"No," she said, "now he's after Pascual's niece."

To him, however, that seemed like a smoke screen. At night he heard stones being thrown near the shack, and a couple of times, when he peeked out from behind the curtain, he'd see Janampa walking along the beach.

"What were you doing at night, looking for sea urchins?" Dionisio asked. Janampa cut the last knot and turned toward the coast.

"It's daybreak!" he said, pointing to the sky. Then, after a pause, he added, "No, I wasn't looking for anything. I had bad thoughts, that's all. Many nights, I couldn't sleep, thinking… But now, everything's all worked out…"

Dionisio looked him in the eyes. He could finally see them, sunk symmetrically into his hard cheeks. They looked like the eyes of a fish or a wolf. "Janampa has eyes like in a mask," his woman had once said. That morning, before he got on the boat, he'd also noticed them. While tussling with his woman outside the shack, something had bothered him. He glanced around without letting go of her adorable braids and caught a glimpse of Janampa leaning on his boat, his arms crossed over his chest, and his rebellious locks sprayed with foam. The nearby campfire painted her with brushstrokes of yellow light, and his slanting eyes stared back with an irksome gaze from far away, which was almost like a hand resting stubbornly on him.

"Janampa is watching us," he said to his woman.

"So what?!" she replied, slapping him on his buttocks. "Let him look all he wants," and grabbing his neck, she pushed him down onto the rocks and they rolled around together. In the midst of the lovers' tussle, he still saw Janampa's eyes, and he watched their resolute approach.

When he grabbed his arm and said to him, "We're going out to sea this morning," he couldn't say no. He barely had time to kiss his woman between her breasts.

"Don't be gone long!" she shouted, waving the fish pan.

Was her voice shaking? Only now did he seem to notice it. Her shout was like a warning. Why didn't he hold her close? Maybe he could still do something. He could get on his knees, for example. He could cut a deal with him. He could, in any case, fight . . . Lifting his face, where fear and fatigue had already dug in their claws, he met with Janampa's leathery, immutable, illumined face. The rising sun formed a halo of light over his mane. Dionisio saw in that detail a prior coronation, a sign of triumph. Lowering his head, he thought that luck had betrayed him, that everything was already lost. At the construction site, whenever they played and he got a bad hand, he'd withdraw without protest, saying, "I pass, there's no way . . ."

"Here you have me . . ." he mumbled and he wanted to add something else, make a cruel joke that would allow him to live those moments with some dignity. But all he could do was mumble, "There's nothing for it . . ."

Janampa got up. Besmirched with sweat and salt and looking like a sea monster.

"Now you can throw the net off the prow," he said, and he handed it to him.

Dionisio took it, turned his back on his rival, then leaned over the prow. The net spread out heavily in the sea. The work was slow and difficult. Dionisio, leaning over the edge of the boat, thought about the coast that was so far away, about the shack, about the campfires, about the women lolling around, about his woman braiding her hair... All of that was far away, very far away; it was impossible to get there swimming.

"Is it okay?" he asked without turning around, spreading the net out more.

"Not yet," Janampa replied behind him.

Dionisio plunged his arms into the sea up to his elbows and, without taking his eyes off the foggy coastline, overwhelmed by an anonymous sadness that didn't even seem to belong to him, he waited with resignation for the stab of the knife.

Paris, 1954

MEETING OF CREDITORS

WHEN SURCO'S bell tower rang at six in the afternoon, Don Roberto Delmar left the doorway of his grocery store and sat down behind the counter, lighting a cigarette. His wife, who'd been spying on him from the back room, poked her head out from behind the curtain.

"What time are they coming?"

Don Roberto didn't answer. He was staring out the front door, where he could see a slice of unpaved road, a front gate, some kids playing marbles.

"Don't smoke so much," his wife said. "You know how nervous it makes you."

"Leave me alone!" he said, bringing his fist down on the counter. His wife disappeared without a word. He kept looking out the door, as if at a fascinating spectacle taking place outside. The representatives would arrive shortly. The chairs were all set up. The mere idea of seeing them sitting there with their watches, their mustaches, and their chubby cheeks, aggravated him. *I must retain my dignity*, he repeated to himself. *It's all I have left*. He quickly scanned the four walls of his shop. On the unpainted wood shelves were an infinite array of foodstuffs. Also on display were stacks of soap bars, pots and pans, toys, notebooks. Dust had accumulated.

At five minutes past six o'clock, a head positioned on the end of an ostentatiously long neck appeared in the doorway.

"Roberto Delmar's grocery store?"

"The one and only."

A tall man entered with a binder under his arm.

"I am the representative of Arbocó Company, Inc."

"My pleasure," Don Roberto said, without moving an inch. The newcomer took a few steps into the shop, adjusted his eyeglasses, then began to look over the merchandise.

"Is this all there is?"

"Yes, sir."

The representative looked disappointed and, once seated, began to leaf through his binder. Don Roberto turned his gaze back to the door. He felt a lively curiosity and wanted to observe the newcomer, but he refrained. He felt that doing so would show weakness, or at least, gracious hospitality. He preferred to remain immutable and dignified, with the demeanor of a man who deserves an explanation rather than must give one.

"Pursuant to the information I possess, your debt to Arbocó, Incorporated, exceeds the amount—"

"Please," Don Roberto interrupted, "I would prefer not to discuss numbers until the other creditors arrive."

A short, fat man wearing a bowler hat crossed the threshold at that very moment.

"Good afternoon," he said and plopped into a chair, where he remained still and quiet as if he had fallen fast asleep. A moment later he took out a piece of paper and began to write numbers.

Don Roberto began to feel cross. The tobacco had left a bitter taste in his mouth. At moments he shot fleeting and rapacious glances at the creditors, as if he wanted to seize them and annihilate them through the mere act of perception. Without knowing anything about their lives, he thoroughly detested them. He was not a subtle man who could make distinctions between a company and its employees. For him, that tall man with glasses *was* Arbocó, Inc., in the flesh, wholesaler of paper products and cookware. The other man, because he was blubbery and seemed very well-nourished, must be La Aurora Noodle Factory, all dressed up in a jacket and a bowler hat.

"I would like to know," began the noodle factory, "how many creditors have been invited to this meeting."

"Five!" replied Arbocó, without waiting for the grocer to answer.

"According to the summons in my portfolio, there are five of us who hold his debt."

The fat man thanked him with a nod then continued, immersed in his numbers.

Don Roberto opened another pack of cigarettes. He thought for a moment that it would have been better to leave the door closed but ajar, because there was always the chance of a customer coming in and sniffing out what was happening. He felt, however, a certain reluctance to stand up, as if the tiniest movement caused him to lose an enormous amount of energy. Immobility was for him at this moment one of the preconditions of his strength.

A boy with books under his arm rushed into the shop. When he saw the strangers, he stopped in his tracks.

"Good afternoon, Father," he said at last and, passing through the curtain, disappeared into the back room. The whispering of hushed voices drifted out.

Don Roberto automatically looked at his left wrist, where there was nothing but a patch of lighter skin. A sudden wave of shame washed over him at the thought that the creditors might have noticed that aborted act. They had, however, begun a tedious conversation among themselves.

"Arbocó?" the fat man asked. "Isn't that on Avenida Arica?"

"No! That's Arbicó," the other replied, clearly offended by the mistake.

The other creditors still hadn't shown up, and Don Roberto began to feel increasingly impatient. They knew how to keep others waiting but were incapable of giving him a grace period of a few months. In his irritation, he was confusing the punctual arrival at a meeting with due dates that were legally binding, the attributes of individuals with those of institutions. He was on the verge of tipping into an even greater muddle when two men entered, carrying on a lively conversation.

"Los Andes Cement Factory," said one.

"Marilú Candies and Chocolates," said the other, and they continued talking as they took their seats.

"Cement...Candies," Don Roberto said automatically and repeatedly, as if they were unknown words and he had to find out what they meant. He remembered the expansion of his store, which he had had to suspend for lack of cement. He remembered those candy jars numbered from one to twenty. He remembered the Italian, Bonifacio Salerno...

"Okay, so who's missing?" asked a voice.

A pathway opened into Don Roberto's interior world. The cement man looked at him, awaiting a response. But Arbocó had consulted his binder before responding.

"According to my documents here, only Ajito is missing. A-j-i-t-o, just like it sounds! He's Japanese, from Callao."

"Thank you," answered the questioner. And, turning to his companion, he added, "You can't attribute *this* to Oriental courtesy."

"On the contrary," answered the other. "Based on his name, that Japanese is more Peruvian than...than *ají* chilies."

The representatives laughed. It seemed as if they needed this quip in order to establish their complicity as creditors. The four struck up a lively conversation about their businesses, their loans, and their jobs. Opening their binders, they showed each other bills of exchange, confidential correspondence, and other documents that they qualified as "certified," endowing the technical nature of the term with a certain voluptuousness.

Don Roberto, seeing all those pieces of paper, felt a sense of muffled humiliation. He had the impression that those four gentlemen were determined to strip him naked in public in order to ridicule him or reveal some horrible defect. In order to defend himself against such an attack, he curled up like a pill bug. He raked through his past, his entire life, trying to find some honorable act, some meaningful experience that would prop up his threatened dignity. He remembered that he was president of the Parent-Teacher Association of Centro Escolar #480, where his children went to school. This fact, however, which used to fill him with pride, seemed to now turn against him. He knew he'd discovered a hidden tip of irony, for it immediately occurred to him that he would need to resign from his position. He had just begun to think about the words he would use in the letter when his son appeared and stepped into the middle of the room. Don Roberto shuddered because the boy was pale and looked angry. After stopping to cast disdainful glances at the creditors, he went outside without saying a word.

"Okay," said one, "I think we should start the meeting."

"Let's wait five minutes," Don Roberto said and was surprised to find that his voice still retained traces of authority.

A shadow appeared in the doorway. The representatives thought it was Ajito; but it was the grocer's son, having returned.

"Father, come here for a second."

Don Roberto got up and walked through the shop on his way out. His son was waiting for him a few feet away from the door, his back turned.

"What does all this mean?" he asked, sharply turning to face him.

Don Roberto didn't answer, silenced by the tone in his son's voice.

"What are all those people doing in the store? Why have you let them in?"

"Listen, son, it's business...you know..."

"I don't know anything! The only thing I know is that if I were you, I'd throw them out! Don't you realize they're laughing at you? Don't you realize they're making fun of you?"

"Making fun of me? Never!" Don Ramon protested. "My dignity—"

"What dignity are you talking about?!" he shouted, beside himself. There was a luxury car parked next to him, probably belonging to one of the creditors. "Your dignity!" he repeated with scorn. "That's the only dignity!" he said, pointing at the car. "When you have one of these, then you can talk about dignity!" Blinded by rage, he kicked one of the tires, which echoed like a drum.

"Calm down!" Don Roberto said, trying to grab his arm. "Calm down, Beto! Everything will work out, I know it will, you'll see..." And, to mollify him, he added, "Want a cigarette?"

"I don't want anything," he said, and began to walk away. A few steps later, he stopped. "Have you got a few bucks?" he asked. "I wanna go to the movies, I can't keep listening to those idiots..."

Don Roberto pulled out his wallet. The boy took the money and walked away quickly without a word of thanks. Don Roberto, disheartened, watched him walk away. The voices of the creditors reached him from inside the shop.

Taking advantage of his absence, they had stood up to "stretch their legs," according to what they said. They poked around the shelves, picking up and examining the merchandise. They smoked, told jokes. Resigned to waiting, they tried to make the best of it. As if having sniffed them out, Arbocó discovered a few bottles of pisco behind a stack of inkwells.

"Aha, a secret stash!" he said, delighted by his find.

When Don Roberto entered, they returned to their seats and to their roles as creditors. Their faces hardened, their hands resting solemnly in their waistcoat pockets.

"The meeting can begin," Don Roberto announced. "The other creditor will be here soon."

There was a short silence. The noodle man finally stood up, opened his binder, and began to read off his outstanding loans. The other creditors nodded, some taking notes. Don Roberto did his best to concentrate, to pretend to pay attention. The memory of his son, however, his sarcastic remarks about dignity, the way he grabbed the money out of his hand, tormented him. At one moment, he thought he should have slapped him. But, what for? He was too big for that kind of punishment. Moreover, he feared that deep down he agreed with his son's words.

"—I'm done," said the fat man and sat down.

Don Roberto woke up.

"Good, good . . ." he said. "Perfect. I agree with everything. Next."

Los Andes Cement started reciting from a long list: a letter of credit for three hundred soles, dated the fourth of August; another for eight hundred, from the sixteenth of the same month . . .

Don Roberto remembered the bags of cement they had brought him in August. He remembered his excitement when he started the expansion. He planned to turn it into a modern grocery store, maybe even open a restaurant. Everything, however, had been left half finished. The few remaining bags had turned hard from the humidity.

The arrival of Bonifacio Salerno had been, for him, the beginning of the end...

"—for a total of 2,800 soles," the cement representative concluded, and sat down.

Marilú Candies and Chocolates stood up, but Don Roberto was no longer listening. Every time he remembered Bonifacio Salerno's face, he felt a burning inside that befuddled him. Within a month of opening his store, just a few doors down from his own, Bonifacio had stolen all his customers. Well organized, better stocked, the competition had been wholly unfair. Don Bonifacio sold on credit and moreover, he had a potbelly, a huge potbelly... Don Roberto clung to this detail with childish glee, mentally exaggerating his rival's defect until he had turned him into a caricature of himself. This was, however, an easy subterfuge he often fell into. He made a concerted effort and managed to return to reality. The candy man was still reading: "...two kilos of chocolates, thirty-five soles..."

"Enough!" Don Roberto said, and when he realized that he had raised his voice, he apologized. "The truth is, reading it out loud makes no sense," he added. "I am acutely aware of my debts. It would be better to move straight to the arrangements."

The man from Arbocó protested. If his colleagues had read theirs, he would, too. It wasn't fair to leave him out!

"My documents are certified!" he shouted, waving his binder.

His colleagues calmed him down, convincing him to abstain from his reading. He was not very happy. Casting his myopic gaze over the shelves, he tried to find a way to take his revenge. The tops of the pisco bottles peaked out inconspicuously.

"Maybe I could pour myself a glass?" he said. "It's a bit cold this afternoon. I suffer from bronchitis."

Don Roberto stood up. In his impatience to conclude the meeting, he was willing to make such concessions. He thought, moreover, that his daughters could arrive at any moment. He lined up four glasses on the counter and filled them.

At that moment a short Asian man, his hat pulled down over his temples, slipped into the shop like a shadow.

"Ajito," he whispered in a barely audible voice. "I am Ajito."

"You've come just in time!" Los Andes Cement exclaimed.

"For the toast!" Marilú Candies said, and they both laughed loudly. It was obvious that the two of them belonged to something like a clandestine society for making stupid jokes. Their spirits were joined in common purpose. One always topped off the other's words, and they split the profits between them.

"I don't drink," the Japanese man said, excusing himself.

"I'll have his," Arbocó said, and poured himself one after another. After clicking his tongue, he returned to his chair. Red spots appeared on both his cheeks.

"Okay," Don Roberto repeated, "I insist we move directly to the arrangements."

"Agreed," the creditors said.

"Agreed!" Arbocó said, standing up. "Yes, I agree. But first I think we need a summation—"

"No summations! Let's cut to the chase!" some voices shouted.

"A summation is indispensable!" Arbocó exclaimed. "We can't do anything without a summation . . . You know, method before all. We need to proceed in an orderly fashion. I have prepared a summation, I have taken notes . . ."

He continued to insist, gained their consent, and soon embarked on a long account in which he arbitrarily mixed anecdotes, articles of the civil code, moral considerations, and by all means possible, little bits of wit. The creditors began to talk to each other under their breath. Ajito stood up and took a look outside. Don Roberto thought again about his daughters. If they arrived right then, how could he explain to them the meaning of this ceremony? It would be impossible to hide the truth from them. Everything could be heard from the back room.

Arbocó, in the meantime, had stopped talking when he saw how little attention was being paid to his words. Disappointed, he went to the counter to pour himself another glass of pisco. The creditors were laughing, surely at some joke. He felt offended, as if he were the butt of the joke. For a moment, he saw everything as black and hostile: his failure as an orator, his bad luck with women, the tragedy of having to travel on the streetcar. It all made him bilious, predisposing him to intransigence.

"Well, if it's a matter of rushing things, let's rush!" he said. "Enough deliberations. Let's cut to the chase!" Collapsing into his chair, he crossed his arms over his chest in a somewhat pretentious show of gravity. Ajito returned to his place. All eyes turned on the host.

Don Roberto stood up. He felt vaguely ill. The idea that his wife would be spying on him from behind the curtain made him more nervous. *Don't give in*, was his watchword. *Maintain your dignity.*

"Gentlemen," he began, "here's my proposal. My debts amount to a total of twenty-five thousand soles. I believe that if you grant me an extension of two months..."

Rumbles of protest began to be heard. Arbocó was the most irate.

"Why not, while we're at it, a whole year?" he shouted. "Yes, why not, while we're at it, a whole year?"

"Let me finish!" Don Roberto said, bringing his fist down on the counter. "Then I'll listen to you. I'm saying that if you grant me a two-month extension and reduce my debt to 30 percent—"

"No way, no way!" shouted Arbocó, and when he saw that his colleagues agreed with him, he stood up, trying to take control of the situation. "No way, Mr. Delmar!" he continued, but then his ideas grew blurry, he couldn't find the precise and solemn words the occasion required, and he was stuck repeating mechanically, "No way, Mr. Delmar! No way, Mr. Delmar!"

Next, the noodle representative stood up. His infectious tranquility calmed things down a notch.

"Gentlemen," he said, "let us assess the situation dispassionately. I consider our debtor's suggestion interesting, but, frankly, unacceptable. The fact is, his debt is long overdue. Some of it was incurred a year ago. If he has not been able to pay any of it in these twelve months, I believe that it will be equally impossible in two more."

"You forgot the reduction," Don Roberto objected.

"That is precisely what I would like to address. Reducing your debt to 30 percent is almost forgiving it. I think that the companies we represent would never accept—"

"My boss? No way!" Arbocó interrupted. "My boss is a very important man!"

"Mine wouldn't, either," said the cement creditor.

"Mine, either!" said the candy one.

Don Roberto remained silent. He had predicted a negative response, though he didn't think he would encounter such energetic solidarity within the group. The four men, still standing up, had also fallen silent, forming a kind of indestructible unit. They looked at him defiantly, clearly ready to drown him in a sea of explanations and numbers if he committed the folly of insisting. Only Ajito remained seated in a corner, separate and apart from the swirl of emotions. Don Roberto gave him an almost friendly look, sensing that he might find in him an ally.

"What about you?" he asked him. "What do you think?"

"I agree, I agree..." he mumbled.

"You agree with who?" Arbocó shouted, stretching his long neck toward him.

"I agree with the debtor."

Arbocó exploded. He raved about disloyalty, a lack of tact, an absence of collegiality. Only when on the attack did he seem to recover a certain modicum of eloquence. He tried to rile up the others against the Japanese, against all Japanese, against the entire Orient.

"It seems those people don't care about money!" he spluttered. "Yes, of course, for them it's a minor issue. They're a clan, they've got entire networks of taverns all over the city, they get help from the government!..."

Ajito remained unperturbed. Don Roberto intervened.

"This is not the time to bring up such things. I'm willing to listen to your counterproposals."

The four creditors—they left Ajito out—formed a tight circle and began their discussion. Disagreement reigned. Arbocó seemed to represent the most extreme position. His voice dominated the group. From time to time he went to the counter and poured himself another glass of pisco. Finally, for the sake of convenience, he kept the bottle with him.

"We must put our feelings aside!" he shouted. "We represent the interests of the company!"

Don Roberto made a great effort to appear indifferent, even though his fate depended on what would be decided then and here. With his eyes glued on the door, he puffed on his cigarette. The beats of a mambo wafted in from the neighbors'. His wife must have felt like he did, standing behind the curtain, her heart in her throat . . . His son, where was his son? Why hadn't he slapped him? . . . And he had to give a speech at the Centro Escolar #480! . . . Bonifacio was probably selling tons of spaghetti . . . The sounds of the mambo grew louder . . . There was a dance party, probably, a dance party at the neighbors' . . . Why didn't he and the creditors and Bonifacio hold hands and join the party and forget all these petty misfortunes?

"Don Roberto Delmar," the fat noodle man began, "we have, in a sense, reached an agreement."

"I dissent!" Arbocó protested. "My opinion . . . !"

"The majority has reached a decision," the fat man continued. "It is as follows: we will grant you a fifteen-day extension and reduce your debt by 50 percent. Do you agree?"

"No!" Don Roberto replied. And this immediate negative was met with deep silence, which Don Roberto prolonged as his heart rate returned to normal and he prepared his response. The mambo started up again. A few curious passers by poked their heads in the door.

"I cannot accept those conditions," he said finally. "No, gentlemen, I cannot," he continued, his voice faltering for the first time. "You people don't know, you don't understand how this all came about. I didn't mean to cheat anyone. I am an honorable shopkeeper. But honor is not enough when it comes to business . . . Do you by any chance know my competitor? He is powerful and fat; he opened a grocery store a few steps away from here and has ruined me . . . If it weren't for him, I'd be selling, and I could've finished expanding my store . . . But he's well-stocked and fat . . . I repeat, gentlemen, fat . . ." The creditors looked at each other with concern. "He has a lot of capital and a lot of belly. I am powerless against him . . . Just to break even, I need two months and thirty percent...You can see in the next room, the construction's at a standstill...If it weren't for Bonifacio, I would've already opened my restaurant, and I'd be selling and paying my debts!...But the competition is terrible, and moreover my children are in high school, and I'm president of the Parent-Teacher Association—"

"In short," Arbocó said, once he saw the strange turn the subject was taking, "you can't?"

"I can't!" Don Roberto concluded.

"There's nothing more to say, then. I will inform my principles."

"But, please, reconsider," the noodle man said. "Our conditions are not draconian."

"I can't!" Don Roberto repeated. "Why would I? In fifteen days, it'll be the same story all over again!"

"So, there's no alternative," Cement and Candies said in unison. "It's bankruptcy!"

"Yes, bankruptcy," Noodles confirmed.

"Bankruptcy!" Arbocó shouted with a certain amount of ferocity, as if he had scored a personal victory.

"Bankruptcy procedures will be initiated."

"Yes, of course, bankruptcy."

Don Roberto looked at them in turn, how the word kept bouncing from one mouth to the other, repeating itself, combining with others, growing, detonating like a firecracker, blending into the notes of the music...

"Okay then, bankruptcy!" he said in turn, and pressed his elbows into the counter with such force that it seemed as if he wanted to nail them into the wood.

The creditors looked at one another. This abrupt surrender to what they considered to be their most powerful threat perplexed them. Arbocó muttered something. The others mumbled under their breath. They were waiting for the shopkeeper to once again confirm his decision. Not daring to ask a question or budge or leave, Don Roberto intervened.

"Gentlemen, the meeting has come to an end," he said, and, crossing his arms over his chest, he stared straight at the ceiling.

The creditors picked up their binders, tossed their cigarette butts on the floor, bowed to each other, and, one by one, walked out the door. Ajito removed his hat before leaving.

Don Roberto pressed his palms into his temples and sat with his head buried between them. The music had stopped. For a moment, the silence was broken by the sound of a car starting.

Then everything went quiet. The idea that he had maintained his dignity began to seem true and to fill him with a strange euphoria. He had the feeling that he had won the battle, that he had forced his adversaries to retreat. The sight of empty chairs, smoldering cigarette butts, and overturned cups produced in him a kind of victorious delirium. For a moment he felt like going into the back room and passionately embracing his wife, but he refrained. No, his wife would not understand the meaning, the nuance, of his victory. The dust-covered merchandise on the shelves insisted he maintain mute discretion. Don Roberto swept his gaze over it and felt distress. That merchandise no longer belonged to him; it belonged to "others"; it had all been left there on purpose to dampen his joy, confound his spirit. Within a few days, it would all be removed and the shop would be empty. Within a few days, the foreclosure would take effect and the shop would be shuttered.

Don Roberto stood up nervously and lit a cigarette. He wanted to revive in his spirit the sensation of victory, but it was no longer possible. He realized that it disfigured reality, coercing his own rationalizations. His wife, at that moment, appeared from behind the curtain, noticeably ashen.

Don Roberto couldn't tolerate her eyes on him and turned his face to the wall. A candy jar returned his image to him from an aberrant angle.

"You have no idea . . . !" he exclaimed, but was unable to utter another word.

His wife shrugged and returned to the back room.

Don Roberto looked at his small and twisted image in the jar. "Bankrupt!" he whispered, and that word took on the entirety of its tragic meaning. Never had a word seemed so real, so atrociously tangible. His business was bankrupt, his home was bankrupt, his conscience was bankrupt, his dignity was bankrupt. Perhaps his own human nature was bankrupt. Don Roberto had the painful sense that he himself was bankrupt, ruptured, broken into pieces, and he thought that he would need to look for all those pieces of himself and pick himself up from every corner.

He kicked over a chair then wrapped his muffler around his neck. Turning off the light in the store, he walked to the door. His wife, who heard him leaving, appeared for the third time.

"Roberto, where are you going? Dinner's almost ready."

"Bah! Where do you think? I'm going out!" and he walked out the door.

Once outside, he hesitated. He didn't know exactly why he'd gone out or where he wanted to go. A few meters away he saw the red lights of Bonifacio Salerno's grocery store. Don Roberto looked away, as if to avoid an unpleasant encounter, and, turning in the opposite direction, he took off walking. Some girls were coming toward him, laughing, and he pressed himself against the wall. He was afraid they were his daughters and would ask him something, want to give him a kiss. Increasing his pace, he reached the corner, where a group of neighbors were chatting. When they saw him, they turned to him and spoke:

"Don Roberto, aren't you joining the procession?"

He answered with a nod and continued walking. A moment later, he reconsidered. It was the procession for the Lord of Miracles. This event, which used to mean so much to him, now left him indifferent, and he even thought it ridiculous. He thought that calamities had their due dates, after which even God couldn't intervene. He was plagued by the bizarre feeling of having been anesthetized, of his skin having turned into bark, of having become a thing. The fact that he was now bankrupt, broke, strengthened that sensation. It was horrible, he thought, that words that had come into being to refer to objects could be applied to people. You can break a glass, you can break a chair, but you can't break a human being, not like that, through an act of will. But those four gentlemen had delicately broken him, what with their bowing and their threats.

When he came to a bar he stopped, then continued walking. No, he didn't want to drink. He didn't want to talk to the bartender or anybody else for that matter. Perhaps the only company he would be able to stand at that moment was his son's. With a certain pleasure he had watched him develop the same black eyebrows and the same pride ... But no. That was absurd. He wouldn't understand, either. He had to avoid him. He had to avoid everybody: those who walked by and looked at him, and those who didn't even bother to do so.

It had grown dark. The scent of the sea saturated the air. Don Roberto thought of the esplanade. It was good to be there. There was a curved balustrade, a row of yellow lanterns, a dark sea that never ceased to strike at the bottom of the cliff. It was a peaceful place where the sounds of the city barely reached, where you could barely feel the hostility of men. In its sanctuary, you could make important decisions. There, he remembered kissing his wife for the first time, so long ago. On that precise border between the earth and the sea, between light and darkness, between the city and nature, it was possible to win everything or lose everything ... His steps grew faster. The stores, the people, the trees rushed by him, as if urging him to stretch out his hand and hold on tight. The salt air stung his nostrils.

There was, however, still so far to go ...

Paris, 1954

from
STORIES UNDER THE CIRCUMSTANCES

THE INSIGNIA

To this day I perfectly remember that afternoon when I was strolling along the esplanade and caught sight of a shiny object in a small trash can. With the curiosity that is naturally part and parcel of my collector's temperament, I leaned over, picked it up, and rubbed it against the sleeve of my jacket. I could then see that it was a small silver insignia, engraved with marks that at that time were utterly incomprehensible to me. Without giving it a second thought, I dropped it in my pocket and continued on my way home. I can't know for certain how long it remained in that jacket, for I wore it infrequently. I only remember that at some point I sent it to the cleaners, and I was greatly surprised when the clerk returned it to me clean, along with a small box, and said to me, "This must be yours, I found it in your pocket."

It was, of course, the insignia, and its unexpected recovery touched me so much that I decided to wear it.

Here commences the chain of really strange events. The first took place in a used bookshop. I was looking through some antique volumes when the proprietor, who had been observing me from the darkest corner of his shop for quite some time, approached, and in a tone of complicity and accompanied by winks and knowing facial expressions, said, "We have a few books by Feifer." I stared at him, intrigued, because I had not asked for books by this author, whom, moreover, and although my knowledge of literature is not that broad, I had never heard of. Immediately thereafter, he added: "Feifer was in Pilsen." As I had still not recovered from my astonishment, the bookseller ended in a tone of revelation, of unambiguous trust: "You must know that they killed him. Yes, they killed him with a blow from a stick at the Prague train station." This said, he retreated into the corner from which he had emerged and remained there in the deepest of silences. I continued to mechanically leaf through several volumes, but my mind was preoccupied with the bookseller's enigmatic words. After buying a book on mechanics, I left the shop, bewildered.

For some time I tried to explain the meaning of this incident, but, unable to solve it, I finally forgot all about it. Soon, however, something else happened that was also quite alarming. I was strolling across a plaza in a suburb, when a small man with an angular, jaundiced face approached me awkwardly and left a card in my hand before I could react, then disappeared without uttering a word. On the white card were written only an address and the words SECOND SESSION: TUESDAY 4. You can well imagine that on Tuesday the fourth I made my way to the address indicated on the card. As I approached, I encountered several strange subjects lurking around who, in a surprising coincidence, were all wearing the exact same insignia. I joined the group and saw that they were all holding out their hands to me as if we were old acquaintances. Shortly thereafter we entered the appointed house and found seats in a large room. A gentleman with a grave demeanor appeared from behind a curtain and, standing on a dais and after welcoming us, began to speak for an interminable length of time. I don't know exactly what the lecture was about, or if, in fact, it was even a lecture. Memories of his childhood were woven into incisive philosophical speculations, and the same expository method was used for digressions about the growing of beets and the organization of the state. I remember that he concluded by drawing red arrows on a blackboard with a piece of chalk he pulled out of his pocket.

When it was over, we all rose and began to leave, enthusiastically praising the success of the lecture. To be polite, I added my praise to theirs, but just as I was about to go out the front door, the speaker called to me and, when I turned around, he gestured to me to approach.

"You're new, aren't you?" he asked, a bit distrustfully.

"Yes," I answered after hesitating for a moment, for I was surprised he was able to pick me out of such a large crowd. "I've just been for a short time."

"Who introduced you?"

Much to my good fortune, I remembered the bookseller.

"I was in the bookshop on Calle Amargura, and the ..."

"Who? Martín?"

"Yes, Martín."

"Oh, yes, he is a great associate."

"I'm an old customer of his."

"What did you talk about?"

"Well ... Feifer."

"What did he tell you?"

"That he was in Pilsen. The truth is ... I didn't know that."

"You didn't?"

"No," I answered, just as calmly as I could.

"You also probably didn't know that he was killed by a blow at the Prague train station?"

"He told me that, as well."

"Oh, it was a terrible thing for us!"

"Indeed," I agreed. "An irretrievable loss."

We continued to converse in a casual and indistinct way, full of unexpected confidences and superficial allusions, such as occurs between two strangers who happen to be sharing a seat on a bus. I remember that whereas I went to great lengths to describe my tonsillectomy, he, with grandiose gestures, proclaimed the beauty of Nordic landscapes. Finally, before I left, he charged me with a task that did not fail to garner my utmost attention.

"Next week," he said, "bring me a list of all telephone numbers that begin with 38."

I promised to do so and proceeded to assemble the list well before the deadline.

"Admirable!" he exclaimed. "You work with exemplary speed."

From that day on, I performed a series of similar tasks, all of the strangest kind. For example, I was told to find a dozen parrots, which

I never saw again. Later, I was sent to a city in the provinces to make a sketch of the city hall. I remember that I also threw banana peels in front of the doors of certain scrupulously marked residences, wrote an article about celestial bodies, which I never saw published, trained a monkey in parliamentary-style gesticulations, and even carried out certain secret missions, such as delivering letters I didn't read to exotic women who always disappeared without leaving a trace.

In this way, and little by little, I commanded more and more respect. In an emotional ceremony a year later, I was promoted. "You have been promoted," I was told by the ranking member of our circle as he embraced me effusively. I then had to give a short speech in which I referred to our common purpose, and although I spoke in vague terms, my words were resoundingly applauded.

At home, however, the situation was unsettling. My family did not understand my unexpected disappearances and my actions enveloped in that air of mystery, and whenever I was questioned I avoided responding because, to tell the truth, I had no satisfactory answers. Some relatives even recommended that I be examined by a psychiatrist, as my behavior was not exactly that of a sensible man. Above all, I remember leaving them very intrigued one day when they surprised me making a gross of fake mustaches, as my leader had assigned me to do.

This domestic belligerence did not prevent me from continuing my dedication to the work of our society with an enthusiasm that I myself found inexplicable. Soon I became rapporteur, treasurer, conference associate, management consultant—and the further I went into the heart of the organization, the greater was my bewilderment, for I had no idea if I belonged to a religious sect or a group of fabric manufacturers.

Three years later they sent me abroad. It was a most intriguing trip. I didn't have a penny, but the ships gave me cabins, at every port there was somebody who met me and lavished me with attention, and hotels offered me their hospitality without asking for anything in return. I made connections with other brotherhoods, learned foreign languages, gave lectures, opened subsidiaries of our group, and watched as silver insignias spread to every corner of the continent. Upon my return after a year of intense human experience, I was just as bewildered as when I entered Martín's bookshop.

Ten years have passed. Due to my own merits, I have been appointed president. When I preside over large ceremonies, I wear a toga rimmed with purple. The members call me Your Excellency. I receive a salary of five thousand dollars, have houses at beach resorts, servants in livery who respect and fear me, and even a charming wife who comes to me each night without me calling her. In spite of all of that, and just like the first few days, I live in total and abject ignorance, and if somebody asked me what the purpose of our organization was, I would not be able to answer. At most, I would confine myself to drawing red arrows on a blackboard, waiting confidently for the results produced in the human mind by any explanation that is inexorably based on a cabal.

Lima, 1952

DOUBLED

AT THE time, I lived in a small hotel near Charing Cross and spent my days painting and reading books about the occult. The truth is, I have always felt an affinity for the occult sciences, perhaps because my father spent many years in India and brought back from the banks of the Ganges a complete collection of treatises on the esoteric—as well as a vicious case of malaria. In one of those books I read a sentence that piqued my curiosity. I don't know if it would be called a proverb or an aphorism, but either way it was a closed-form expression that I have never been able to forget: "Each of us has a double who lives in the antipodes, but finding him is difficult because doubles always tend to carry out the contrary movement."

If the statement interested me it was because I had always been tormented by the idea of having a double. I had had only one experience of it, when I boarded a bus and had the misfortune of sitting and facing an individual who looked very much like me. For a while, we sat and stared at each other, both of us obviously curious, until I became quite uncomfortable and had to get off several stops before my destination. Although I never had another similar experience, I embarked on a mysterious quest, and the idea of the double became one of my favorite subjects of speculations.

My thinking was that, considering the millions of people populating the globe and through a simple calculation of probabilities, it would not be so strange for some features to recur. After all, with one nose, one mouth, two eyes, and certain other accessory details, there are not an infinite number of combinations. The case of body doubles corroborated my theories, in a way. At that time, it was fashionable for statesmen or movie stars to hire people who looked like them, and to have them run all the risks of being a celebrity. This, however, did not entirely satisfy me. My idea of a double was more ambitious. I thought that having identical features should correspond to having an identical temperament and—why not—destiny. The few body doubles I had the opportunity to see combined a vague physical similarity—often enhanced with makeup—and a complete absence of spiritual connection. In general, the body doubles of the great financiers were humble men who had invariable failed their math classes. Without a doubt, the double constituted for me a more encompassing, and much more fascinating, phenomenon. My reading of the text I have just quoted not only helped confirm my idea but also enhanced my conjectures. Sometimes I thought that in another country, on another continent, in the antipodes, in short, there was a person exactly like me, one who did what I did, had my defects, passions, dreams, and obsessions, and this idea beguiled me while also causing me great distress.

With time, I became obsessed with the idea of a double. For many weeks I couldn't work and did nothing but repeat that strange formula, expecting perhaps that through some kind of sorcery, my double would rise out of the center of the earth. I soon realized that I was torturing myself futilely, and if those lines proposed a riddle, they also suggested the solution: a journey to the antipodes.

At first, I rejected the idea of taking the trip. During that time, I had a lot of projects to finish. I had just begun a Madonna and had received, in addition, an offer to design the inside of a theater. Nonetheless, I walked by a shop in Soho and saw a beautiful globe in the window. Without a second thought, I bought it and that night I studied it meticulously. To my great surprise, I saw that the antipode of London was the Australian city of Sydney. The fact that this city belonged to the Commonwealth seemed to be a magnificent omen. I remembered, moreover, that in Melbourne I had a distant aunt, whom I could visit. Many other equally harebrained excuses occurred to me—such as a sudden passion for Australian goats—but the fact is, three days later, and without saying a word to the proprietor of my hotel so as to avoid any indiscreet questions, I boarded an airplane to Sydney.

Shortly after landing, I realized the absurdity of my decision. On the flight, I had returned to reality; I felt ashamed of my chimeras and was tempted to return on the same plane. To top things off, I found out that my aunt in Melbourne had died years before. After a long internal debate, I decided that it was worth it to stay a few days to rest after such an exhausting trip. I ended up staying for seven weeks.

To begin, I will say that the city was quite big, much bigger than I had expected, so I immediately abandoned my search for my supposed double. How, I asked myself, would I ever find him? It was simply ridiculous to stop every passerby on the street and ask them if they knew anybody who looked just like me. They would think I was mad. In spite of that, I confess that every time I was in a crowd, whether leaving a theater or in a public park, I felt a constant uneasiness, and despite my willpower, I would carefully examine people's faces. On one occasion, I spent an entire hour in a state of abject anxiety on the heels of a subject who was my height and had my manner of walking. What drove me to despair was his stubborn refusal to turn his face to me. Finally, unable to stand it any longer, I spoke to him. Upon turning, he showed me a pale, inoffensive countenance full of freckles that—why not admit it?—restored my peace of mind. If I remained in Sydney for a monstrously long seven weeks, it was definitely not to continue these investigations but rather for reasons of a different nature: I fell in love. A rare occurrence for a man over thirty, above all for an Englishman devoted to the occult.

I fell head over heels in love. The woman's name was Winnie, and she worked in a restaurant. Without a shadow of a doubt, this was the most interesting experience I had in Sydney. She seemed to feel almost instantly attracted to me, too, which surprised me, for I have never had much luck with women. From the very beginning she accepted my attentions, and a few days later, we took a walk around the city. It is futile to try to describe Winnie; I will say only that she was rather eccentric. At times she treated me with extreme familiarity; at others, she was disconcerted by some of the expressions or words

I used, but far from angering me, I found this enchanting. Having decided to cultivate this relationship under more comfortable conditions, I decided to leave the hotel, and, after a phone conversation with an agency, I found a furnished house in the suburbs.

I cannot avoid a powerful rush of romantic feelings when I remember this small villa. Its peace and quiet and the tastefulness of its decor captivated me from the very first moment. I felt utterly at home. The walls were adorned with a marvelous collection of yellow butterflies, for which I acquired a sudden fondness. I spent my days thinking about Winnie and chasing those gorgeous Lepidoptera in the garden. At a certain point I decided to settle there permanently, and I was about to acquire the necessary supplies I needed to paint, when a singular and perhaps inexplicable accident occurred, to which I insisted on attaching exorbitant significance.

It was a Saturday, and Winnie, after putting up fierce resistance, decided to spend the weekend at my house. The afternoon passed cheerfully with the usual oases of affection. Toward evening, something about Winnie's behavior began to worry me. At first I didn't know what it was, and in vain I studied her face, trying to discover some change that would explain my malaise. Soon, however, I realized that what made me uncomfortable was the familiarity with which Winnie moved around the house. Several times she found a light switch without even looking. Was I jealous? At first I felt a kind of dark rage. I was truly attached to Winnie, and if I had never asked her about her past, it was because I was already forging certain plans about her future. The possibility that she had been with another man didn't hurt me as much as the idea that it had taken place in my house. Filled with anxiety, I decided to verify my suspicions. I recalled that one day, while looking around in the attic, I had found an old oil lamp. Immediately I used the pretext that we should take a stroll in the garden.

"But we don't have anything to light our way," I muttered.

Winnie got up and stood hesitantly in the middle of the room. Then I saw her move with determination toward the stairs and climb them. Five minutes later she appeared with the lamp lit.

The next scene was so violent, so painful, that I find it difficult to relive. The truth is, I blew up, flew into a rage, lost my cool, and behaved cruelly. With one blow I knocked the lamp out of her hand—at the risk of starting a fire—and, throwing myself on her, I tried to extract an imaginary confession with brute force. Twisting her wrists, I asked her with whom and when she had been in this house. The only thing I remember is her incredibly pale face, her bulging eyes looking at me as if I were a madman. Her discomposure made it impossible for her to utter a word, which only increased my rage. In the end, I insulted her and threw her out. Winnie picked up her coat and ran out the door.

All night I berated myself for my behavior. I never thought I could be so excitable, and I attributed it in part to my scant experience with women. Upon reflection, Winnie's actions, which had so riled me, seemed completely normal. All those country houses are similar, and it is only natural that there would be a lamp in a country house and that this lamp would be in the attic. My explosion had been unjustified, and even worse: in very bad taste. To find Winnie and offer her an apology seemed the only decent recourse. It was in vain: I was never able to talk to her again. She had quit the restaurant, and when I went to her house, she refused to let me in. One day, after I continued to insist, her mother came out and told me quite rudely that Winnie wanted absolutely nothing to do with a madman.

Madman? There is nothing more terrifying to an Englishman than to be called mad. I spent three days in my country house trying to put my feelings in order. After patient reflection, I began to realize that this whole story was petty, ridiculous, and despicable. The very origins of my trip to Sydney were ludicrous. A double? What senselessness! What was I doing there: lost, anxiety-ridden, thinking about an eccentric woman whom I maybe didn't even love, wasting my time collecting yellow butterflies? How could I have abandoned my brushes, my tea, my pipe, my walks in Hyde Park, my beloved fog over the Thames? My sanity returned; in the blink of an eye I packed my bags, and the next day I was on my way back to London.

I arrived in the evening and from the airport went straight to my hotel. I was truly exhausted, with an enormous desire to sleep and recover my energy for my pending projects. What joy to be again in my own room! At moments it felt like I had never left. I sank into my armchair and remained there for a long time, savoring the pleasure of finding myself among my own things once again. My eyes passed over each and every familiar object and caressed each one with gratitude. Leaving is a great thing, I told myself, but returning is truly marvelous.

What was it that suddenly drew my attention? Everything was in its place, exactly how I had left it. I nevertheless began to feel a sharp sense of discomfort. In vain I tried to discover the reason. Rising from my chair, I inspected the four corners of my room. There was nothing out of place, but I could feel, smell, a presence, a vestige, something that was about to disappear...

Knocks on the door. I opened it a crack, and the bellboy poked in his head.

"They've called you from the Mandrake Club. They say that yesterday you forgot your umbrella in the bar. Would you like them to send it over or will you go pick it up?"

"Have them send it over," I replied automatically.

Immediately I realized the absurdity of my answer. The evening before I had been flying, probably over Singapore. When I looked at my brushes I shuddered: they had fresh paint on them. Rushing over to the easel, I pulled off the sheet: the Madonna I had left as a sketch had been finished with the skill of a master, and her face, odd as it may seem, was Winnie's.

I fell, defeated, into my armchair. A yellow butterfly was flying in circles around the lamp.

Paris, 1955

from
OF BOTTLES AND MEN

THE SUBSTITUTE TEACHER

TOWARD evening, while Matías and his wife were sipping sad tea and complaining about the impoverishment of the middle class, the need to always wear a clean shirt, the price of transportation, the tax increases, on the whole, what poor couples talk about at the end of the day, they heard some loud knocks on the door, and, when they opened it, Dr. Valencia burst in, cane in hand, suffocating under his stiff collar.

"Matías, my dear man! I come bearing great news! From this day forth, you will be a teacher. Wait! Don't say no ... I have to go abroad for a few months, and I've decided to have you teach my history classes at the high school. It's not an important position, and the remuneration isn't great, but it's a magnificent opportunity for you to start teaching. With time, you will pick up more classes, and doors will open for you at other high schools; maybe you'll even get to the university ... That depends on you. I've always had the greatest confidence in you. It's so unfair that a man of your quality, an erudite man, one who has finished the university, has to earn his living as a debt collector ... No, sir, it's not right, and I'm the first one to admit it. Your place is in education ... Don't give it a second thought. I'll call the principal right now to tell him that I've found a replacement. There's no time to lose, a taxi is waiting for me out front ... Give me a hug, Matías, and tell me I'm your friend!"

Before Matías had time to express an opinion, Dr. Valencia had called the school, spoken to the principal, hugged his friend for the fourth time, and was off like a shot, without having even removed his hat.

For a few moments, Matías stood there thinking, rubbing his lovely bald head, the delight of children and the terror of housewives. With an energetic gesture, he prevented his wife from getting a word in edgewise, silently walked over to the cupboard, poured himself a glass of port wine reserved only for visitors, and savored it slowly, after having held it up to the light of the streetlamp and looked at it carefully.

"None of this surprises me," he said finally. "A man of my quality could not remain buried in oblivion."

After dinner, he shut himself up in the dining room, had a pot of coffee brought to him, brushed the dust off his old textbooks, and told his wife not to let anybody interrupt him, not even Baltazar and Luciano, his colleagues, with whom he usually met in the evenings to play cards and even crack lewd jokes about their bosses.

At ten the next morning, Matías left his apartment. He had memorized his inaugural lecture and now fended off with slight impatience his wife's anxious attentions as she ran after him through the corridors of the apartment block, picking the last bits of lint off his best suit.

"Don't forget to put up the card on the door," Matías reminded her before leaving. "Make sure it reads MATÍAS PALOMINO, HISTORY PROFESSOR."

On his way, he went over the paragraphs of his lesson plan in his mind. The previous night he had not been able to avoid a little shiver of joy when he had discovered "The Hydra" as an epithet for Louis XVI. It had been in vogue in the nineteenth century and had fallen a bit out of use, but Matías—his demeanor and his readings—still belonged to the nineteenth century, and his intelligence, no matter how you cut it, had also fallen into disuse. For the last twelve years, after failing his qualifying exams twice in a row, he had not opened a single textbook or presented a single reflection to the slightly languid passion of his spirit. He always attributed his academic failings to the malevolence of the judges and a kind of sudden amnesia that would attack him mercilessly every time he was required to display his knowledge. Though he had not been able to pursue his legal studies, he had chosen the prose style and the bowtie of a notary; if not in expertise than at least in appearance, he always remained within the confines of the profession.

When he arrived in front of the school, he came to a sudden stop and stood there, somewhat baffled. The big clock on the front of the building told him that he had arrived ten minutes early. Excess punctuality seemed inelegant to him, and he decided it would be best to take a stroll to the corner. As he passed in front of the school gate, he saw a doorman with a rather surly face and his hands crossed behind his back, who was keeping his eye on the sidewalk.

At the corner of the park he stopped, took out his handkerchief, and wiped his forehead. The day was a bit warm. A pine tree and a palm tree, their shadows mingling, reminded him of a poem, whose author he tried in vain to recall. He was about to return—the city clock had just struck eleven—when he saw a pale man behind the window of the record shop spying on him. To his surprise, he realized that the man was none other than his own reflection. Watching himself out of the corner of his eye, he winked, as if to dissipate the slightly gloomy look the long night of studying and coffee had stamped upon his features. But that look, rather than disappear, displayed new vestiges, and Matías saw that his bald spot lay forlornly between the tufts of hair at his temples, and that his mustache fell over his lips in an expression of total defeat.

A bit mortified by these observations, he yanked himself away from the window. The stifling summer morning made him loosen his satin bow tie. But when he arrived in front of the school, an enormous doubt assailed him without any apparent provocation: at that instant he could not be certain if the hydra was a marine animal, a mythological monster, or an invention of that selfsame Dr. Valencia, who employed similar images to demolish his enemies in Parliament. Confused, he opened his briefcase to look at his notes just as he noticed that the doorman had not taken his eyes off him. That glare from a uniformed man aroused sinister associations in his small taxpayer consciousness, and unable to stop himself, he continued walking until he reached the opposite corner.

There he stopped, out of breath. By now, the problem of the hydra no longer mattered: that doubt had brought in its wake many much more urgent ones. Now, everything in his head was becoming confused. He turned Colbert into an English minister, placed Marat's humpback on the shoulders of Robespierre, and through some trick of the imagination, Chénier's fine alexandrine verses came to rest on the lips of Samson, the executioner. Terrified by such slippage, he searched madly for a grocery store. He was overwhelmed by a thirst that could not be ignored.

For a quarter of an hour he dashed through the adjacent streets, but in vain. There were nothing but hair salons in that residential neighborhood. After an infinite number of turns, he happened upon the record shop, and his own image again rose up out of the depths of the window. This time, Matías examined it carefully: around his eyes had appeared two black rings that subtly configured a circle, which could be none other than the circle of terror.

Flustered, he turned around and stood contemplating the park. His heart knocked against his chest like a caged bird. Despite the hands of the watch continuing to turn, Matías stood stock-still, stubbornly concentrating on insignificant things, such as counting the branches on a tree, then deciphering the letters of an advertisement obscured behind some foliage.

The bell on the parish church brought him around. Matías realized that he was still on time. Grasping at all his virtues, even those ambivalent ones like obstinacy, he managed to pull together something that could pass as a conviction, and, baffled by the loss of so much time, he rushed toward the school. His courage increased with movement. When he saw the gate, he adopted the deep and occupied air of a businessman. He was just about to pass through it when, upon lifting his eyes, he saw next to the doorman a conclave of gray-haired and enrobed men who were watching him uneasily. This unexpected constellation—which reminded him of the judges of his youth—was enough to unleash a profusion of defensive reflexes and, swerving quickly, he fled toward the main avenue.

After twenty steps he realized that someone was following him. A voice rang out behind him. It was the doorman.

"Excuse me," he said, "aren't you Mr. Palomino, the new history teacher? The brothers are waiting for you."

Matías turned around, red with rage.

"I'm a debt collector!" he answered harshly, as if he had been the victim of an embarrassing confusion.

The doorman apologized and withdrew. Matías continued along his way, reached the avenue, turned toward the park, walked aimlessly among the shoppers, stumbled over a curb, almost knocked down a blind man, then finally collapsed onto a bench—overheated, thwarted, as if his brain were made of cheese.

When the children began to leave school and romp around him, he woke from his lethargy. Still confused, under the impression that he had been the victim of a humiliating scam, he rose and started home. Unconsciously, he chose the most roundabout route. He lost his way then found it. Reality escaped through the cracks in his imagination. He thought that one day he would become a millionaire through a stroke of good luck. Only when he arrived at the apartment block and saw his wife waiting for him at the door of their apartment, her apron tied around her waist, did he become aware of his enormous frustration. Nonetheless, he pulled himself together, attempted a smile, and prepared to greet his wife, who was already running down the hallway with her arms held open.

"How did it go? Did you teach class? What did the students say?"

"It was fantastic! ... Everything was fantastic!" Matías stammered. "They applauded me!" but when he felt his wife's arms encircling his neck and looked into her eyes, for the first time on fire with invincible pride, he violently dropped his head and began to cry in desolation.

Antwerp, 1957

A NOCTURNAL ADVENTURE

AT FORTY, Arístides would be wholly correct in considering himself a man "excluded from the banquet of life," as they say. He had no wife or girlfriend, he worked in the basement of the city hall recording civil registry certificates, and he lived in a tiny apartment on Avenida Larco, cluttered with dirty clothes, broken-down furniture, and photos of movie stars stuck on the walls with thumbtacks. His old friends, now married and prosperous, would drive by in their cars while he waited in line for the bus, and if by chance he ran into one of them in a public place, they gave him a quick handshake through which slipped a certain dose of revulsion. For Arístides was not only the moral symbol of failure but also the physical image of neglect: he dressed poorly, shaved carelessly, and smelled of cheap food from seedy taverns.

Without family and without memories, Arístides was a regular at the neighborhood movie houses and the ideal occupier of public benches. At the movies, out of the glare of the light of day, he felt both concealed and accompanied by the legions of shadows laughing or tearing up around him. In parks he could strike up conversations with the old men, the cripples, or the beggars, and thus feel part of that immense family of people who, like he, wore on his lapel the invisible badge of loneliness.

One night, forsaking his favorite spots, Arístides started walking aimlessly through the streets of Miraflores. He walked the entire length of Avenida Pardo, reached the esplanade, kept going up the coast, then snaked around the San Martín barracks through increasingly deserted streets, neighborhoods still in their infancy and that most likely had not yet witnessed a single funeral. He walked past a church, a half-built movie house, past the church a second time, and finally became lost. A little after midnight, he happened upon a wholly unfamiliar residential neighborhood where the first apartment buildings of the seaside resort were in the initial stages of construction.

He noticed a café with a completely deserted and enormous terrace full of small tables. Coming to a standstill, he pressed his nose against the glass and looked inside. The clock said one. He didn't see a single customer. Behind the counter, standing next to the cash register, he could just make out a fat woman wearing a fur wrap, smoking a cigarette, and absentmindedly reading a newspaper. The woman lifted her eyes and looked at him with an expression of moderate complacency. Arístides, totally unnerved, continued on his way.

A hundred steps away he stopped and looked around: the modern buildings were fast asleep and had no history. Arístides felt like he was treading on virgin soil, wrapping himself in a new landscape that touched his heart and retouched it with invincible zeal. Retracing his steps, he cautiously approached the café. The woman was still sitting in the same place, and when she saw him, she reproduced her slightly cheerful expression. Arístides walked abruptly away, stopped in the middle of the street, hesitated, turned back, peeked in again, and finally pushed open the glass door, walking in and sitting down at a small red table, where he sat absolutely still, his eyes downcast.

He waited there for a moment, not exactly sure what for, and observed a wounded fly laboriously dragging itself into the abyss. Then, unable to control the trembling in his legs, he timidly lifted one eye: the woman was staring at him over her newspaper. Stifling a yawn, she spoke in a thick, somewhat manly voice: "The waiters have all gone home, sir."

Arístides picked up the sentence and stored it inside him, seized by a sudden joy: a strange woman had spoken to him late at night. He immediately understood that the sentence was an invitation to engage. Suddenly confused, he stood up.

"But I can serve you. What will you have?" the woman said, as she made her way toward him with a slightly awkward gait, which one could not deny contained a certain amount of majesty.

Arístides sat back down.

"A coffee. Just coffee."

The woman had reached the table and was leaning her chubby bejeweled hand on the edge.

"The machine's off. I can serve you a drink."

"Okay, then, beer."

The woman returned to the bar. Arístides took the opportunity to observe her. He had no doubt that she was the proprietress. Judging from the look of the place, she must have a lot of money. With quick movements, he straightened out his old tie and smoothed down his hair. The woman returned. Along with the beer, she brought a bottle of cognac and a glass.

"I'll join you," she said, sitting next to him. "I have the habit of always having a drink with the last customer."

Arístides thanked her with a nod. The woman lit a cigarette.

"Beautiful night," she said. "Do you like to walk? I'm a bit of a night owl myself. But people in this neighborhood go to bed early, and after midnight I'm always completely alone."

"It's a little sad," Arístides stammered.

"I live above the bar," she said, pointing to a small door at the very back of the room. "At two I close the shutters and go to sleep."

Arístides summoned the courage to look her in the face. The woman blew the smoke out elegantly and smiled at him. The situation exhilarated him. He would have loved to pay for his drink and dash out, grab the first passerby, and tell him this marvelous story about the woman who made disconcerting advances in the middle of the night. But the woman had already stood up: "Do you have one sol? I'll put on a song."

Arístides hurriedly handed her a coin.

The woman put on some soft music and returned. Arístides looked outside: not a single shadow could be seen. Encouraged by this detail and seized by a sudden bout of courage, he asked her to dance.

"With pleasure," the woman said, leaving her cigarette on the edge of the table and taking off her fur wrap, exposing flabby freckled shoulders.

Only when he had grabbed her around the waist—taut and swathed under his untried hand—did Arístides have the conviction that he was living one of his oldest dreams, a poor bachelor's dream: to have an affair with a woman. That she was old and fat didn't matter. His imagination would soon pluck her clean of all her defects. Looking at the shelves filled with bottles that were swirling around him, Arístides was reconciled to life; splitting off from himself, he mocked that other Arístides, already distant and forgotten, who trembled from joy for a week after a stranger asked him the time.

When they finished dancing, they returned to the table, where they conversed for a few moments. The woman offered him a glass of cognac. Arístides even accepted a cigarette.

"I never smoke," he said. "But I will now, I don't know why."

His sentence sounded banal to him. The woman started laughing. Arístides suggested another dance.

"First, let me close the blinds," the woman said, walking toward the terrace.

They continued to dance. Arístides saw that the clock on the wall said two. But the woman didn't make any move to leave. This seemed like a good omen, and he, in turn, offered her a cognac. He began to feel a bit cocky. He asked some rather indiscreet questions, hoping to create a more intimate atmosphere. He found out that she lived alone, that she was separated from her husband. He had taken her by the hand.

"Okay," the proprietress said, standing up, "it's time to close."

Stifling another yawn, she walked over to the door.

"I'm staying," Arístides said, in an imperious tone that surprised him.

Halfway there, the woman turned around. "Of course. We've agreed on that," she said and continued on her way.

Arístides pulled on the cuffs of his shirt then stuffed them back because they were frayed, poured himself another glass, lit a cigarette, put it out, then lit it again. From the table he watched the woman, and lost his patience with the slow pace of her movements. He watched as she picked up a glass and took it to the counter. Then she did the same thing with an ashtray, then with a cup. When all the tables were clean, he felt enormous relief. She walked to the door and, instead of closing it, stood leaning on the frame, looking outside.

"What's the matter?" Arístides asked.

"The tables on the terrace have to be put away."

Arístides stood up, cursing between his teeth. Puffing out his chest, he walked toward the door and declared: "That's a man's job."

When he reached the terrace, he suffered a shock: there were more than thirty tables and their respective arrays of chairs and ashtrays. He figured it would take at least a quarter of an hour to put it all away.

"If we leave them out they'll get stolen," the proprietress said.

Arístides got down to work. First he collected the ashtrays. Then he began with the chairs.

"But not just any which way!" the woman protested. "They have to be stacked neatly so the kid can clean in the morning."

Arístides obeyed. Halfway through his labors, he was sweating copiously. He stacked the tables, made of iron and weighing a ton each. The landlady, still wearing her apron, had a loving expression on her face as she watched him work. Sometimes, as he walked past her panting from the effort, she reached out her hand and stroked his head. That gesture lent Arístides renewed strength, giving him the illusion that he was the husband fulfilling his conjugal duties so that later he could enjoy his privileges.

"I can't go on," he complained when he saw the terrace still full of tables, as if they were under a spell and kept multiplying.

"I thought you'd have more stamina," the woman said bitingly.

Arístides looked her in the eyes.

"Buck up, there's not much more to go," she added, winking at him.

A half hour later, Arístides had cleared the entire terrace. He took out his handkerchief and wiped the sweat off his brow. He wondered if all that effort would compromise his virility. Good thing he had the entire bar at his disposal and could recover his strength with a shot. He was about to enter, when the woman stopped him. "My flowerpot! Are you going to leave that outside?"

He had not moved the flowerpot. Arístides looked at the gigantic artifact at the entrance to the terrace, where a vulgar geranium was losing its leaves. Summoning up his strength, he went over and picked it up. Doubled over with effort, he made his way to the door, and by the time he lifted his head, he saw that the woman had just shut it. From behind the glass, she was still looking at him with a cheerful expression on her face.

"Open up!" Arístides whispered.

The landlady made a negative though charming gesture with her finger.

"Open up! Can't you see my back is about to break?"

The woman again refused.

"Please, open up, this isn't a joke!"

The woman pushed the bolt, made a gracious curtsey, and turned her back. Arístides, without dropping the flowerpot, watched her turn off the lights and pick up the glasses as she slowly walked away then disappeared behind the door at the back. When everything had grown dark and silent, Arístides lifted the flowerpot over his head and dashed it to the ground. The sound of the pottery smashing brought him to his senses: in every shard he recognized a piece of his broken dream. And he felt a terrible sense of shame, as if a dog had just urinated on him.

Lima, 1958

from
THREE ELEVATING STORIES

AT THE FOOT OF THE CLIFF

to Hernando Cortés

WE ARE like the *higuerilla*, the wild castor bean plant that germinates and spreads in the steepest and least hospitable places. Look how it grows out of the sand, along riverbanks, in vacant lots, in garbage dumps. It doesn't ask anyone for any favors, just a tiny bit of space to survive. It never gets any respite, not from the sun or the salt from the sea winds, and men and tractors trample it, but the higuerilla keeps growing, propagating, feeding off rocks and garbage. That's why I say that we are like the higuerilla; we poor folks. Wherever a man from the coast finds a higuerilla, that's where he builds his house, because he knows that he, too, will be able to live there.

We found one at the bottom of the cliffs, where the Magdalena baths used to be. We were fleeing the city like bandits because the pencil pushers and the police had thrown us out of one shanty, one tenement after another. We saw that plant there, growing in all its humility among the ruins, among the many dead ducks and the many rockslides, and we decided that was where we'd build our home.

People said those baths had once been famous, in the days when men wore booties and women bathed in the sea wearing long shifts; when the beach resorts of Agua Dulce and La Herradura didn't yet exist. They also say that the last concessionaires couldn't hold out against the competition from other resorts or the solitude or the rockslides, and that's why they hauled away everything they could: they took doors, windows, guardrails, and plumbing. Time did the rest. That's why, when we arrived, we found nothing but ruins, everywhere, ruins and—in the middle of it all—higuerillas.

At first we didn't know what to eat, and we walked up and down the beach looking for clams and winkles. Then we started collecting those sand crabs called *muy muy* and boiled them to make a strong broth, which made us drunk. Later, I don't remember when, we discovered a fisherman's cove about a kilometer from there, where my son Pepe and I worked for a while, while Toribio, my youngest, did the cooking. That's how we learned to fish. We bought lines and hooks, and we started to work on our own, catching *toyos*, sea bass, tunas, which we sold at the fish market in Santa Cruz.

That's how we started, I and my two sons, the three of us all on our own. Nobody helped us. Nobody ever gave us a crumb, and we never asked for one. But a year later we already had our house at the base of the ravine, and it didn't matter to us that there above us, the city was growing and filling up with palaces and policemen. We had set our roots down in the salt.

I have to admit, our life was hard. Sometimes I think that Saint Peter, the patron saint of fishermen, helped us. Other times I think that he was laughing at us and turning his back, his wide back, on us.

That morning, when Pepe came running up to our embankment, his hair standing on end, as if he'd seen the devil himself, I got scared. He had been to where the fresh water seeps out of the cliff wall. He grabbed me by the arm and dragged me to a slope above our house and showed me an enormous crack that reached all the way down to the beach. We didn't know how it came about, or when, but there it was. I dug around with a shovel, trying to find out how deep it went, and then I sat down on a pile of pebbles to give it some thought.

"We're idiots!" I cursed. "What were we thinking when we built our house here? Now I understand why nobody has ever wanted to build here. The cliff collapses every certain amount of time. It won't happen today or tomorrow, but any day now it will collapse and bury us like cockroaches. We have to leave this place!"

That very morning we walked the length of the beach, looking for new shelter. I say "the beach," but you have to know what this beach is like: it's little more than a thin lip between the cliff and the sea. When the sea is high, the waves creep up the shoreline and crash against the bottom of the cliff. Then we climbed up the ravine that leads to the city and we looked in vain for a level area. It's a narrow ravine, more like a gulch, and it's full of garbage, and truck drivers block it when they dig into it to take cement.

The truth is, I started to despair. But my son Pepe had an idea.

"That's it!" he said. "We need to build a retaining wall to hold back the rockslides. We'll put up some beams, then some mainstays to hold them up, and that way the cliff will hold."

The work took several weeks. We found timbers in the old bathing huts buried under the rubble. But once we had the timber we realized we didn't have any iron bars to shore them up. In the city, they wanted to charge us an arm and a leg for every piece of rail. But the sea was right there. You never know what the sea might contain. Just as the sea gave us salt, fish, clams, polished stones, iodine that burned the skin, it also gave us iron.

When we first arrived, we saw those black iron rods appear at low tide, about fifty meters from the shore. We said to ourselves: "A ship must have run aground here a long time ago." But that wasn't it. The people who built the baths had sunk three barges there to form a breakwater. Twenty years of surf had flipped, sunk, shaken, tossed, and moved around those vessels. All the wood had rotted away (even now, some splinters wash ashore), and the nails were gone, but the iron remained, hidden under the water like a reef.

"We'll get those iron rods," I told Pepe.

Very early in the morning we would enter the water naked and swim out to the sunken barges. It was dangerous because the waves came in groups of seven and churning eddies formed when they hit the rods. But we persisted, and for weeks we tore our hands apart using all our strength to pull with ropes from the beach, dragging out a few rusty girders. Then we scraped them and painted them; then with the wood we built a wall against the slope; then we shored up the wall with the rods. This is how the retaining wall was built and our house protected from the rockslides. When we saw all the rocks piled up against our barrier, we exclaimed, "May Saint Peter protect us! Not even an earthquake could hurt us now."

In the meantime, our house had been filling up with animals. At first, it was just the dogs, those poor stray dogs that the city discards, farther and farther away, just like the people who don't pay rent. I don't know why they came here: maybe because they could smell the cooking or simply because dogs, like some people, need a master in order to live.

The first one arrived along the beach from the fishermen's cove. My son Toribio, who is shy and of few words, fed him and the dog became his slave. Later, a German shepherd came down, and when he turned fierce, we had to tether him to a stake every time strangers climbed down to the beach. Then two scrawny dogs arrived together; they had no breeding, no job, and seemed willing to perform any noble deed for a miserable piece of bone. Three tabby cats also settled in, running back and forth along the cliff, eating rats and small snakes.

At first, we shooed the animals away with sticks and stones. It was hard enough for us to keep our own bodies and souls together. But the animals always returned, in spite of all the perils, and you should have seen the gratitude they expressed with their sad snouts. No matter how tough you are, something always gives, softens, when you meet with humility. That's how we ended up taking them in.

But somebody else arrived around that time: the man who carried his shop in a sack.

He arrived in the afternoon, silently, as if no ravine could keep any secrets from him. At first we thought he was deaf, or maybe an imbecile, because he didn't talk and didn't respond and did nothing but wander up and down the beach, picking up sea urchins and squishing jellyfish. It wasn't till a week later that he opened his mouth. We were frying fish on the terrace, and breakfast smelled good. The stranger appeared from the beach and stood there, staring at my shoes.

"I'll fix them," he said.

Without knowing why, I handed them over to him, and in a few minutes, with a skill that left us with our mouths hanging open, he changed the worn and holey soles.

In return, I held out the fish pan to him. He picked out a piece with his fingers, then another, then a third one, and soon devoured the entire fish with such ferocity that a bone got stuck in his throat, and we had to give him a piece of bread and some slaps on the back to dislodge it.

From that moment on, without either me or my sons giving him anything, he started working for us. First he fixed the locks on the doors, then he sharpened the hooks, then he built an aqueduct with palm fronds that brought the spring water right to the house. His sack seemed to be bottomless because he took the strangest tools out of it, and those he didn't have he fabricated out of junk from the garbage dump. He fixed everything that was broken and invented something new out of every broken object. Our home grew richer, filled with things small and large, with things that were useful and things that were beautiful, all thanks to this man who was bent on changing everything. And he never asked for anything in return for his work: he was happy with a piece of fish and for us to leave him in peace.

When summer arrived, we found out only one thing about him: his name was Samuel.

On summer days, the gulch became lively. Poor folks who couldn't make it to the big sand beaches would come down to bathe in the sea. I would watch them cross over our embankment and spread themselves along the rocky shore, lie down next to the sea urchins and among the pelican feathers, as if they were in a garden of their choosing. For the most part they were the children of workers, public school students on vacation, or craftsmen from the outskirts of the city. They all lay in the sun until it set. As they were leaving, they would walk past the house and say, "Your beach is a little dirty. You should get it cleaned up."

I don't like to be criticized, but I did like it that they called it my beach. That's why I made an effort to clean it up a little.

Toribio and I spent some mornings picking up the paper, shells, and dead grebes, who would come, already sick, to bury their beaks in the rocks.

"Very nice," the beachgoers would say. "Things are looking better."

After cleaning the beach, I built a lean-to so the swimmers would have a little shade. Then Samuel built a waterhole with fresh water and four stone steps down the steepest part of the gulch. More and more came. Word spread. They'd say, "It's a clean beach where they even give us shade for free." Around the middle of summer, hundreds were coming. That was when it occurred to me to charge an entry fee. The truth is, I hadn't planned it: it just came to me, suddenly, without thinking.

"It's only fair," I told them. "I made stairs, I've put up shade, I give you drinking water, and in addition, you have to pass through my place to get to the beach."

"We'd pay if there was a place to change," they said.

The old bathing huts were there. We scraped the cement off them and exposed a dozen.

"Everything's ready," I said. "I'm charging only ten centavos."

The beachgoers laughed.

"One thing is still missing. You have to remove those iron rods in the sea. Don't you see, we can't swim out there. We have to stay close to shore. It just isn't worth it, not the way it is."

"Okay, we'll remove them," I said.

And, in spite of the summer being over and the beachgoers becoming fewer and fewer, I made the effort, with the help of my son Pepe, to pull the iron rods out of the sea. We already knew how to do it because we had removed some for our retaining wall. But now we had to get all of them, even those that had taken root among the seaweed. Using hooks and picks, we attacked them from every angle, as if we were sharks. We lived an underwater life, one that seemed odd to the strangers who, in the fall, sometimes came down there to watch the sunset from closer up.

"What are those men doing?" they would say. "They spend hours underwater just to bring some scrap metal back to shore."

It seemed that Pepe had committed his honor to the battle against the iron rods. Toribio, on the other hand, like the strangers, watched indifferently as he worked. He had no interest in the sea. He had eyes only for the people who came from the city. The way he looked at them always worried me, how he followed them and returned home late, his pockets full of bottle caps, or spent light bulbs, or other nonsense in which he thought he saw a path to a better life.

When winter arrived, Pepe continued to wage war against the rods in the sea. They were days filled with the white fog that arrived at daybreak, crept up the cliff, and occupied the city. At night, the lighthouses along the Costanera were transformed into halos, and from the beach we could see a milky blotch that extended from La Punta to Morro Solar. Samuel had difficulty breathing during this period and said that the humidity was killing him.

"I like the fog," I'd tell him. "The temperature is just right at night, and it's a pleasure to work the ropes."

But Samuel coughed, and one afternoon he announced that he was going to move to the upper part of the cliff, to the flat area where the truck drivers had dug into the promontory to take cement. He started to move stones there to build his new place. He lovingly collected them along the beach, choosing them for their shapes and colors, placing them in his sack, then started up the slope, singing softly, stopping every ten steps to catch his breath. My sons and I watched this labor with amazement. We said to ourselves: Samuel is capable of clearing the entire coastline of stones.

The first migration of guano birds went squawking by along the horizon; Samuel was already raising the walls of his house. Pepe, for his part, had almost finished the job. Eighty meters from the shore there was still the skeleton of a barge that was impossible to remove.

"Don't try for that one," I told him. "We'd need a crane to get it out."

But Pepe, after fishing and selling our catch, would swim out there, balance on the iron rods, and dive down, trying to find the right spot to hit. At nightfall, he'd return tired and say, "When there's not a single piece of iron left, hundreds of beachgoers will come. Then the money will rain down on our heads."

It's so strange: I didn't feel anything, didn't even have any nightmares. I was so relaxed that when I returned from the city I hung around the upper part of the ravine talking with Samuel, who was putting a roof on his house.

"They'll come, for sure!" Samuel told me, pointing to some stones that were thrown on the ground. "Today I saw people poking around here. They've left those stones as markers. My house is the first one, but soon others will follow suit."

"Better," I answered, "then I won't have to go into the city to sell my fish."

When it started getting dark, I made my way down to the house. Toribio was pacing back and forth across the embankment and looking out to sea. The sun had set a while ago and all that remained was an orange line, far away, a line that continued behind San Lorenzo Island and then on toward the northern seas. Maybe that was the warning, the one I had waited for in vain.

"I don't see Pepe," Toribio said. "He went in a while ago and I don't see him. He went out with the saw and the pole."

At that moment, I felt fear. It was a violent thing that tightened my throat, but I gathered my wits.

"Maybe he's diving," I said.

"He couldn't last that long under water," Toribio said.

Again, I felt fear. In vain I scanned the sea, looking for the skeleton of the barge. I could no longer see the orange line. Large waves came and winded around and crashed against the base of the embankment.

To give myself time, I said, "Maybe he swam to the cove."

"No," Toribio answered. "I saw him go toward the barge. His head came out to breathe several times. Then the sun went down and I didn't see anything."

At that moment I started taking off my clothes, faster and faster, then even faster, pulling the buttons off my shirt, the laces off my shoes.

"Go get Samuel!" I shouted, as I dove into the water.

When I started to swim, everything was already black: black was the sea, black the sky, black the land. I swam blindly, smashing against the waves, not knowing what I wanted. I could barely breathe. Currents of cold water hit my legs, and I thought they were *toyos* trying to bite me. I realized I couldn't continue because I couldn't see anything and because at any moment I would crash into the rods. I turned around, almost with shame. As I returned, the lights of the Costanera started going on, an entire necklace of lights that seemed to wrap around me, and at that moment I knew exactly what I had to do. When I reached the shore, Samuel was already there waiting for me.

"To the cove!" I shouted. "Let's go to the cove!"

We both started running down the dark beach. I felt my feet being torn by the rocks. Samuel stopped to give me his shoes, but I didn't want anything and I swore at him. I was looking ahead, trying to find the lights of the fishermen. Finally I stopped from exhaustion and collapsed on the shore. I couldn't get up. I started to cry with rage. Samuel pulled me into the sea and dunked me a couple of times in cold water.

"We're almost there, *Papá* Leandro!" he said. "Look, there are the lights."

I don't know how we made it. Some of the fishermen had already gone out to sea. Others were getting ready to launch.

"I beg you, on my knees!" I cried. "I've never asked you for anything, but this time I'm begging you! Pepe, my oldest, hasn't come out of the sea for an hour. We have to go look for him!"

Maybe there is a way to speak to men, a way to reach their hearts. I could see, this time, that they were all with me. They surrounded me, asked me questions, offered me sips of pisco. Then they left their nets and their ropes on the beach. Those who had just launched returned when they heard the shouts. We took off in eleven boats. We went in a line toward Magdalena, our torches lit, lighting up the sea.

When we reached the sunken barge, we formed a circle around it. While some held the torches, others dove into the water. We were diving till midnight. The light didn't reach the bottom of the sea. We bumped against each other under the water, we scratched ourselves on the iron rods, but we didn't find anything, not the pick or his sailor's cap. I didn't feel tired anymore, I wanted to keep searching till dawn. But they were right.

"He must have gotten caught in the undertow," they said. "We have to look past the shoal."

First we went in, then we came out. Samuel had a pole that he sank into the sea every time he thought he saw something. We kept going around and around in a line. I felt sick to my stomach and like an idiot, maybe because of the pisco I'd drunk. When I looked back toward the cliffs, I saw up there, behind the railing on the esplanade, the lights of automobiles and the heads of the curious. Then I said to myself: "Damned rubberneckers! They think we're throwing a party, lighting torches for our own amusement." Of course, they didn't know that I was shattered, and that I would have been capable of swallowing all the water in the sea to find my son's body.

"Before the *toyos* bite him!" I kept whispering to myself. "Before they bite him!"

Why cry, when tears neither kill nor feed. As I said to the fishermen, "The sea gives, the sea also takes."

I didn't want to see him. Someone found him, floating belly up in the sun-drenched sea. It was already the next day, and we were wandering along the shore. I had slept for a bit on the rocks until the noon sun woke me up. Then we took off for La Perla, and when we returned, a voice shouted: "There he is!" I could see something, something that the waves were pushing toward the shore.

"That's him," Toribio said. "Those are his pants."

Several men went into the sea. I saw them pushing through the rough waves and I watched them, almost without sorrow. The truth was, I was exhausted, and I couldn't even feel upset. It took several of them to pull him out, bring him to shore, swollen, to me. They told me he was blue, and the *toyos* hadn't bitten him. But I didn't see him. When they were close by, I left without looking back. All I said before leaving was: "Bury him on the beach, under some morning glories." (He always loved those flowers that grew on the cliffs, which are, like geraniums, like nasturtiums, miserable flowers, the ones nobody wants, not even for their funerals).

But they didn't listen to me. They buried him the next day in the cemetery in Surquillo.

To lose a son who works is like losing a leg or like a bird losing a wing. I was like a cripple for many days. But life reclaimed me because there was a lot to do. We had a stretch with bad catches, and the sea had become stingy. Those with boats went farther out to sea and came back in the mornings with rings under their eyes and four bonitos in their nets—barely enough to make soup.

I had smashed the statue of Saint Peter with rocks, but Samuel put it back together and placed it at the entrance to my house. Under the statue he placed a collection box. That way, people who used my ravine saw the statue and, since they were fishermen, they left five or ten centavos. That's what we lived on till summer.

I say summer because we have to name things. In these parts all the months are the same: during some periods, there might be more fog, during others, the sun is hotter. But, deep down, it's all the same. They say we live in eternal springtime. For me, the seasons aren't in the sun or in the rains but rather in the birds who pass overhead or the fish who leave or return. During some periods it's harder to live, that's all.

That summer was difficult because it was sad, because there was little warm weather and very few beachgoers. I put up a sign at the entrance that said GENTLEMEN: 20 CENTAVOS. LADIES: 10 CENTAVOS. Those who came, paid, it's true, but there weren't many. They dove in, shivered a little, then climbed back up the hill, cursing, as if it was my fault that the sun wasn't warmer.

"There are no rods anymore!" I shouted at them.

"Right," they said, "but the water's cold."

That summer, though, something important happened: they started building houses on the upper part of the cliff.

Samuel hadn't been wrong: those who left rocks as well as many others who arrived soon enough. They came alone or in groups, they looked at the esplanade, walked down the ravine, sniffed around my house, breathed in the sea air, walked back up, always looking up and down, pointing, pondering, until suddenly they'd rush to build a house with whatever they could find. Their houses were made of cardboard, dented sheet metal, rocks, reeds, burlap sacks, mats, anything that can enclose a space and separate it from the world. I don't know what those people lived off, because they knew nothing about fishing. The men left early for the city, or lay around at the doors to their shacks, watching the vultures fly overhead. The women, on the other hand, went down to the beach in the afternoons to do their laundry.

"You're lucky," they'd say to me. "You knew how to pick a spot for your home."

"I've been living here for three years," I'd answer them. "I lost a son to the sea. I have another who doesn't work. I need a woman to keep me warm at night."

They were all married or had somebody. At first they didn't pay any attention to me. Then they laughed at me. I set up a stand to sell drinks and sandwiches, so I could get by.

That's how another year passed.

August is the windy month when street urchins run through open fields flying kites. Some climb onto the *huacas*, the ancient burial mounds, so their kites will fly higher. I've always felt a little sad watching this game because at any moment the string can break, and the kite, that beautiful colorful kite with a long tail, gets tangled in the electrical wires or lost on the rooftops. Toribio was like that: I was holding onto him by a string, and I felt him getting farther and farther away, getting lost.

We talked less and less. I said to myself: "It's not my fault he lives on a cliff. Here, at least, we have a roof over our heads, a kitchen. There are people who don't even have a tree to lean against." But he didn't understand this; he had eyes only for the city. He never wanted to fish. Several times he told me: "I don't want to drown." That's why he preferred to go with Samuel to the city. He accompanied him into the seaside resorts, helping him install windows, fix plumbing. With the money he earned he went to the movies and bought adventure magazines. Samuel taught him to read.

I didn't want to see him idling about and I told him as much.

"If you like the city so much, learn a trade and go get a job. You're eighteen years old. I don't want to support slackers."

That was a lie: I would have supported him all my life, not only because he was my son but because I was afraid of being alone. In the afternoons I had nobody to talk to, and my eyes, when there was a moon, were drawn to the waves and searched for the barges, as if a voice were calling me from the depths.

Once Toribio said to me, "If you'd sent me to school I would know what to do and I could earn a living."

That time I smacked him because his words hurt me. He was gone for several days. Then he returned, without saying a word to me, and spent some time eating my bread and sleeping under my roof. From then on, he always went to the city, but he also always returned. I didn't want to ask. Something must have been going on for him to keep returning. Samuel opened my eyes: he came back for Delia, the tailor's daughter.

Several times I'd invited Delia to come sit on our embankment and have a glass of lemonade. I had noticed her among the women who came down to do laundry, because she was round, buzzing and happy, like a bee. But she had no eyes for me, only for Toribio. It's true, I could have been her father, and I was all shriveled up as if I'd been steeped in brine, and I had so many wrinkles from squinting so hard in the glare of the sun.

They met secretly in some of the many nooks and crannies around the place, behind vines, in the freshwater grottos, because what had to happen, happened. One day Toribio left, as usual, but Delia went with him. The tailor came down, furious, threatening to bring the police, but he ended up breaking down in tears. He was a poor old man, already blind, who mended things for the people in the shanty-town.

"I raised my son well," I told him, to comfort him. "He doesn't know anything now, but life will teach him how to work. Moreover, they'll get married if they get on well, just as God wishes."

The tailor was reassured. I realized that Delia was a burden for him, and that all his fuss was a show. From that day on he sent a tin can with the washerwomen so I'd give him a little soup.

It's true, it's sad to be left alone like that, with just the animals to look at. They say I talked to them and to my house and that I even talked to the sea. But maybe people lied, maybe out of envy. The only true thing was that when they came from the city and climbed down to the beach, I shouted loudly because I liked to hear my voice echoing through the ravine.

I did everything myself: I fished, I cooked, I washed my clothes, I sold the fish, I swept the embankment. Maybe that's why solitude taught me many things, such as, for example, to know my own hands, every single one of their wrinkles, their scars, or to see the many shapes of twilight. Those summer twilights were, for me, mostly like a party. I could watch them and predict their fortune. I could know what color would come next and at what spot in the sky a cloud would turn completely black.

In spite of all my work, I had a lot of extra hours, hours meant to be spent in the company of others. That was when I told myself that I had to build a boat. That's why I brought Samuel down, so he would help me. Together we went to the cove and we looked at the other boats. He made drawings. Then he told me what wood we needed. We talked a lot during that period. He asked after Toribio and said, "He's a good boy, but he did wrong to get involved with a woman. Women. What good are they? They make us curse, and they put hatred in our eyes."

The boat was coming along; we built the keel. It was pleasant to spend time on the beach, smoking, telling stories, and building something that would make me a master of the seas. When the women came down to wash clothes—there were more and more of them all the time!—they'd say to me, "Don Leandro, you're doing such good work. We need you to go out to sea and bring us something cheap to eat."

Samuel said, "The esplanade is full! Not a single person more can fit and they keep coming. Soon they'll build their houses down in the ravine, and they'll get all the way to where the waves crash."

This was true: the shanties descended like a deluge.

If the boat got only half built it was because some strange things happened that summer.

It was a good summer, that's true, full of people who came to the beach, turned red, peeled, then turned black. They all paid their entry fee, and for the first time I saw money raining down on us, as my late son Pepe would say. I kept it in two baskets under my bed, and I locked my door with two padlocks.

I said that some strange things happened that summer. One morning, while Samuel and I were working on the boat, we saw three men, wearing hats, climbing down the cliff face, holding out their arms, trying to balance so they wouldn't fall. They were clean shaven and wore shiny shoes that the dust rolled off and ran away from. They were city people.

When Samuel saw them, I could see the fear in his eyes. Lowering his head, he stared at a piece of wood, I don't know why because there was nothing to look at there. The men walked past my house and continued to the beach. Two of them were holding onto each others' arms, and the other was talking to them and pointing at the cliffs. They were walking around like this for a while, from one end to the other, as if they were in the hallways of an office building. Finally, one of them came up to me and asked me several questions. Then they left as they had come, all in a row, helping each other through the more difficult spots.

"I don't like those folks," I said. "Maybe they're going to charge me some tax."

"Neither do I," Samuel said. "They're wearing bowler hats. Bad sign."

From that day on, Samuel was nervous. Every time somebody came down the ravine, he looked up warily, and if it was a stranger, his hands would shake and he'd begin to sweat.

"I'm coming down with a fever," he said, wiping the sweat off his face.

Not true: he was trembling from fear. And for good reason, because a while later they took him away.

I didn't see it happen. They say there were three policemen and a patrol car waiting on top, at Pera del Amor. They told me that he came running down to my house, and halfway down the ravine, that man who never took a false step, slipped on a boulder. The cops grabbed him and took him away, twisting his arm and hitting him with their clubs.

There was a huge uproar because nobody knew what had happened. Some said that Samuel was a thief. Others, that many years before he had put a bomb in the house of a famous person. Since we didn't buy newspapers, we didn't know anything until a few days later when, by accident, one fell in our hands. Five years before, Samuel had killed a woman with a carpenter's chisel. He stabbed her, this woman who'd cheated on him, eight times. I don't know if it was true or it was a lie, but I do know that if he hadn't slipped, he would have come running to my house, and with my teeth I would have dug a cave in the cliff to hide him, or I would have hidden him under some rocks. Samuel was good to me. I don't care what he did to others.

The German shepherd, who had always lived with him, came to my house then walked up and down the beach howling. I petted his wide back and understood his sorrow and added my own to it. Because I'd lost everything, even the boat, which I sold, because I didn't know how to finish it. I was a crazy old man, crazy and tired, but why? I liked my house and my little piece of ocean. I looked at the railing, and I looked at the reed-covered hut, I looked at everything I'd made with my own hands, and the hands of my people, and I said to myself, "This is mine. Here I have suffered. Here I should die."

The only thing missing was Toribio. I thought that one day he had to come, it didn't matter when, because children always end up coming even if it is only to see if we are old enough, and if we only have a little time left before we die. Toribio came just when I started to build a big room for him, a beautiful room with a window facing the sea.

He was skinny and pale, with that worn-out face of young men who eat poorly and don't know what to do with their lives.

"Give me five hundred soles," he said. "I've lost one child, and I don't want the same thing to happen to the one who's on his way."

Then he left. I didn't want to detain him, but I kept building his room. I painted it with my own hands. When I got tired, I climbed up to the shantytown and chatted with the folks there. I tried to make friends, but they were all wary of me. It's difficult to make friends when you're old and live alone. People say, "There must be something wrong with that man if he's alone." The poor little kids, who don't know anything about this world, sometimes followed me and threw rocks. It's true: a man alone is like a dead body, like a ghost who walks among the living.

Those men with the hats and the patent leather shoes came several more times and walked up and down the beach. I didn't like them because I blamed them for Samuel's fate. One day I said to them, "The man helping me build the boat was a good Christian. You were wrong to turn him in. He must have had a good reason to kill his wife."

They started laughing.

"You don't know what you're talking about. We aren't the police. We're from the municipality."

They must have been, because shortly thereafter came the notification. A commission came to me from the shantytown to show me. They were up in arms. Now they treated me well, and called me "*Papá* Leandro."

Of course, I was the oldest and the most skilled, and they knew I would help them. The piece of paper said that all the inhabitants of the ravine had to leave within three months.

"It's your problem!" I said. "As for me, nobody's throwing me out of here. I've been here for seven years."

They pleaded with me so much, I ended up listening to them.

"We'll find a lawyer," I said. "This land doesn't belong to anybody. They can't kick us out."

When the lawyer came, we met at my house. He was a short little man, who wore glasses and a hat and carried a very well-worn briefcase full of papers.

"The city wants to build a new bathing establishment," he said. "That's why they need to clear out the area, to build a new path. But this land belongs to the state. Nobody can kick you out of here."

Then he made each head of household give him fifty soles, and he left with some signed papers. Everybody congratulated me. They said, "We don't know what we would do without you!"

The truth is, the lawyer gave us courage and we were happy.

"Nobody," we said, "nobody will kick us out of here. This land belongs to the state."

Several weeks passed. The men from the city didn't come back. I'd finished Toribio's room and put glass in the window. The lawyer sometimes came to lecture us and make us sign papers. I strutted around among the people in the shantytown, and said, "You see? You should never disrespect the old folks! If it weren't for me, you would already be nailing your stakes into the desert."

However, on the first morning of winter, a group came running down the ravine and into my house, shouting.

"They're here! They're already here!" they said, pointing up.

"Who?" I asked.

"The crew! They've started plowing a road!"

I climbed up immediately and arrived when the workers had knocked down the first abode. They had a lot of machinery. There were some policemen standing with a tall man and another shorter one, who was writing in a large notebook. I recognized this last one: even those pencil pushers made their way to our shacks.

"These are our orders," the workers said, as they broke down the walls with their equipment. "We can't do anything about it."

It's true, you could see through the cloud of dust that their work gave them sorrow.

"Orders from who?" I asked.

"The judge," they answered, and pointed to the tall man.

I went over to him. The policemen wanted to stop me, but the judge motioned to them to let me pass.

"There seems to be a mistake here," I told him. "We live on state property. Our lawyer says that nobody can throw us out of here."

"That's it precisely," the judge said. "We're removing you because you are living on land that belongs to the state."

People started shouting. The policemen cordoned off an area around the judge while the pencil pusher—as if nothing was going on—looked calmly at the sky, the landscape, and continued writing in his notebook.

"You people must have relatives," the judge said. "Anybody left without a home today should go live with relatives. Then you'll work things out from there. I'm very sorry, believe me. I'll try to help you out."

"At least let us call our lawyer!" I said. "The workers shouldn't do anything until our lawyer arrives."

"You can call him," the judge said, "but the work will continue."

"Who's going to come with me to the city?" I asked.

Several wanted to come, but I chose a few who were wearing shirts.

We took a taxi to the city center and went up the stairs together. The lawyer was there. At first he didn't recognize us, but then he started shouting.

"Cases are either won or lost! There's nothing more I can do. This isn't a shop where we return your money if the product is bad. This is a lawyer's office."

We argued for a long time, but finally we had to leave. We didn't talk on the way back, we didn't know what to say. When we reached the cliffs, the judge had already left but the police were still there. The people of the shantytown greeted us angrily. Some said the whole thing was my fault, that I had made a deal with the lawyer. I paid no attention to them. I saw that Samuel's house, the first one built on the site, had come down and all the rocks were scattered on the ground. I recognized one white stone, one that had been on the shore for a long time, near my house. When I picked it up, I saw that it was cracked. How strange: that stone, which the sea had polished and rounded for years, was now cracked. The pieces fell apart in my hands, and I went down to my house, looking at one piece and then the other, while the people hurled insults at me, and I felt a strong urge to cry.

"Those people!" I said to myself the following days. "Let them be crushed, splattered! As for my house, it won't be so easy for them to bring their machinery here. There's too much cliff to cut through!"

It was true: the crew worked slowly. When nobody was watching, they dropped their tools and smoked, chatting among themselves.

"It's a real pity," they'd say, "but those are our instructions."

In spite of the insults, I also thought it was a pity. That's why I didn't go up there, so as not to see the destruction. To get to the city, I used the ravine in La Pampilla. There I ran into the fishermen and told them: "They're throwing the shantytown out to sea."

They merely said, "It's an outrage."

We knew it, of course, but what could we do? We were divided, fighting among ourselves, we didn't have a plan, everybody wanted different things. Some wanted to leave, some wanted to protest. Some, the poorest ones, those who had no work, joined the crew and destroyed their own homes.

But most went farther down the ravine. They built their houses twenty meters from the tractors so that, the next day, they could collect what was left from them and build them again ten meters farther away. This is how the shantytown came to me, falling one stretch farther down every day, till it seemed that I would soon have to carry it on my shoulders. Four weeks after the work began, the shantytown had reached my doorstep: destroyed, defeated, full of dusty men and women who said to me, over the railing, "Don Leandro, we have to come to your embankment! We'll stay there till we find something else."

"There's no room!" I answered them. "That big room you see there is for my son Toribio, who's going to live there with Delia. Anyway, you folks never lifted a finger to help me. Go to hell! Or to the desert, for all I care!"

But that was unfair. I knew very well that the women's bathing huts, made of wood, and the men's huts, made of reeds, could shelter those who'd been evicted. I turned this idea over in my head. It was winter, so the huts were empty. But I didn't want to say anything, perhaps so they'd really know what suffering is. Finally, I gave in.

"The women who are pregnant can come." (Almost all of them were pregnant, because in the arid shantytowns, among so much that is shriveled and wilted, the only things that always flower, that are always on the verge of ripening, are the bellies of our women.) "They can stay in the wood huts and manage there!"

The women came. But the next day I had to let in the children and then the men, because the crew kept advancing, patiently, that's true, but accompanied by the terrible racket of machinery and falling rocks. My house was filled with shouts and arguments. Those who couldn't fit went to the beach. It looked like a campground for people without hope, people waiting to be executed.

We lived like that for a week, I don't know why, since we knew they were going to come. One morning the crew appeared behind the railing with all its machinery. When they saw us, they stopped, not knowing what to do. Nobody made a move to give the first blow of the crowbar.

"You want to throw us into the sea?" I said. "You will not pass. Everybody knows very well that this is my house, that this is my beach, that this is my sea, that I and my sons have cleaned everything here. I've been living here for seven years and those who are with me, all of them, are my guests."

The supervisor tried to convince me. Then came the engineer. We stood our ground. We were more than fifty strong, and we were armed with all the rocks of the sea.

"You will not pass," we said, looking at each other with pride.

The machines were stopped all day. Sometimes the supervisor came down, sometimes we went up to discuss things. In the end, the engineer said he would call the judge. We believed there would be a miracle.

The judge came the next day, accompanied by the police and other gentlemen. Leaning on the railing, he spoke to us.

"We're going to work this out," he said. "Believe me, I'm very sorry about it. They can't throw you into the sea, that's obvious. We're going to find you a place to live."

"He's lying," I said later to my people. "They'll cheat us. They'll end up throwing us into a ditch."

That night, we stayed up late discussing our options. Some started to weaken.

"Maybe they'll give us a good piece of land," those who were afraid said. "Anyway, the police have their clubs, their guns, and they can shoot us."

"We can't give in," I insisted. "If we stay united, they won't be able to throw us out."

The judge returned.

"Those who want to go to Pampa de Comas, raise your hands!" he said. "I have arranged for them to give you twenty plots of land. Two trucks will come to pick you up. The city is doing you a favor."

At that moment, I felt lost. I knew they would all betray me. I wanted to protest, but I couldn't find my voice. In the midst of the silence, I saw one hand rise, then another, then another, and soon all but a small group of hands were raised, as if begging for alms.

"There's no water where they're taking you!" I shouted. "There's no work! You'll only have sand to eat! You'll have no choice but to let the sun kill you!"

But nobody paid any attention to me. They'd already begun to roll up their mattresses, quickly, eagerly, as if they were afraid of missing this last opportunity. All afternoon they paraded up the cliff through the ravine. When the last men had left, I stood in the middle of the embankment and looked at the crew, resting behind the railing. I looked at them for a long time, not knowing what to say to them, because I realized they felt sorry for me.

"You can start," I said finally, but nobody paid any attention to me.

Picking up a crowbar, I added, "Look, I'll set the example."

Some laughed. Others got up.

"It's late," they said. "The work day is over. We'll come back tomorrow."

And they left, too, leaving me humiliated though still master of my meager belongings.

That was the last night I spent in my house. I left at dawn so as not to watch. I carried everything I could toward Miraflores, followed by my dogs, always along the beach, because I didn't want to be separated from the sea. I wandered aimlessly, for a while watching the waves, then looking at the cliffs, tired of life, actually, tired of everything, as the day dawned.

When I reached the big culvert that carried all the filthy water from the city, I thought I heard somebody calling me. When I turned, I saw somebody running down the beach. It was Toribio.

"I heard they threw you out!" he said. "I've been reading the papers. I wanted to come yesterday but I couldn't. Delia is waiting for us on the embankment with our belongings."

"Go away," I answered. "I don't need you. You're no good for anything."

Toribio grabbed my arm. I looked at his hand and I saw that it was worn, that it was already the hand of a real man.

"Maybe I'm no good for anything, but you'll teach me."

I kept looking at his hand.

"I have nothing to teach you," I said. "I'll wait for you. Go get Dalia."

By the time the three of us started down the beach, there was enough light. The air we breathed was good, but we walked slowly because Delia was pregnant. I was looking, always looking, from one side to the other, for the right place. Everything looked so dry, so neglected. No morning glory or nasturtium were growing anywhere. Suddenly, Toribio, who'd gone on ahead, let out a shout: "Look! A higuerilla!"

I ran to him, and there, up against the cliff, in between the white shells, a higuerilla was growing. I looked for a long time at its rough leaves, its coarse stem, its pods covered in spikes that cut any hand that tries to caress them. My eyes clouded over.

"Here," I said to Toribio. "Hand me that crowbar!"

And, digging through the rocks, we raised the first timber of our new home.

Huamanga, 1959

from
CAPTIVES

BARBARA

I KEPT Barbara's letter for ten years. During one period, I carried it around in my pocket with the hope of finding somebody to translate it for me. Then I left it in a folder along with other old papers. Finally one afternoon, prey to one of those sudden bouts of destructiveness in which one turns a certain kind of ferocity on the annihilation of all traces of one's past, I tore it up along with everything one tears up under these circumstances: train tickets from a long journey, receipts from a hotel where we were happy, the program notes of a forgotten play. Nothing, then, remained of Barbara, and I will never know what she said to me in that letter written in Polish.

It was in Warsaw, years after the end of the war. Out of the ruins the Poles had built a new capital, a rather ugly one, riddled with concrete buildings that an architect might call totalitarian. I was among thirty thousand young people who attended one of those Youth Festivals, which later fell on harder times. In those days, we were gullible and optimistic. We believed that all we had to do was gather young people from all over the world in one city for fifteen days, have them travel, talk, dance, eat, and drink together, and that would bring peace to the world. We knew nothing of man or history.

I first saw her at one of those friendship visits—encounters, they were called—that Polish young people made to the foreign delegations. Her head was perfectly round and golden; she was tiny, agile, and slim; and her profile was so delicately drawn that it was frightening to look at it for long, as if the gaze would use it up and demolish it. We made friends using sign language. During the encounter, which was also a celebration of folklore and an exchange of virtuosities, someone danced, and Barbara sang us an enigmatic and wild song that left us smitten.

She worked in a laboratory where I went several times to pick her up. In Lenin Square, in front of the Palace of Culture, we danced every night with thousands of other young people to the music of several orchestras whose rhythms melded together. After dancing, we would all go to a dark nearby park, where, in the name of universal solidarity, we would make out. That first time, I pressed her against me so brutally that she gasped for breath then folded, as if broken, in my arms.

Unlike other young men who quickly turned their friends into lovers—at night, on the way back to our hostel, cigarettes were lit and stories of violent and vile fornications were recounted—my relationship with Barbara was rather ambiguous and slow moving. To a large extent this was due to the fact that we didn't understand each other. Barbara spoke Polish and Russian and I, Spanish and French. Reduced to facial expressions and hand gestures, our friendship was limited, even more so because we lacked the love that invents all the rest. From me there was only desire, but it was a desire that required the assistance of words to find its way, words that in this case were impossible.

One night we drank beer, a repugnant brew in a bar that pretended to be like in the West, and I saw that Barbara wanted to communicate something to me. On other occasions I had seen her making a similar motion, but now it was more explicit: she grabbed the skirt of her dress, stroked the fabric, and pulled its hem toward her knees or lifted it to carelessly show me part of her divine thigh. What did Barbara want? Had she finally managed to understand what I desired? I laughed to see her so eager and struggling with such disarming determination to communicate to me what she was thinking. Only after a lot of fuss did I understand that she wanted to tell me the following: I live outside the city, one day we will go to my house, we have to take the train.

Beautiful Barbara had finally surrendered. She understood! One night I, too, would arrive at the hostel to light my cigarette and tell my story, the one about the Latin macho claiming his small piece of this Central European garden, a story to make you laugh, to remember later and boast about, until life would take charge of voiding it of all content and reducing it to a rather paltry incident.

At long last, one hot afternoon, we set out on the trip. It had been postponed several times, I assumed because there had been one obstacle or another to us being alone at her house. I had left the strategy around this country tryst totally in Barbara's hands, but I feared that the festival would end before we managed to carry it out.

But on that hot afternoon, Barbara led me to believe that the moment had come, and we started to walk far away from Lenin Square till we reached a train station. There were just three train cars that ran regularly between one of Warsaw's ports and the suburbs to the south, and they were crammed with proletarians. When I boarded I realized that I was probably the only foreigner who dared depart from the more or less official itinerary to which we were restricted. The trip therefore became, in addition to a love escapade, a forbidden act.

The train rode through suburbs, then through farm fields, and twenty minutes later it stopped in a village, where Barbara had me get off. We picked up two communally owned bicycles from a depot at the station and continued on our way, in what became for me, from that point on, a trip tinged with unreality. We rode along dirt paths lined with trees and garden walls; we rode past old and ancestral homes surrounded by gardens and orchards; we passed peasants who stopped to watch us go by; we roused rural dogs who barked wildly behind fences; and we rode fast, Barbara in front of me, pedaling furiously, and I behind her, fascinated by her round head and her golden ponytail.

Finally, she stopped in front of a rather small house with a wooden gate that opened onto the road. I followed her, and together—laughing, happy, sweaty, and pushing our bicycles—we entered the front garden. Barbara took my hand and we ran up the wood stairs that led to the front door. She pulled a key out of her purse and opened it. We entered a dark foyer, then a living room, which I quickly examined—old, country furniture—looking for which sofa we would rest on for a moment, to prepare the mood, to speak however we could, words no longer mattered to me, my hands would be eloquent, and I felt so confident that I didn't give a damn about the man with a big mustache who was watching me from a carved wooden door-frame, and Barbara saying *boom-boom*, cutting her leg with her hand, then doing *tac-tac-tac-tac*, explaining that this was her father, a disabled war veteran and railroad employee.

But we didn't stop in the living room. Barbara was in a headlong rush, for once again she dragged me by the hand down the hallway, pushed open a door, and we found ourselves in a bedroom, where the first thing I saw was a rather narrow bed covered with a flowery cretonne bedspread. A bed. How long the road had been from our first meeting to this small space, as plain as a tomb, but so perfectly adequate, where our bodies would finally be able to speak a common language!

Barbara took off her dress and approached the bed, but instead of lying down on it she walked around it, in quite a hurry to get to an enormous wardrobe, all the time speaking to me in Polish without caring if I understood, then abruptly opened its doors.

Inside were half a dozen skirts on hangers. Barbara took them out and tried them on one by one, pointing to their printed designs, their clasps and zippers, explaining something about their cut and style, speaking that demonic language that I now understood without comprehending, full of excitement, until finally, not taking off the last one, she grew quiet in front of the garments piled on the bed and stared at me eagerly.

"Many skirts," I said, finally.

But she seemed to be waiting for something else and continued to interrogate me with her gaze.

"Pretty skirts," I added, "*bonitas*, *molto bellas*, beautiful, many skirts, pretty skirts."

She understood and smiled. Sighing, she took a moment to look at her garments and then, slowly, she placed them back on their hang-ers and hung them up in the wardrobe. She took out a blouse and put it on. As she closed the wardrobe doors, she kept smiling and indicated that it was time to leave. We didn't stop in the living room this time, either—out of the corner of my eye, I saw the mustachioed man's gaze, surly, fierce—and found ourselves in the garden picking up our bicycles. I was woozy, addled, dragging along behind her like a rag doll; I got on the bike and again found myself pedaling down the flowery lane on the way back to the station, behind the round head and the flamboyant ponytail.

We left the bicycles in the same room at the station, and minutes later we were on the suburban train back to Warsaw. Barbara wasn't talking, but I sensed neither boredom nor sadness in her silence, but rather something more akin to relief, satisfaction, and delightful serenity. Every time she looked at me, she smiled as if at her dearest pal, one who shared all her secrets and who had earned the right to contemplate, rather than her nakedness, her belongings.

The next day we left for Paris. The train cars were packed to the brim with young people drinking, singing, and bidding farewell through the windows to their ephemeral lovers. In vain I looked for Barbara among the people on the platform.

It was months later when I received her letter.

Paris, 1972

RIDDER AND THE PAPERWEIGHT

To VISIT Charles Ridder I had to travel across the width of Belgium by train. Considering the size of that country, it was like traveling from a city center to a more or less distant suburb. Madame Ana and I took the express from Antwerp at eleven in the morning, and a little before noon, after making one connection, we found ourselves on the platform in Blankenberge, a remote town on a graceless plain near the French border.

"We walk from here," Madame Ana said.

And off we went across the flat terrain, recalling that moment in Madame Ana's library when I randomly picked up one of Ridder's books and didn't put it down until I'd finished reading it.

"Then you didn't want to read anything but Ridder."

That was true. I spent a month reading his books. Timeless, they took place in a country with no name and no borders, and were as likely to feature a flamenco carnival as a Spanish jamboree or a Bavarian beer festival. Through their pages strode burly men, charlatans, and heavy drinkers who laid maidens low in meadows and challenged each other to single combat, in which strength usually triumphed over skill. His books were devoid of elegance, but they were colorful, violent, and lewd, and had the strength of a peasant's hand crushing a clod of clay soil.

Noting my enthusiasm, Madame Ana told me that Ridder was her godfather, hence our stroll through a field on our way to his home in the countryside to pay a prearranged visit. Not far away I caught sight of the gray, turbulent sea, which looked to me at that moment as if it had been excerpted from my country's landscape and inserted here. It was rather strange; maybe it was the sand dunes, the grass smothered by the sand, and the tenacity with which the waves crashed against the arid coastline.

When we turned onto another path, we caught sight of the house, a banal house like many local farmhouses, built behind a corral and surrounded by a stone wall. We reached the door, preceded by an entourage of dogs and chickens.

"I haven't seen him for at least ten years," Madame Ana said. "He lives in complete isolation."

We were greeted by an old woman, who could have been his housekeeper or his nursemaid.

"The gentleman is expecting you."

Ridder was sitting in an armchair in his living room/study, a blanket draped over his legs, and when he saw us he didn't move a muscle. Based on the size of the armchair and the shape of his boots, I could see that he was an extremely burly man, and I immediately understood that there was not so much as a crack between him and his work, that this old corpulent man—ruddy, gray, his mustache yellowed by tobacco—was the model, now probably broken-down, for his collection of colossi.

Madame Ana explained to him that I was a friend from South America and that I had wanted to meet him. Ridder indicated that I should sit down facing him while his goddaughter gave him news of the family, of everything that had happened during the long years they had gone without seeing each other. Ridder listened to her, bored, without offering a single word in response, staring at his own two enormous weather-beaten and freckled hands. Only every once in a while did he lift an eye to look at me from under his gray eyebrows, a quick blue glance, which only at those moments seemed to take on an irresistible sharpness. He would then fall back into his absent-mindedness, his lethargy.

The housekeeper had brought a bottle of wine with two glasses and tea for her employer. Our offer of a toast found no response in Ridder, who was now playing with his thumb and not touching his tea. Madame Ana kept talking, and Ridder seemed, if not pleased, at least accustomed to this chatter that furnished the silence and kept all possible interrogation under wraps.

Taking advantage of a pause in Madame Ana's account, I finally managed to slip in a sentence.

"I've read all your books, Mr. Ridder, and have truly enjoyed them. I think you are a great writer. I don't think I exaggerate: a great writer."

Far from thanking me, Ridder merely riveted his blue eyes on me, this time with a certain degree of astonishment, then pointed vaguely to the library in his living room, which took up an entire wall from floor to ceiling. In his gesture I thought I understood his response: *So much has been written.*

"But tell me, Mr. Ridder," I continued, "what world do your characters live in? What era, what place?"

"Era? Place?" he asked and, turning to Madame Ana, he asked her about a dog who had apparently belonged to someone in the family.

Madame Ana told him the story of the dog, dead now many years, and Ridder seemed to derive a special pleasure from the story, for he tasted his tea and lit a cigarette.

At that point the housekeeper entered with a small rolling table, lunch was served, and we would eat in the living room so the gentleman would not have to get out of his chair.

Lunch was painfully boring. Madame Ana, having exhausted her repertoire of news items, didn't know what to say. Ridder opened his mouth only to guzzle his food, with a voracity that stunned me. I was thinking about the disappointment, about the ferocity with which life destroys the most beautiful images we can make of it. Ridder possessed the size of his characters, but not the voice, not the inspiration. Ridder was, I now saw, a hollow statue.

Only when we came to dessert, and after drinking half a glass of wine, did he feel like talking a little. He told a story of a hunt, though the telling was convoluted, incomprehensible, for it took place in Old Castile as well as on the plains of Flanders, and the protagonist was alternately Phillip II and Ridder himself. In the end, a completely idiotic tale.

Then came the coffee and the boredom grew denser. I looked at

Madame Ana out of the corner of my eye, almost begging that we leave already, that she find an excuse to get us out of there. Ridder, moreover, addled by the food, was nodding off in his armchair, paying absolutely no attention to either of us.

Just to do something, anything, I stood up, lit a cigarette, and took a few steps around the living room/study. It was only then that I saw it: cube-shaped, blue, transparent, with beveled edges, it was on Ridder's desk behind a bronze inkwell. It was the same exact paperweight that had accompanied me from my earliest childhood until I was twenty years old, its exact replica. It had belonged to my grandfather, who had brought it from Europe at the end of the last century; he had left it to my father, and I had inherited it along with his books and papers. I could never find another one like it in Lima. It was heavy, but at the same time diaphanous, truly useful. One night in Miraflores, I was awoken by a concert of cats who were prowling on the rooftop. I went out into the garden and shouted at them threateningly. But when they continued to make a racket, I returned to my room and looked for something to throw at them, and the first thing I saw was the paperweight. I picked it up, went back out to the garden, and threw it against the bougainvillea, where the cats were yowling. They ran off, and I was able to sleep peacefully.

The first thing I did the next day when I rose was to go to the roof to retrieve my paperweight. Impossible to find. I searched the rooftop inch by inch, pushing aside the branches of the bougainvillea one by one, but there was no trace of it. It was lost, gone forever.

But now I was looking at it again, shining in the semidarkness of this Belgian interior. I walked over and picked it up, weighed it in my hands, examined its scratched edges, held it up to the light of the window, discovered its tiny air bubbles captured in the crystal. When I turned to Ridder to ask him about it, I saw that he had woken up from his nap and was staring at me anxiously.

"This is odd," I said, showing him the paperweight. "Where did you get it?"

Ridder rubbed his thumb for a moment.

"I was in the corral, about ten years ago," he said. "It was night, there was a moon, a marvelous summer moon. The chickens were making a racket. I thought it was the neighbor's dog prowling around the house. Suddenly, an object flew over the fence and landed at my feet. I picked it up. It was this paperweight.

"But, how did it get here?"

This time Ridder smiled. "You threw it."

Paris, 1971

NOTHING TO BE DONE, MONSIEUR BARUCH

MONSIEUR Baruch was wholly unaware that the postman kept pushing advertising circulars under the door. In the last three days, one had come from the Electrotherapy Society, and on the first page was a photograph of a man with the face of an imbecile under a headline that read: "Thanks to Dr. Klein's method, I am now a happy man"; there was also a flyer for Ajax detergent, offering a discount of five cents per family-size package if bought in the next ten days; finally, there came illustrated circulars offering the memoirs of Sir Winston Churchill, payable in fourteen monthly payments; a complete tool kit for home carpentry, whose pièce de résistance was an electric carpenter's brace; and finally a flyer in particularly bright colors on *The Art of Writing and Composition*, which the mailman pushed in with such prowess that it was on the verge of falling directly into Monsieur Baruch's hand. But he, in spite of being close to the door and with his eyes facing it, found little interest in any of these subjects, as he had been dead for three days.

Precisely three days earlier, Monsieur Baruch had woken up in the middle of the afternoon, after a night of total insomnia during which he had tried to remember in order all the beds he had slept in over the last twenty years and all the songs that had been popular in his youth. The first thing he did when he got up was go to the sink in the kitchen to check if it was still clogged, and if—as on the previous few days—in order to wash, he would need to fill a pot with water and rinse his fingers and the tip of his nose.

Then, without going to the trouble of changing out of his pajamas, he threw himself, out of habit, into a problem that had preoccupied him ever since Simón had let him live in that house one year earlier, and that he had never managed to solve: which of the two rooms in the apartment would be the dining room/living room and which the bedroom/office? Since his arrival, he had weighed the pros and cons of both options, and every day new objections arose that prevented him from settling on one. His puzzlement arose from the fact that both rooms were absolutely symmetrical with relation to the front door—which opened onto a tiny entryway only large enough for a coat rack—and both were furnished in similar fashion, with a sofa bed, a table, a wardrobe, two chairs, and a nonworking fireplace. The only difference was that the room on the right led into the kitchen and the one on the left into the lavatory. To have his bedroom on the right meant that the lavatory would be beyond his immediate reach, and an old problem with his bladder forced him there with unusual frequency; having it on the left implied more distance from the kitchen and his nocturnal cups of coffee, which had become a necessity of an almost spiritual order.

For all those reasons, Monsieur Baruch had slept alternatively in one or the other room and eaten at one or the other table ever since he first arrived in that house, depending on the successive and always provisional solutions he found to his dilemma. This kind of nomadic lifestyle that he led in his own home had produced a paradoxical feeling: on the one hand, he had the impression that he lived in a much bigger house, for he could imagine that he had two dining rooms and two bedroom/offices; but at the same time he realized that the similarities between the two rooms actually reduced the size of his house, for it meant the useless duplication of space, as can be derived from a mirror, for in the second room he could find nothing that wasn't in the first, and to try to add one to the other would be cheating, like someone who, while counting the books in his library, counts separately two exact editions of the same text.

Monsieur Baruch was unable to resolve the problem that day, either, and leaving it up in the air once more, he returned to the kitchen to prepare his breakfast. With his steaming cup of coffee in one hand and his dry toast in the other, he sat down at the nearest table, took meticulous stock of his frugal meal, then moved to the table in the contiguous room, where a folder with writing paper awaited him. He picked up a single sheet and wrote a few brief lines, then placed this in an envelope. On it he wrote: *Madame Renée Baruch, 17 rue de la Joie, Lyon.* Underneath, with a fountain pen and red ink, he added: *Personal and Urgent.*

Leaving the envelope in a place on the table where it could be seen, Monsieur Baruch mentally surveyed the rest of his day and chose two actions that he customarily carried out before he had to once again confront the night: buy a newspaper and make another cup of coffee and dry toast. While waiting for night to fall, he wandered from one room to the other, looking out their respective windows. The one on the right gave onto the hallway of a factory, where he never knew what they fabricated, but it must have been a place of penitence for it was only ever frequented by black, Algerian, and Iberian workers. The one of the left looked out on the roof of a garage, behind which, if he made an effort, he could glimpse a sliver of the street down which cars always drove with their lights already on. A fire truck also went by with its siren blaring. Far away, a house was on fire.

Monsieur Baruch prolonged his wanderings more than usual, convincing himself that it was time to give up his newspaper habit. Besides the help wanted ads, he never finished reading it, and he didn't understand what was being talked about anyway: What did the Vietnamese want? Who was that Carlos Lacerda person anyway? What was an electronic computer? Where was Karachi? And while he was wandering, and as night was falling, he again heard that tiny noise inside his head, which did not come, as he had discovered, from Madame Pichot's television set or from Mr. Belmonte's water heater or from the typewriter Mr. Ribeyro wrote on in the attic. It was a sound reminiscent of a wagon uncoupling from a standing train and taking off on its own unforeseen journey.

In the now dark apartment, he stood for a moment next to the light switch, wondering. What if he did go out for a walk? He barely knew the neighborhood. Since he had arrived he had studied the shortest route to the bakery, the Metro station, and the grocery store, and had restricted himself scrupulously to it. Only one time did he dare to diverge from his regular route, and he ended up in a horrible square, which he soon found out was called Reunion Square: a mound of dirt with dirty trees, broken benches, stray dogs, crippled old men, groups of unemployed Algerians, and houses, for god's sake, chancrous houses, without joy or mercy, that glared at each other in terror, as if they were suddenly going to shout and disappear in an outburst of shame.

The walk now also ruled out, Monsieur Baruch turned on the light in the room where he had left the letter, checked to make sure that it was still in its place and, crossing through the other darkened room, entered the kitchen. He shaved carefully in five minutes, put on a clean three-piece suit, and returned to examine his face in the bathroom mirror. There was nothing out of the ordinary. His long diet of coffee and toast had sunken his cheeks, it's true, and his nose, for which he always had a certain amount of commiseration due to its tendency over the years to curve downward, hung now between his cheeks like a flag lowered in a gesture of surrender. But his eyes had the same expression as always, the one that reflected his fear of traffic, air drafts, movie theaters, beautiful women, nursing homes, hoofed animals, and unaccompanied nights, and that made him startle and protect his heart with his hand whenever a stranger stopped him in the street to ask him the time.

It must have been time for the after-dinner movie, for a male voice was heard from the neighbor's television set, a voice that could have belonged to Jean Gabin at the police station speaking in slang with a cigarette hanging off his lips, but Monsieur Baruch, indifferent to the emotions surely flooding Madame Pichot, did nothing but rinse his razor, remove the blade, and turn off the light. Fully dressed, he climbed into the shower—a metal stall in a corner of the kitchen—and opened the cold-water tap to wet his head, his neck, and his three-piece suit. Holding the razor blade firmly between his thumb and index finger of his right hand, he lifted his jaw and made a short but deep incision in his throat.

The pain he felt was less sharp than he had expected, and he was tempted to repeat the operation. But, in the end, he decided to sit down in the shower with his legs crossed, and there he began to wait. His already wet clothes made him shiver, so he lifted his arm to turn off the tap. When the last drops stopped falling on his head he experienced in his chest a sensation of warmth and almost well-being, which made him remember sunny mornings in Marseille, when he would go from bar to bar in the port offering ties to sailors, without much luck, or those other mornings in Genoa, when he would help Simón in his fabric store. Then there were his plans to travel to Lithuania, where they told him he had been born, and to Israel, where he had close relatives, whom he imagined to be numerous, sketching his own features over their blank faces.

Far away, another fire truck went by with its siren blasting, and then he told himself it was absurd to be inside that dark wet stall, like someone purging a sin or hiding from a bad deed (but hadn't his whole life been one bad deed?), and that it would be better to stretch out on the sofa in either of the rooms and thereby establish a new room in his home, the mortuary chapel, a room he had known potentially existed ever since he arrived, stalking him through that symmetrical space.

He had no difficulty standing up and walking out of the shower, but just as he was about to leave the kitchen, he felt a retching that doubled him over, and he began to vomit so violently that he lost his balance. Before he could lean against the wall, he found himself lying on the ground under the lintel of the doorway, his legs in the kitchen and his trunk in the adjoining room. In the next room, a light had been left on, and from his prone position Monsieur Baruch could see the table, and on the edge of the table, the spine of the folder that held the writing paper.

He mentally scrutinized his body, hunting for a pain, a crack, a serious impairment that would reveal that his human mechanism was definitively out of order. But he felt no discomfort. The only thing he knew was that it was impossible for him to stand up, and that if something had finally happened, it was that from then on he would have to give up living a vertical life and make do with the slow existence of worms and their flat chores, their lack of prominence, their penitence skimming the ground, the dust from which they had arisen.

He then took off on a long journey across the floor strewn with circulars and old newspapers. His arms were heavy and in his effort to move forward, he began to use his jaw, his shoulders, to bend at the waist, at his knees, to scrape along the floor with the tips of his shoes. He stopped for a bit while trying to remember where he might have left that long bandage he wrapped around his waist in winter to fight his sciatica. If he had left it in the wardrobe in the first room, he would only have to advance four meters to get to it. Otherwise, his journey would become as improbable as his return to Lithuania or his voyage to the Kingdom of Zion.

While he was summoning his memory, and while he was fighting the sensation that the air had turned into something bitter and unbreathable, and while he recalled his actions of the last few weeks and the objects he kept in all the drawers in the house, Monsieur Baruch once again heard the sirens of the fire trucks, but this time they were accompanied by the clattering of the wagon uncoupling and increasing its acceleration as it struck out into the open field, without schedule or destination, obliviously passing provincial stations, beautiful sites marked by a cross on tourist maps, disconnected, intoxicated, with no consciousness other than its own speed and its condition of being something broken, separate, condemned to finish up on a forgotten track, where nothing but rust and oblivion awaited it.

Perhaps his eyelids fell or his exposed eyeballs were flooded with an opaque substance, because he ceased to see his home, his wardrobes, and his tables, and instead he saw clearly, this time, indeed, and unexpectedly, by the light of an internal projector, a magic spell, the beds he had slept in for the last twenty years, including the last double bed in the shop in Le Marais, where Renée would curl up on one side and not allow him to cross the imaginary and geometric line that divided the bed in half. Beds in hotels, boardinghouses, hostels, always narrow, impersonal, rough, and hard, and each one came punctually in its own time, not a single one was skipped, and they gathered in the space shaping up into a nocturnal and infernal train, onto which he had crawled, like now, to spend long nights, alone, seeking refuge from his fear. But what he couldn't make out were the songs, other than a disharmonious clatter, as if dozens of radio stations were playing all at the same time, fighting to drown each other out, and managing only to articulate single words, perhaps from the titles of pop tunes, words like *betrayal*, *infidelity*, *treachery*, *solitude*, *anyone*, *anguish*, *revenge*, *summer*, words without melody, words that fell hollow on his ear like tokens, and gathered there, proposing, perhaps, a charade or constituting a concise account, in chapters, of a passion that was mediocre but nonetheless catastrophic, like those in the crime section of the newspapers.

The humming stopped abruptly, and Monsieur Baruch realized that once again he could see, that he could see the lamp that was out of reach in the next room and under the lamp the inaccessible folder of writing paper. And the silence in which familiar objects now floated was worse than blindness. If it would at least start to rain on the corrugated iron or if Madame Pichot would turn up the volume on her television set or if Mr. Belmonte would decide to take a late bath, some sound, no matter how soft or loud, would rescue him from that world of silent and present things, which seemed hollow when deprived of sound, deceptive, meted out with artifice by some clever stage designer to make him believe that he was still in the realm of the living.

But he heard nothing and could not even manage to remember in which corner of the house he might have left the bandage for his sciatica, and all he could do was continue on his journey, though without much faith, for the newspapers crumpled under his effort, creating undulations and obstacles that he felt incapable of overcoming. By squinting he could read the headline, SHEILA'S ACCUSATIONS, and underneath, in smaller type, LORD CHALFONT GUARANTEES THE STRENGTH OF THE POUND STERLING, and next to it a box announcing, "A typhoon sweeps through the north of the Philippines," and then, with almost imperceptible lettering—and how tenaciously he worked to make it out—"Monsieur and Madame Lescène are pleased to announce the birth of their grandson Luc-Emmanuel." And then he felt warmth, an agreeable breeze in his chest, and immediately he heard Bernard's voice telling Renée that if they didn't raise his salary he would leave the shop in Le Marais, and Renée's that said that the young man deserved a raise, and his own voice recommending that they wait a while and the creaking of the stairs the first time he climbed down on tiptoe to spy on how they talked and joked behind the counter, between purses and umbrellas and gloves and that ripping sound that could be none other than the message Renée wrote on notebook paper before she left and that he tore to pieces after reading several times, thinking idiotically that by destroying the proof he would destroy what it proved.

The voices and sounds grew distant or Monsieur Baruch gave up tuning them in, for as he turned his eyeballs he corroborated a circumstance that forced him to immediately change his plans: the front door was closer to him than the wardrobes in both rooms and his improbable bandage. Through the crack underneath he could see the light in the stairwell. He then began to turn onto his belly—with extreme difficulty for he needed to change the entire orientation of his initial itinerary and while he was trying to do so the light on the stairway turned on and off several times, accompanied by footsteps on the stairs though probably ones that moved in circles or on the lower floors or in the basement because they never ended up approaching.

After the effort he had made to change direction, his head ceased to be supported by his jaw and fell heavily to one side, where it remained, resting on one ear. The walls and ceiling were now spinning, the fireplace passed several times in front of his eyes, followed by the wardrobe, the sofa, and the other pieces of furniture, and in the background a lamp and all those objects were chasing one another in an ever more boundless circle. Monsieur Baruch then summoned a final resource, which he had until that moment held in reserve, and tried to shout, but in all that chaos, who could assure him where to find his mouth, his tongue, his throat? Everything was scattered, and the relationship he retained with his body had become so vague that he didn't really know its shape, how big it was, how many extremities it had. By now the whirlwind had stopped, however, and what he saw in front of his eyes was a piece of newspaper on which he read, "Monsieur and Madame Lescène are pleased to announce the birth of their grandson Luc-Emmanuel."

Then he gave up all his efforts and surrendered on top of the dusty newspapers. He could just barely feel the presence of his body floating in an aqueous space or submerged in the depths of a tank. He was now swimming skillfully in a sea of vinegar. No, it was not a sea of vinegar, it was a becalmed lake. A bird was trilling in the crown of a snow-covered tree. Water flowed down a green ravine. The moon appeared in a diaphanous sky. Cattle grazed in a fertile meadow. By some odd route he had reached the pleasant landscape of the classics, where everything was music, order, light, reason, and harmony. Everything could now be explained. Now he understood, without any rationale, apodictically, that he should have had his bedroom in the place where he had left the bandage and he should have left the bandage in the place that would be his bedroom and he should have thrown Bernard out of the shop and turned Renée in for having run off with the money and chased her down in Lyon begging on his knees for her to return and he should have told Renée to leave without Bernard knowing and he should have killed himself the night she left so as not to suffer an entire year and then paid a murderer to stab Bernard or Renée or both of them or himself on the steps of a synagogue and he should have gone alone to Lithuania and left Renée in poverty and when he was young he should have married the employee of the boardinghouse in Marseille who had only one breast and he should have kept his money in the bank instead of in the house and made where he was lying the bedroom and not have gone on the first date Renée asked him for at the Café des Sports and he should have shipped out on that merchant marine ship on its way to Buenos Aries and at some point he should have sported a thick mustache and kept the bandage in the wardrobe that was closest so that now that he was dying, now so far away from that pleasant corner, having fallen to the bottom of a filthy ravine, he could have attempted an emergency rescue, given himself a stretch of time, carried on, torn up the letter, written it the next morning or the following year and continued to wander around that house, in his sixties, tired, without skill or art or ability, without either Renée or the business, watching the enigmatic factory or the roof of the garage or listening to how the water flowed through the pipes from the attic or how Madame Pichot turned on her television set.

And everything, moreover, was possible. Monsieur Baruch stood up, but in reality he continued lying down. He shouted, but he only bared his teeth. He lifted one arm, but he managed only to open his hand. That's why three days later, when the policemen knocked down the door, we found him stretched out, looking at us, and if not for the black puddle and the flies we would have thought that he was performing a pantomime, waiting for us there on the floor, his arm outstretched, anticipating our greeting.

Paris, 1967

THE FIRST SNOWFALL

THE ITEMS Torroba left were easily assimilated into the disorderly panorama of my room. Altogether, they consisted of a few pieces of dirty clothes wrapped in a shirt and a cardboard box containing some papers. At first I didn't want to store these odds and ends because Torroba had a well-earned reputation as a pickpocket, and everyone knew that the police couldn't wait to dump him on the other side of the border as an undesirable alien. But Torroba asked me in such a way, bringing his myopic and mustachioed face right up to mine, that I had no choice but to agree.

"My friend, it's just for one night! Tomorrow, I promise, I'll come get my things."

Needless to say, he didn't. His things remained there for several days. Out of sheer boredom I examined his dirty clothes and amused myself looking through his papers. There were poems, drawings, pages of a personal diary. The truth was, there were rumors in the Latin Quarter that Torroba had a lot of talent, a tentative and exploratory talent that could be applied to a range of materials, but above all to the art of living. (Some of his verses were moving: *Soldier in winter's stubble, hands and nails blue from cold.*) This may be why I developed a certain amount of interest in this vagabond bard.

A week after his initial visit, he showed up again. This time, he was carrying a suitcase held together with a rope.

"Sorry, but I still haven't found a room. You're going to have to keep my suitcase. Do you possibly have a razor I can use?"

Before I could answer, he had deposited his suitcase in a corner, gone over to the sink, and picked up my personal items. He stood in front of the mirror and whistled while he shaved, not taking the trouble to remove his sweater, his muffler, or his beret. When he finished, he dried himself off with my towel, told me some neighborhood gossip, and left, saying that he would return the next day to pick up his belongings.

The next day he did, in fact, return, but not to pick them up. On the contrary, he left me a dozen books and two teaspoons, probably stolen from a student restaurant. This time he didn't shave, but he had the nerve to eat a large chunk of my cheese and ask me to lend him a silk tie. I don't know why, because he never wore button-down shirts. Similar visits continued throughout the fall. My hotel room turned into something like a compulsory stop in his Parisian vagrancy. There he found everything he needed: a good chunk of bread, cigarettes, a clean towel, writing paper. I never gave him any money, but he made up for that in kind. I put up with him but not without a certain apprehension, and I waited eagerly for him to find a garret, where he could take refuge along with all his junk.

The inevitable finally occurred: one day Torroba arrived at my room fairly late and asked if he could spend the night.

"Right here, on the rug," he said, pointing to the rug with holes through which the hexagonal brick floor could be seen.

Although my bed was fairly wide, I agreed that he could sleep on the floor. I did so with the intention of making him uncomfortable and thereby preventing him from adopting bad habits. Apparently, however, he was used to that kind of hardship, because while I lay awake, I heard him snoring the whole night long, as if he were sleeping on a bed of roses.

And there he lay, stretched out, until almost noon. I had to jump over him to prepare breakfast. He finally rose, placed his ear to the door, then ran to the table and gulped down a cup of coffee.

"Time to leave! The landlord is upstairs."

And he was gone in a flash, and without having said goodbye.

From then on, he came every night. He arrived late, when the landlord was already snoring.

There seemed to be a tacit agreement between us, for without requesting or demanding anything, he would appear in my room, make coffee, then lie down on the threadbare rug. He rarely spoke except when he was slightly drunk. What was most disturbing was his smell. It wasn't a particularly unpleasant smell, but it was a different smell from my own, the smell of a stranger who occupied the room and gave me the sensation, even when he wasn't there, of having been invaded.

Winter came and frost began to accumulate on the windowpanes. Torroba must have lost his jacket in the course of one or another of his adventures because he now went around in his shirtsleeves, shivering. I pitied him somewhat, seeing him lying there on the ground without any blankets. One night his cough woke me up. We spoke in the darkness. He asked me, then, if he could lie down on my bed because the floor was too cold.

"Okay," I said, "just for tonight."

Unfortunately his cold lasted for days, and he took advantage of it to claim a piece of my bed. It was an emergency measure, true, but it ended up becoming the norm. By the time his cough was gone, Torroba had won the right to share my pillow, my sheets, and my blankets.

To give your bed to a vagabond is a sign of surrender. From that day on, Torroba ruled supreme over my room. He gave the impression of being the occupant, and I, the clandestine guest. Many times I returned home to find him in my bed, reading and marking up my books, eating my bread, and spilling crumbs on the sheets. He even took some surprising liberties, like wearing my underwear and painting eyeglasses on my delicate Botticelli prints.

Most worrisome to me, however, was that I didn't know if he felt any gratitude. I never heard the words *thank you* pass his lips. It's true that at night, when I ran into him at one of those sordid dives, like Chez Moineau, surrounded by Swedish lesbians, Yankee queers, and potheads, he'd invite me to his table and pour me a glass of red wine. But perhaps he did that to have a laugh at my expense, so he could say, when I left, "That guy's an imbecile I now totally own." It's true, I was somewhat fascinated by his temperament, and many times I found comfort in telling myself: "Maybe I have an unknown genius staying in my room."

Finally, something extraordinary occurred. It was midnight and Torroba hadn't shown up. I went to bed a bit worried, thinking that maybe he'd had an accident. On the other hand, I felt like I was breathing the sweet air of freedom. At two in the morning, a pebble hit the window and woke me up. When I looked out and leaned over the windowsill, I saw Torroba standing in front of the door to the hotel.

"Throw down the key, I'm freezing to death!"

The landlord always locked the door at midnight. I threw him the key wrapped in a handkerchief and went back to bed to wait for him to enter. It took him a long time; he appeared to be climbing the stairs with great caution. Finally, the door opened and Torroba appeared. But he wasn't alone: this time he was accompanied by a woman.

I looked at them in astonishment. The woman, who was made up like a mannequin and had the long fingernails of a Mandarin, didn't bother to greet me. She took a theatrical turn around the room and finally removed her coat, revealing a delicious body.

"That's Françoise," Torroba said. "She's a friend of mine. She'll sleep here tonight. She's a bit stoned."

"On the rug?" I asked.

"No, in the bed."

As I seemed hesitant, he added, "If you don't like that plan, you can sleep on the floor."

Torroba turned off the light. I sat on the bed, watching the two of them moving around in the darkness. They had probably got undressed because the smell—this time a new and unfamiliar smell—enveloped me, penetrated my nostrils, and pierced my stomach like a dart. When they got into bed, I jumped up, grabbed a blanket, and lay down on the floor. I couldn't sleep all night. The woman didn't speak (she may have fallen asleep), but Torroba, on the other hand, shook and bellowed till dawn.

They left at noon. The whole time, we didn't exchange a single word. Once alone, I locked the door and started pacing around among my papers and my disorder, smoking incessantly. Finally, as evening began to fall, I closed the curtains and started methodically throwing all of Torroba's belongings into the hallway. Outside the door to my room there formed a pile of his socks, poems, books, crusts of bread, boxes, and suitcases. When there was no longer a single trace of him in my room, I turned off the light and lay down on my bed.

I started to wait. Outside, a mighty wind was blowing. After a few hours I heard Torroba's footsteps climbing the stairs, then a long silence in front of my door. I imagined him in shock, staring at his scattered belongings.

First came a hesitant knock, then several irate knocks.

"Hey, are you there? What happened?"

I didn't answer.

"What's the meaning of this? Have you moved?"

I didn't answer.

"Quit joking and open the door!"

I didn't answer.

"Don't pretend you don't hear! I know you're there. The landlord told me you were."

I didn't answer.

"Open up, I'm getting pissed!"

I didn't answer.

"Open, it's snowing, and I'm all wet!"

I didn't answer.

"I'll just have a coffee then leave."

I didn't answer.

"Here, just a minute, I want to show you a book!"

I didn't answer.

"If you open up, I'll bring Françoise here tonight so you can sleep with her!"

I didn't answer.

For half an hour he kept shouting, begging, threatening, and insulting me. Every once in a while, he would back up his shouts with a kick that shook the door. His voice was growing hoarse.

"I came to say goodbye. Tomorrow I'm leaving for Spain. I'll invite you to my house. I live on Calle Serrano, hard as that is to believe! I have servants who wear livery!"

In spite of myself, I'd gotten up from bed.

"This is how you treat a poet? Look, I'll give you that book you saw, the one I wrote and illustrated by hand! They've offered me three thousand francs for it. I'll give it to you, it's yours!"

I went up to the door and rested my hands on the wood. I felt confused. In the darkness I groped around for the handle. Torroba kept begging. I was waiting for a sentence, a decisive one, *the* sentence that would impel me to move the handle my hands had found. But there was a long pause. When I pressed my ear to the door, I heard nothing. Perhaps Torroba, on the other side, was mirroring my position. A little while later I heard him pick up his things, then they fell out of his arms, then he picked them up again. Then, his footsteps down the stairs . . .

I ran over to the window and pushed aside a corner of the curtain. For once Torroba hadn't lied: it was snowing.

Large snowflakes fell obliquely against the façade of the hotel. People were running by on the white street, pulling down their hats and buttoning up their thick coats. The café terraces were lit and full of customers drinking mulled wine and enjoying the first snow behind the protection of the transparent partitions.

Torroba appeared on the sidewalk. He was wearing a shirt and carrying in his hands, under his arms, over his shoulders, and on his head, his heteroclite property. He lifted his face and looked up at my window, as if he knew I was there spying on him and wanted to show how forsaken he was in the blizzard. He must have been saying something because his lips were moving. He then began a hesitant stagger, full of detours, retreats, doubts, and stumbles.

By the time he crossed the boulevard on his way into the Arab neighborhood, I felt that I was suffocating in this room that seemed now too big and protected to shelter my solitude. Throwing the window open, I leaned half my body out the window and over the railing.

"Torroba!" I shouted. "Torroba, I'm here! I'm in my room!"

Torroba kept walking away through the throng of pedestrians who slipped silently along on the silent snow.

"Torroba!" I insisted. "Come, there's room for you! Don't go, Toooorrooobaaa!"

Only at that moment did he turn and look up at my window. But just when I thought he was going to return, he raised his arm with his fist clenched in a gesture that was, more than a threat, an act of revenge, then he disappeared forever in the first snowfall.

Paris, 1970

NEXT MONTH I'LL SET THINGS STRAIGHT

THE WARDROBE, OLD FOLKS, AND DEATH

THE WARDROBE in Father's room was not merely another piece of furniture but rather a house within the house. Inherited from his grandparents, it was gigantic and cumbersome and had accompanied us through all our moves, until it found its permanent place in the paternal bedroom in Miraflores.

It took up nearly half the room and almost reached the ceiling. Whenever my father wasn't there, my brothers and I would enter it. It was a genuine baroque palace, full of knobs, moldings, cornices, medallions, and columns, every last detail carved by some demented eighteenth-century woodworker. It had three chambers, each with its own physiognomy. The door on the left was heavy, like a portal, and from its escutcheon hung an enormous key, which was itself a protean toy, for we employed it interchangeably as a gun, a scepter, and a truncheon. Behind this door, my father kept his suits and an English overcoat he never wore. It was the obligatory entryway to that universe scented with cedar and naphthalene. The central chamber, our favorite because of its variety, had four large drawers at the bottom. When father died, each of us inherited one of those drawers and established over it a jurisdiction as jealously protected as the one Father had maintained over the entire wardrobe. Above the drawers was an alcove that housed approximately thirty well-chosen books. The central chamber was topped off by a high square door, always locked, and we never knew what it contained; perhaps those papers and photos that one carries around from one's youth and doesn't destroy out of fear of losing part of a life that, in reality, is already lost. Finally, the chamber on the right had another door, this one covered with a beveled-glass mirror. The drawers at the bottom contained shirts and linens, and above them was a space without shelves, large enough to stand up in.

The chamber on the left communicated with the one on the right through a high overhead passageway situated behind the alcove. One of our favorite games was to enter the wardrobe through the solid wood door and appear a short while later through the mirrored one. The upper passageway was an ideal hiding place: our friends could never find us when we used it. They knew we were in the wardrobe, but they couldn't imagine that we had scaled its architecture and were lying supine over the central chamber, as if in a coffin.

My father's bed was located directly in front of the right-hand chamber, so that when he was propped up on his pillows to read the newspaper, he could look at himself in the mirror. He would look at himself, but more than just at himself, he would look at all those who had looked at themselves. He would muse: "Here Don Juan Antonio Ribeyro y Estada looked at himself and tied his bow tie before going to the Council of Ministers," or "Here Don Ramón Ribeyro y Álvarez del Villar looked at himself before teaching his class at the University of San Marcos," or "How many times did my father, Don Julio Ribeyro y Benites, look at himself here while dressing to give a speech before Congress?" His ancestors were captives there, in the depth of the mirror. He saw them and saw his own image superimposed upon theirs in that unreal space, as if once again, by a miracle, they inhabited the same time. Through that mirror, my father penetrated the world of the dead, but he also made it possible for his grandparents to find their way, through him, into the world of the living.

We marveled at the intelligent way summer was expressing itself, its days always clear and available for pleasure, play, and happiness. My father, who had stopped smoking, drinking, and visiting with his friends after he got married, became more accommodating, and since the fruit trees in his small orchard had offered up their greatest gifts, ripe for admiration, and since a decent dinner service had finally been acquired for the household, he decided from time to time to invite over one of his old buddies.

The first was Alberto Rikets. He was a version of my father in reduced format. As a precaution, nature had gone through the trouble to edit the copy. They shared the same pallor, the same slender physique, the same gestures, and even many of the same facial expressions. All of this because they had attended the same high school, read the same books, spent the same sleepless nights, and suffered from the same long and painful illness. During the ten or twelve years that they had not seen each other, Rikets had made a fortune working doggedly in a pharmacy, which he now owned, as opposed to my father, who had only ever managed to scrape together enough money to buy the house in Miraflores.

In those ten or twelve years, Rikets had done something else: he had had a son, Albertito, whom he brought with him on his inaugural visit. Since the children of friends rarely end up being friends among themselves, we welcomed Albertito with some apprehension. We thought he was scrawny, dimwitted, and, at moments, frankly idiotic. While my father was giving Alberto a tour of the orchard, showing him the orange tree, the fig tree, the apple trees, and the grapevines, we took Albertito with us to play in our bedroom. Albertito didn't have any siblings, so he knew nothing of the collective games we played at home, was inept in the role of Indian, and much more inept when the sheriff riddled him with bullets. He had a very unconvincing way of falling down dead and was incapable of understanding that a tennis racket could also be a machine gun. For all these reasons we refused to share our best game with him, the wardrobe game, and focused instead on perfunctory and petty pastimes, which left everyone to their own devices, such as pushing around toy cars or building castles out of wood blocks.

We played while waiting for lunch, peering out the window at my father and his friend, who were now walking through the garden, for this was the season to admire the magnolia, the geraniums, the dahlias, the carnations, and the wallflowers. Years ago my father had discovered the delights of gardening and the profound truth in the shape of a sunflower or the blooming of a rose. Rather than spend his free days as he used to, reading wearisome texts that forced him to meditate on the meaning of existence, he spent them on simple tasks, such as watering, pruning, grafting, or weeding, tasks in which he invested true intellectual passion. His love of books had deviated to a love of plants and flowers. The entire garden was his oeuvre and like a character from Voltaire, he had reached the conclusion that happiness lies in cultivation.

"One day, I'll buy myself a piece of land in Tarma, not like this, a real farm, and then you'll see, Alberto, then you'll really see what I'm capable of doing," we heard my father say.

"My dear Perico, instead of Tarma, Chaclacayo," his friend responded, alluding to the luxury mansion he was building there. "Almost the same climate and only forty kilometers from Lima."

"Yes, but my grandfather didn't live in Chaclacayo, he lived in Tarma."

Again, his ancestors! And his childhood friends called him Perico.

When Albertito's toy car rolled under the bed, he crawled after it, and then we heard him let out a victory shout. He had found a soccer ball. Until that moment and while struggling to entertain him, we had been wholly unaware that if that frail and solitary child had one secret passion, one obsession, it was to kick around a leather ball.

He had received the imaginary pass and was preparing to kick it on, but we stopped him. Playing in the room was pure madness, playing in the garden was strictly forbidden, so we had no choice but to go out to the street.

That street had been the scene of dramatic matches that we played for years against the Gómez brothers, matches that lasted four or five hours and ended when it was pitch-dark, when we could no longer see goals or rivals, at which point they turned into ghostly contests, fierce and blind battles that allowed for cheating, insults, and fouls. No professional team ever invested as much hatred, fury, and vanity as we did in those childhood encounters. That's why when the Gó-mezes moved away, we forsook soccer, knowing that nothing could ever compare to those feuds, and we stashed the ball under the bed. Until Albertito found it. If he wanted soccer, we'd give him soccer, no holds barred.

We set up a goal next to the wall of the house so the ball would bounce off it, and we made Albertito the goalkeeper. He bravely blocked our first shots. But then we bombarded him with low-flying kicks, just to have the pleasure of seeing him sprawled on the ground, stretched out and defeated.

Then it was his turn to kick, and I was goalie. For such a wimp he kicked like a mule, and though I blocked his first strike, my hands were left smarting. His second kick, from the side, was a perfect goal, but the third was truly prodigious: the ball passed through my arms, flew over the wall, slipped through the branches of the climbing jasmine, soared over the crown of the cypress tree, bounced off the trunk of the acacia, and disappeared into the depths of the house.

For a while we sat and waited on the sidewalk for the maid to return the ball, which is what usually happened. But nobody appeared. Just as we were about to go look for it, the back door opened, and my father emerged, carrying the ball. He looked paler than usual and didn't say a word, but we saw him walk resolutely toward a worker who was whistling on the sidewalk across the street. When he reached him, he handed him the ball and returned to the house without even looking at us. It took the worker a moment to realize that he had just been given that ball, and when he understood, he ran off so fast that we could never have caught up with him.

Based on the dejected expression on my mother's face, which awaited us at the door when she summoned us to the table, we real-ized that something very serious had happened. With one sharp movement of her hand, she ordered us into the house.

"How could you do such a thing!" were the only words she spoke as we walked past her.

But when we noticed that one of the windows in my father's bedroom, the only one without bars, was open, we suspected what had happened: Albertito, with that masterful kick that neither he nor anybody else could repeat even if they spent their entire life trying, had managed to send the ball on an insane trajectory, which, in spite of walls and trees and bars, had hit the wardrobe mirror right in its heart.

Lunch was painful. My father, incapable of reprimanding us in front of his guest, swallowed his rage in a silence that nobody dared break. Only over dessert did he show a bit of graciousness, regaling us with a few anecdotes that cheered everybody up. Alberto followed his lead and the meal ended with laughter. This did not, however, erase the general impression that the lunch, the invitation, my father's good intentions to take up with his old friends, which he never did again, had been a total fiasco.

The Riketses left in due time and to our great terror, for we feared that our father would take the opportunity to punish us. But the visit had exhausted him, and without saying a word to us, he went to take his nap.

When he woke up, he called us to his room. He had rested and was calm, leaning back on his pillows. He had opened the windows wide so that the afternoon light would enter the room.

"Look," he said, pointing to the wardrobe.

It was truly regrettable. Having lost its mirror, the wardrobe had lost its life. Where before had been glass, there was now merely a rectangular piece of dark wood, a gloomy space that neither reflected nor said anything. It was like a shimmering lake whose waters had suddenly evaporated.

"The mirror where my grandfathers looked at themselves!" he said, sighing, and dismissed us with a wave of his hand.

From that day on, we never again heard mention of his ancestors. The disappearance of the mirror had made them disappear, as well. His past ceased to torment him and instead, curiously, he leaned into his future. Perhaps because he knew that soon he would die and that he no longer needed the mirror to reunite him with his grandparents, not in a different life, for he was a nonbeliever, but in the world that already enthralled him, as the world of books and flowers had before: the world of nothingness.

Paris, 1972

SILVIO IN EL ROSEDAL

SILVIO IN EL ROSEDAL

EL ROSEDAL was the most coveted hacienda in the valley of Tarma, not because of its size, for it was a mere five hundred hectares, but because of its proximity to the town, the fertility of its land, and its beauty. Wealthy Tarma ranchers, who owned enormous pastures and potato fields in the high cordillera, had always dreamed of owning this small estate, which, besides a place of repose and relaxation, could be turned into a model dairy, capable of supplying milk to the entire region.

But destiny conspired to deprive them of the property, for when its owner, the Italian Carlo Paternoster, decided to sell it and move to Lima, he chose a fellow countryman, Don Salvatore Lombardi, who had never, moreover, set foot in the mountains. Lombardi was also the only bidder who was able to pay Paternoster in cash and up-front. The ranchers in the mountains were much wealthier than he, and millions passed through their hands every year, but it was all invested in crops and livestock, and involved as they were in the complexity of credits and debits, they were usually able to enjoy the fruits of their fortune only in the abstract shape of bills of exchange and lines of credit.

Don Salvatore, on the other hand, had worked for forty years at a hardware store in Lima, one that he eventually purchased, and he had amassed a respectable bit of capital by squirreling away one bill at a time. His dream was to return to Tyrol, in the Italian Alps, buy a farm, show his *paesanos* that he had made a lot of money in America, and die in his native land respected by the locals and above all envied by his cousin, Luigi Cellini, who as a child had punched him in the nose and broken it, as well as stolen one of his girlfriends, but who had never set foot outside that alpine terrain, nor owned more than ten cows.

Unfortunately, it was not a good time to return to Europe, where the Second World War had just broken out. Besides, Don Salvatore had developed a lung disease. His doctor recommended that he sell the hardware store and find a peaceful place with a good climate where he could spend the rest of his life. Through mutual friends he found out that Paternoster was selling El Rosedal, so he gave up his dream of returning to Tyrol and moved to the Tarma hacienda, leaving his son in Lima to settle his affairs.

As fate would have it, he swept through El Rosedal like a summer cloud: three months after moving there and starting renovations on the manor house, after buying a hundred head of cattle and bringing furniture and even a pasta-making machine from Lima, he choked on a peach stone and died. Hence Silvio, his only heir, came to be the exclusive proprietor of El Rosedal.

The property fell upon Silvio like an elephant from a fifth-story window. Not only did he lack all skills necessary to manage a dairy ranch or anything else, but the idea of burying himself in the provinces gave him gooseflesh. The only thing he had ever wanted to do since childhood was be a virtuoso violinist and stroll along Lima's Jirón de la Unión, wearing a hat and a plaid vest, like some elegant Limeño gentlemen he had seen. But Don Salvatore had sacrificed him to his accursed idea of returning to Tyrol and wreaking revenge on his cousin Luigi Cellini. Tyrannical and miserly, he put his son to work in the store before he'd finished high school, right after his mother died, and kept him there behind the counter like any other employee— though with an allowance instead of a wage—wearing a canvas apron and dispensing screws, pliers, feather dusters, and cans of paint. He never made friends, had a girlfriend, cultivated his most secret desires, or found a place for himself in a city where he did not exist: to the wealthy Italian community, engaged in banking and industry, he was the son of an unknown hardware store owner; and to the native society, he was just another immigrant without status or power.

The only moments of happiness he had known as a child were when his mother was still alive. An extremely refined woman, she sang opera, accompanied herself on the piano, and for four years paid for violin lessons for her son out of her own savings. Then there were a few youthful nocturnal escapades in the city, where he looked for something without knowing what it was, hence never found, which cultivated in him a certain appetite for solitude, introspection, and reverie. Then came the routine at the store, his entire youth buried in the buying and selling of lackluster objects, and the progressive elimination of his most intimate hopes, until he turned into a man devoid of initiative and passion.

For him then, at forty years old, to take on the responsibility of an agricultural estate in addition to his own life seemed way beyond the pale. It was one or the other. His first thought was to sell the hacienda and live off the proceeds until they ran out. Whatever remnants of prudence he still had, however, encouraged him to hold on to the property, place it in the hands of a good administrator, and enjoy the profits, thereby freeing him up to do whatever he wished, if he ever wished to do anything. For this, he would have to go to Tarma and figure out in situ how to carry out his plan.

He had seen the hacienda only once, and fleetingly, when he had come at a moment's notice to pick up Don Salvatore's body and bring it back to Lima for burial.

Now that he returned with more time, he was impressed by the beauty of his property. It consisted of a series of ensembles that arose one out of the other, unfolding in space with the precision and elegance of a musical composition.

First of all: the house. This old two-story colonial mansion was built in the shape of a U surrounding a large dirt courtyard, with a stone arcade on the ground floor and a veranda with an enclosed glass balcony and wooden colonnades on the second, topped by a gable roof. From the middle of the central wing there rose a kind of turret, topped by a square, tiled mirador, a rather strange construction that partially ruptured the unity of the enclosed space but at the same time lent it a spiritual air. Upon entering the courtyard through the large gate that opened onto the road, one felt immediately embraced by the wings on either side and sucked into what could only be an enigmatic, serene, and delightful existence.

The servants lived on the ground floor. The upstairs, the living quarters of the masters, consisted of a series of spacious rooms, among which Silvio identified three drawing rooms, a dining room, a dozen bedrooms, an old chapel, a kitchen, a bathroom, and several other empty rooms that could be used as a library, a pantry, or something else. All the rooms were covered with old wallpaper, quite faded though still elaborate and distinctive—hunting scenes, landscapes, still lifes of fruit, or portraits of famous people of bygone times—that invited perusal rather than contemplation. And, fortunately, the rooms still had their old furnishings, for Don Salvatore had not had time to replace them with the mass-produced items still sitting in boxes in a storeroom downstairs.

Behind the house was the rose garden, *el rosedal*, for which the hacienda was named. It was an enchanted spot, where all the roses in the world, and surely since time immemorial, blossomed throughout the year. There were white roses and red roses and yellow, green, and purple roses, there were wild roses and hybrid roses, roses that looked like celestial bodies, mollusks, a tiara, the mouth of a coquette. Nobody knew who had planted them, what criteria they had used, or for what purpose, but the result was a multicolored labyrinth where the eyes could exult and wander.

Next to the garden was an orchard, with a few fig and pear trees but a full five hectares of peaches. The trees were low-growing, but their branches succumbed to the weight of the pink fleshy fruit covered in their adorable fuzz, which were a delight to the touch before being a gift to the tongue. Now Silvio understood how his father, motivated by an urge both aesthetic and gluttonous, had devoured one of those fruits whole, stone and all, paying with his life for his impulsive act.

And, passing through the gates of the orchard, the open countryside. First, the alfalfa fields, stalks growing as tall as a boy along both banks of the Acobamba River, followed by the pastures, as flat as could be, always swathed in damp grass, and along the edges of the property, a forest of eucalyptus trees that started in the flats and continued for a short way up the mountainside, where they gave way to broom, succulents, and prickly pears.

Silvio congratulated himself on not giving in to his initial impulse and selling the hacienda, and since he liked it just the way it was, he immediately gave orders to suspend the renovations that Don Salvatore had undertaken. He agreed only for them to finish repainting the light pink façade and repair the plumbing, the leaks in the roof, the wood floors, and the locks. He also refused to hire a steward and left the management of the entire place in the hands of the old foreman, Eleodoro Pumari, who, thanks to his experience and his thirty-odd descendants, was the most qualified person to fully realize the potential of his inheritance.

These minor duties required that he delay his return to Lima, though the thought that winter was in full swing on the coast weighed heavily on his decision. There was nothing Silvio hated more than winter in Lima, with its endless drizzle, never a star in the sky, and that sensation of living at the bottom of a well. In the mountains, on the other hand, it was summer, the sun shone all day long, and the cold air was dry and invigorating. He therefore decided to strike up a more intimate relationship with his property and try for a budding one with his new city.

At first, the people of Tarma gave him a reticent welcome. Not only was he not a local, but his parents were Italian, making him an outsider twice over. They soon realized, however, that he was an unassuming, healthy, sane, and serious man, as well as a bachelor. This last attribute was the best argument for them to open the doors into their clan. A bachelor was vulnerable and by definition soluble into local society.

The clan consisted of a dozen families who owned all the land in the province, all except El Rosedal, which continued to be an island apart in the sea of their power. At its head was the wealthiest and most powerful landowner, Don Armando Santa Lucía, the mayor of Tarma and the president of the social club. He was the first to invite Silvio to one of their gatherings, and the rest of the clan soon followed suit.

Silvio accepted this first invitation out of politeness and a touch of curiosity, and was gradually swept up into a round of banquets, outings, and horseback rides, which were linked one to the next according to the laws of emulation and compensation. He spent the entire summer at one hacienda or another, accepting one invitation after another. Some of these gatherings lasted for days, turning into itinerant and ever-growing parties, with new contingents continually joining in. Silvio remembered dining one Sunday at the home of Armando Santa Lucía with five other landowners, then leaving the gathering on Thursday, near the province of Ayacucho, after having breakfast with some forty landowners.

As he had little fondness for drink and ate sparingly, he turned down several of these invitations in the hopes of breaking the chain, but the rainy season had begun and gatherings took on a more intimate and tolerable aspect, now circumscribed to dinners and dances at homes in Tarma. If summer was the season for masculine escapades, winter was the empire of women. Silvio soon realized that he was surrounded by spinsters, female cousins, daughters, nieces, and goddaughters of landowners, all of whom were brazenly courting him. These mountain-dwelling families were tireless, and each always had a batch of women in reserve, whom they opportunistically placed into circulation for their ambiguous purpose. The image Silvio retained of his mother was too vivid, and his ideal of feminine beauty too refined, for him to suffer much temptation, hence the frequency of his visits slowly dwindled until he had stoically secluded himself in his hacienda.

Every day he spent there, he felt better, so much so that he kept postponing his return to Lima, where, truth be told, he had nothing at all to do. He loved walking under the stone arcade, eating a peach under a tree, watching the Pumaris as they milked the cows, leafing through old newspapers as if they referred to a nonexistent world, but above all, walking through the rose garden. Rarely did he pick a flower, but he smelled them and could identify a different species in each perfume. Every time he left the garden he felt an immediate desire to return to it, as if he had forgotten something. Several times he did just that, but he always left with the impression of having paid an imperfect visit.

Thus, several years passed. Silvio had by now fully settled into country life. He had gained a bit of weight and had the tendency to spend the entire day in his pajamas. His strolls around the hacienda became increasingly limited to the house and the rose garden, and finally he took it into his head to not leave the veranda for days and then only to go to his bedroom, where he took his meals and met with his foreman. He made so few trips to Tarma, and then only for particularly urgent matters, that the landowners stopped sending him invitations, and rumors began to circulate that questioned his mental stability or his manhood.

He traveled to Lima two or three times, usually to attend a concert or buy equipment for the hacienda, and he always returned after completing his task. Upon each return, he resumed his wanderings, recognizing his hackneyed memories of each spot though no longer deriving the same pleasure from them. One morning while shaving he thought he noticed the source of his malaise: he was growing old in a barren, lonely house without ever having really done anything besides enduring. Life couldn't possibly be that thing that is forced on us, and that we pay off, like a mortgage, without protest. What, then, could it be? In vain he looked around, searching for a clue. Everything seemed to be in its place. But there should be a sign, a clue, something that would allow him to break through the barrier of routine and indolence and finally gain access to some knowledge, to true reality. Such ephemeral restiveness! He calmly finished shaving and his skin felt fresh, in spite of his age and even if, in the depths of his eyes, he noticed a restless, supplicating flicker.

One afternoon, exceedingly bored, he picked up his binoculars and set out to do the one thing he had never done: climb the mountains of his hacienda. They rose out of the far end of the meadows, and their lower slopes were covered with eucalyptus trees. Making his way along the banks of the river and through the alfalfa fields and pastures, into the forest, he began the ascent under the blazing sun. The slope was steeper than he had expected, and it was full of cacti, magueys, and prickly pears, aggressive and harsh plants that obstructed his way with walls of thorns. The ground was rocky and inhospitable. In half an hour, he was exhausted, his hands swollen, his shoes torn, and he still hadn't made it to the ridge. With great effort he continued until he reached one peak. This was, of course, only the first, for the mountains, after a brief descent, continued to rise into the blue sky. Silvio was dying of thirst and berated himself for not having brought his canteen; giving up on the idea of continuing to climb, he sat down on a rock to contemplate the view. He was high enough up to be able to see, spread out at his feet, the entirety of his hacienda, and beyond, very far away, the rooftops of Tarma. On the other side he could make out the peaks of the eastern mountain range, the Cordillera Oriental, which formed the boundary between the mountains and the jungle beyond.

As Silvio breathed in deeply the pure mountain air, he saw that the hacienda was shaped like a triangle, the house situated in the most acute angle, which unfurled like a fan toward the rest of it. With his binoculars he could see the meadows, where a sparse sprinkling of cows was grazing, the orchard, the house, and finally, the rose garden. The binoculars were not very strong, but through them he could vaguely make out what looked like a multicolored carpet in which certain shapes tended to repeat themselves. He saw circles, then rectangles, then more circles, and everything was arranged with such

precision that he lowered his binoculars in order to get a more pan-
oramic view of the garden. But he was too far away, and with the
naked eye he saw nothing but a polychromatic blotch. Adjusting the
binoculars again, he continued his observations: the shapes were
there, but he saw them only partially and successively and from an
angle that did not allow him to reconstruct the entirety of the image.
It was very strange: he never imagined that in that motley rose garden
there existed any order at all. Once he had recovered from the ascent,
he put away his binoculars and initiated his descent.

A few days later he took a short trip to Lima to attend a performance
of *Aida* by an Italian opera company. Then he tried to have some fun,
but it was winter on the coast, it was drizzling, people walked around
wearing scarves and coughing, the city seemed to have closed its doors
against intruders; so he grew bored, missed his hermetic life at the
hacienda, and abruptly returned to El Rosedal.

Upon entering the courtyard, he was disturbed by the presence
of the turret rising from the main wing, having suddenly become
fully aware of the aberrant nature of this minaret, to which he had
never ascended due to its rotten staircase. It was clearly out of place,
fulfilled no function, and at the slightest tremor would collapse, even
if perhaps at one time it served to scan the horizon in search of an
invisible enemy. But maybe it had another purpose; whoever ordered
its construction must have had a specific goal. And, of course—how
could he not have thought of this sooner?—it could serve as a privileged vantage point to contemplate one very particular thing: the
rose garden.

He immediately instructed one of Pumari's sons to repair the
staircase and do whatever else was necessary to make it possible to
reach the observatory. As it was already late in the day, Calixto had
to work half the night replacing stairs, tying rope, hammering in
hooks, so that the next morning the way would be clear, and Silvio
could climb to the top.

He had eyes for nothing but the rose garden, nothing existed for him but to confirm what he had seen partially from the mountain: the rose beds, which seemed to be arbitrarily placed when viewed from the ground, actually composed a series of shapes. Silvio could clearly make out a circle, a rectangle, two more circles, another rectangle, and two final circles. What could this mean? Who had decided that the roses should be planted in these patterns? He retained the drawing in his head, and as soon as he descended, he reproduced it on paper. For long hours he studied this simple and asymmetrical drawing without understanding anything. Until finally he realized that he was not looking at an ornamental drawing but rather a code, one sign that pointed to another sign: the Morse code. The circles were dots and the rectangles were dashes. In vain he searched for a dictionary or other book that could confirm this. The old man, Paternoster, had left only treatises on veterinary science and growing fruit trees.

The following morning he rode on the milk cart to town and searched futilely through Tarma's only bookstore for the illuminating text. The only thing left to do was go to the post office and consult the telegraph operator. He was very busy—it was the busiest time of day—and he promised to send a copy of the Morse code alphabet with the milkman the following day.

Silvio had never waited so anxiously for anything. The milk cart usually returned around noon, but Silvio was already standing at the gateway to the hacienda much earlier, watching the road. He had only just barely heard the wheels creaking around the curve when he rushed to grab the piece of paper out of Esteban Pumari's hand. It was in an envelope, and as soon as he got to his bedroom, he tore it open. He picked up paper and pencil and turned the dots and dashes into letters to find the word RES.

A small word that left him confused. What was *res*? In Spanish, it was a beast, a head of cattle, like those that abounded on the hacienda. Of course. The original owner, a fanatic rancher, had undoubtedly wanted to represent in the garden the name of the animal species that he raised on his land and upon which his fortune depended: *res*, either a cow, a bull, or a calf.

Disappointed, Silvio threw the piece of paper on the table. He really felt like laughing. And he did laugh, but without joy, noticing that the wallpaper in his bedroom depicted flower arrangements in addition to still lifes. RES. The word had to mean something else. In Latin, of course, according to what he remembered, *res* meant "thing." But, what was a thing? A thing was everything. Silvio tried to dig deeper, to wriggle his way into the depths of this word, but he saw nothing and everything, from a jellyfish to the towers of the cathedral in Lima. Everything was a thing, but it didn't do him any good to know that. Wherever he looked, this word led him to the infinite sum of all things contained in the universe. He pondered it for a few more minutes, then, sick of the futility of his investigations, he decided to forget about it. Surely he had started down the wrong path.

In the middle of the night, however, he woke up and realized that he had been dreaming about climbing up to the tower, about the rose garden, about the drawing. His mind had not stopped working on it. There it was, in his mind's eye, written in the garden and on that piece of paper, the word RES. And what if he turned it around? By reversing the letters it spelled *ser*. Silvio lit a lamp, ran to the table, and wrote SER in big letters. This discovery filled him with jubilation, but he soon realized that *ser* was as vague and broad a word as "thing" and much more so than *res*. *Ser*, in Spanish, meant "being" or "to be." But what? *Ser* was everything, too. Should he understand this word, moreover, as the noun or as the infinitive? He racked his brains for a while. If it was the noun, it had the same infinite meaning and was therefore just as useless as "thing." If it was the infinitive, it lacked an object, not indicating what it was necessary to be. This time, he sank deep into a disillusioned slumber.

In the following days, he went into Tarma quite frequently in the afternoons and without any precise purpose, to take a stroll around the plaza, wander into a store, or see a movie. The residents, surprised by his reappearance after his many months of reclusion, greeted him warmly. They noticed that he was more sociable and seemed to be wanting diversion. He even accepted an invitation to a ball that Don Armando Santa Lucía was giving at his home to celebrate having won the prize as the region's best potato grower. As always at such gatherings, Silvio found the best of Tarma society and the most select visitors to the region, as well as the single women from years past who, now more dried-up and wrinkled, had reached that twilight stage of maturity that foreshadowed a prompt descent into despair. Silvio enjoyed chatting with the landowners, listening to their advice about renewing his herds and improving the distribution of his milk, but just as the dancing began, a cunning idea came to mind, an idea that burst forth like a firecracker from the depth of his being and blinded him: it wasn't a word that was hidden in the garden, they were initials.

Without anybody understanding why, he abruptly left the gathering and took the last bus up the mountain, which could drop him off at his hacienda on the way. Upon arrival, he sat down at his desk and once more wrote out the word RES. As nothing came to mind, he reversed it and wrote SER. Immediately he thought of the sentence *Soy Excesivamente Rico*, I am exceedingly wealthy. But this was obviously a false lead. He was not a wealthy man, much less exceedingly so. The hacienda gave him enough to live on but only because he was single and frugal. He went back and studied the letters and came up with *Serás Enterrado Rápido*, you will be buried quickly, which gave him a start, despite it seeming like an unfounded prediction. He kept coming up with other sentences, fleshing them out. *Sábado Entrante Reparar*, to take notice next Saturday. Of what? *Sólo Ensayando Regresarás*, only rehearsing will you return. Where to? *Sócrates Envejeciendo Rejuveneció*, Socrates rejuvenated as he aged, which was a stupid and contradictory phrase. *Sirio Engendró Rocío*, a doubtfully poetic phrase as well as being ambiguous, for he didn't know if it meant that the star Sirius or an inhabitant of Syria engendered dew. There were an infinite number of sentences one could compose out of words beginning with these three letters. Silvio filled several pages of his notebook with sentences, including some as enigmatic and nonsensical as *Sálvate Enfrentando Rio*, save yourself facing river, *Sucedióle Encontrar Rupia*, he happened to find a rupee, or *Sóbate Encarnizadamente Rodilla*, fiercely rub knee, all of which meant simply replacing one code for another.

Without a doubt he had embarked on a futile journey. Out of sheer doggedness, he continued to try other sentences. All of them led to the ludicrous.

For months he buried himself in routine, that simulacrum of happiness. He slept late, drank several cups of coffee accompanied by their respective cigarettes, took a turn under the arcade, gave instructions to the Pumaris, went down to Tarma from time to time on futile errands, and when he grew truly bored, he traveled to Lima, where he became even more bored. As he still didn't know anybody in the capital, he'd wander through the downtown streets among the thousands of rushing pedestrians, buy trifles in the shops, treat himself to a good meal, sometimes even pluck up the courage to go to a cabaret, and on very rare occasions fornicate with a lady of the night, from which he always departed unsatisfied and dejected. And he'd return to Tarma with a vacuum in his soul, only to roam around his land, smell a rose, taste a peach, leaf through old newspapers, and wait anxiously for the shadows to arrive and carry away forever the debris of the wasted day.

One morning, while strolling through the rose garden, he ran into Felícito Pumari, who took care of the garden, and he asked him what he did to keep it so flourishing, how he watered, where he planted, how he chose which roses to plant, when and why. The lad told him only that he replaced and replanted the bushes that died. And it had always been like that. That's what his father had taught him, and his father, and his father before him.

Silvio thought he had heard something encouraging in this response: there was an order that had always been respected, a message had been transmitted, nobody dared transgress, tradition was perpetuated. This sent him back to his decoding, back to the beginning, and he made a great effort to find, if not an explanation, at least a purpose.

Res was a very unambiguous word and did not require any explanation. Motivated by the characteristics of his property and the advice of the landowners, he decided to increase his herd; he obtained expensive studs and quality cows, and after some wise crossbreeding, his herd's productivity improved considerably. Milk production increased by one hundred percent, he had to buy new carts to keep up with distribution, and his herd's renown spread throughout the region. After a while, however, the hacienda had reached its limit, and stagnated. As did Silvio's mood, for he derived no particular pleasure from having achieved a model dairy operation. His efforts had brought him a bit more profit and prestige, but that was all. He was still an obsolete bachelor who had buried his musical vocation early on and was still asking himself why the hell he had come into this world. So he abandoned his livestock breeding operation and stopped micromanaging his herd. Out of pure idleness he had let grow a scraggly and reddish beard. Also out of idleness, he returned with renewed interest to his clues, which remained undeciphered on his desk. RES = THING.

THING. Good. Maybe it meant he should acquire many things. So he made a list of everything he didn't have, and he realized he had nothing. An airplane, for example, a racehorse, a Hindu butler, a tie with red polka dots, a magnifying glass, and so on indefinitely. Once again he found himself face-to-face with infinity. He then decided that he should make a list of the things he had and began in his bedroom: a bed, a nightstand, two sheets, two blankets, three lamps, a wardrobe, but he had filled just two sheets in his notebook when he encountered unsolvable problems: the figures in his wallpaper, for example, were they one or several things? Did he have to write down and describe each one? And when he went into the orchard, did he have to count the trees, and worse, the peaches, and even worse, the leaves? It was nonsensical, but from that angle he could also approach the infinite. He even had the thought that if the only thing he possessed was his own body, he would have spent years counting each pore, each hair, and cataloging these things, for they belonged to him. He therefore threw his inventory up in the air and looked again at his formula, reversed it, then leaned his elbows on the table in front of the word SER.

This time, he found it luminous. *Ser* was not only the infinitive of the verb and a noun, but was also an imperative, an order: Be! That's precisely what he should do. Then he asked himself what he should be and discovered that what he never should have been was what he was being at that moment: a pathetic fool surrounded by cows and eucalyptus trees who spent whole days shut away in a barren house playing with letter combinations in a notebook. A few ideas of what he should be passed through his head. "To be" one of those dandies strolling down the Jirón de la Unión, tossing out compliments to the lovely ladies. "To be" an excellent javelin thrower and surpass even by a few centimeters that horse-faced kid at school who would throw any object whatsoever whether round, short, or sharp, farther than anybody else. Or "to be"—why not?—what he had always wanted to be: a violinist like Jascha Heifetz, for example, whose photo he saw many times as a child in *Life* magazine, dressed in an impeccable tuxedo playing his instrument with his eyes closed in front of an orchestra to a rapturous audience.

The idea didn't sound so bad, so he dug out his instrument, removed it from its case, and began to do the exercises from his childhood. He applied himself to this task with a discipline that surprised him. Within a few months, practicing five or six hours a day, his fingering became quite skillful, and months later he could play solos and sonatas with unusual virtuosity. But he had reached a plateau and needed a teacher. The idea of traveling to Lima for lessons disheartened him. Fortunately, as was not uncommon in the provinces, there was a little-known violinist who played at church, burials, and weddings, who was a brilliant musician and performer but had failed to attract universal admiration because he was only 1.3 meters tall and had always lived in an Andean town. Rómulo Cárdenas was thrilled at the prospect of giving him lessons, and he saw therein the possibility of fulfilling his own lifelong dream, impossible until that moment because he was the only violinist in Tarma: to one day perform the Concerto for Two Violins, by Johann Sebastian Bach.

But there he was, Silvio Lombardi. For weeks Rómulo came every day to El Rosedal and the two shut themselves up in the old chapel, worked with dogged determination, and managed to perfect the dreamed-of concerto. The Pumaris could not understand how these two gentlemen could forget even to eat in order to rub a bow against a few strings and produce a sound that, for them, didn't resonate in their souls anywhere nearly as deeply as did a good *huayno*.

Silvio thought that it was time to move from secrecy to severity, and he made a decision: to give a concert with Cárdenas and invite all of Tarma's notables to El Rosedal as a way of repaying them for all their attentions. He had invitations printed fifteen days ahead of time and passed them out to landowners, government officials, and visitors of quality. Paulo Pumari repainted the old chapel, set up benches and chairs, and converted the ancient chamber into an ideal concert hall.

The landowners of Tarma were puzzled when they received the invitations. Lombardi hosting at El Rosedal? And to listen to him play a violin duo with that midget, Cárdenas! The invitation didn't say if there would be food or dancing. Many tossed the invitation into the trash, thinking they'd tell him later that they hadn't received it, but others decided to attend the Saturday event at Silvio's hacienda. It was an opportunity to take a look at that elusive property and see how the Italian lived.

Silvio had prepared a meal for a hundred people, but only twelve showed up. The huge table he had had set up under the arcade had to be disassembled, and everybody ended up in the dining room on the second floor. After coffee, they moved to the chapel for the concert. While playing the concerto, Silvio saw out of the corner of his eye that there were only eleven people, and he was never able to figure out who the twelfth one was who had escaped or remained in the dining room having another drink or a second helping of dessert. But the concert was unforgettable. Without the help of an orchestra, Silvio and Rómulo outdid themselves; each bent over his instrument, they created a sonorous structure that the wind carried away forever, lost in infinite galaxies. At the end, the guests applauded without much enthusiasm. It was obvious that an artistic event of universal value had gone right past them without them even realizing it. Later, over drinks, they congratulated the musicians with hyperbolic phrases, but they hadn't heard a thing. Johann Sebastian Bach had walked right by them and they hadn't seen the smallest of his ringlets.

Silvio kept seeing Cárdenas and playing with him in the chapel, under the arcade, and in the middle of the rose garden, solitary concerts, true incunabula of the musical arts, with no audience other than the pigeons and the stars. But he slowly distanced himself from his colleague, finally stopped inviting him, and buried his violin at the bottom of his wardrobe. He did it without joy but also without bitterness, knowing that for those few days of inspired creativity he had been something, perhaps only fleetingly, a voice lost in sidereal space and sunk, like light, into the realm of shadows. Around that same time, he lost a tooth and, a short time later, another one, and out of laziness, or apathy, he didn't have them replaced. One morning he realized that the hair on the right side of his head had gone almost totally gray. Most of the windows enclosing the veranda were broken. Under the arcades he came across two basins full of spoiled milk. Why, dear God, wherever he looked, did he see signs of decomposition, decrepitude, and ruin?

A package from Lima shook him momentarily out of his musings. During his period of frenzied cryptography he had ordered several books, and now they had finally arrived: dictionaries, grammars, language teaching manuals. He looked through them cursorily and discovered something that amazed him: RES in Catalan meant "nothing." He spent days commandeered by this word. His interior life was spent scrutinizing it from all angles, but he failed to find anything more than the obvious: the negation of being, emptiness, absence. A sad harvest after so much effort, for he already knew that nothing was he, nothing was the rose garden, nothing was his property, nothing was the world. In spite of this certainty, he continued to throw himself into his daily chores, to which he devoted heroic resolve: to eat, dress, sleep, wash, go into town, in short, to endure, and it was like being forced every day to read the same page of a book that was poorly written, lacking in any and all charm.

Until one day he read, literally, a different page. It was a letter from Italy: his cousin Rosa was informing him of the death of her father, Don Luigi Cellini, the distant uncle that Don Salvatore had so despised. Rosa had been left destitute and with a young child, for her husband, one Lucas Settembrini, had abandoned her years before. She asked Silvio to receive her at the hacienda, promising to take up as little room as possible and to do any work required of her.

If old man Salvatore hadn't already been dead, he would have exploded in rage upon reading this letter. To think he had crushed his own soul for forty years so that in the end his property would harbor and support the family of that bully, Luigi. But these were not the considerations that made Silvio postpone his response; rather, it was his own apprehensions about having relatives living in the house. He would have to say goodbye to his bachelor life; he would have to shave, change out of his pajamas, eat properly, et cetera. But, as he didn't know what excuse to give when denying his cousin's request, he decided to lie and tell her that he was going to sell the hacienda and embark on a long journey around the world, which would end—for this seemed to be a fitting finale to his tall tale—in a monastery in the Far East, where he could spend the rest of his life in meditation.

Once he had decided how he would respond, he picked up his cousin's letter to find the address, and reread it. Only at the end of the missive did he notice something that made him tremble, as if in a reverie: his cousin signed her name Rosa Eleonora Settembrini. What was so special about this signature? He had no need to rack his brains: her initials spelled the word *res*.

Silvio wavered, bewildered, not knowing if he should give importance to his discovery and carry his inquiries further. Might he finally be in possession of the true meaning of the sign? He had pursued so many avenues followed by so many disappointments! Finally, he decided once again to submit to chance, and he answered the letter in the affirmative, sending, moreover, and as his cousin had requested, the money for the journey.

The Settembrinis arrived in Tarma three months later, having traveled on a cargo ship that stopped at every port in the world. Silvio had set up two upstairs bedrooms in a separate wing for their use. The two appeared at El Rosedal unannounced, with Lavander, the machinist, who on rare occasions used his truck as a taxi. Silvio was spending the afternoon in a lounge chair on the veranda and stroking his reddish beard, tormented by one of the many problems his insipid life offered him: should he or shouldn't he sell one of his studs to Don Armando Santa Lucía? They had just entered the gateway and stopped in the dirt courtyard, followed by Lavander carrying their luggage, when Silvio, impelled by an irrepressible urge, stood up, looked out, then leaned against the wood banister so as not to fall.

It was not his cousin or, of course, Lavander, who had rattled him but rather the sight of his niece, standing apart from the others and admiring the old mansion, her head tilted a bit to one side. This secret realm of his, this decrepit and wild kingdom, was finally welcoming its princess. Such a figure as hers could have come only from a celestial hierarchy, where replicas and fakes are impossible.

Roxana was fifteen years old. Silvio discovered in amazement that his Italian, not spoken since his mother died, was in perfect working order, as if it had been held in reserve since then, destined to become, in keeping with the circumstances, a sacred language. His cousin Rosa, despite her promise otherwise, took over the entire hacienda, house and land, from the very first day. Embittered and worn down by poverty and her husband's abandonment, she realized that El Rosedal was bigger than her village in Tyrol, that here one could own more than one hundred cows, and she devoted herself with vindictive passion to its management. One of the first things she ordered was the repair of Silvio's teeth—for he formed part of the hacienda—as well as all the broken glass on the veranda. Silvio never again saw dirty shirts tossed on the floor, cans with spoiled milk in the passageways, or piles of peaches under the trees being devoured by flies. El Rosedal began to produce cheeses and jams and, emerging from its stagnation, entered a new era of prosperity.

Roxana had turned fifteen on the ship, and it seemed as if she kept turning fifteen and would never stop turning fifteen. Silvio hated night and sleep because he saw it as time taken away from contemplating his niece. From the moment he opened his eyes, he was on his feet, begging Etelvina Pumari to bring the whitest milk, the freshest eggs, the warmest bread, and the sweetest honey for Roxana's breakfast. When, in the mornings, she accompanied him on his daily walk through the orchard, he would enter the realm of the ineffable. Everything she touched shimmered, every word she uttered became memorable, her old dresses were jewels in the crown, wherever she passed were left traces of an preternatural event and the perfume of a visitation from the divine.

Silvio's enchantment redoubled when he discovered that Roxana's middle name was Elena, and because her last name was Settembrini, her initials also spelled RES, a word now charged with so much meaning. Everything became perfectly clear: he was reaping the rewards for his sleepless nights, had finally deciphered the enigma of the garden. One night, out of sheer joy, he played an entire violin concerto by Beethoven for Roxana, without skipping a single note; he took care to ride his horse well, dyed the right side of his hair black, and memorized Rubén Darío's longest poems, all while Rosa became more and more entrenched in the management of the hacienda, with the assistance of the disconcerted tribe of Pumaris, which allowed her cousin to take delight in the education of her daughter.

Silvio made grandiose plans: to found and finance a university in Tarma, with a pleiad of richly compensated professors, so that Roxana could be the only student; to send her measurements to dressmakers in Paris so that they could regularly send her their most expensive designs; to hire a world-renowned chef and assign him the express mission of inventing a new dish for his niece every day; to invite the

Pope for every religious holiday to celebrate Mass in the hacienda's chapel. Naturally, however, he had to adapt these plans to the modesty of his resources and instead hired a Spanish teacher and a singing teacher, sent for her dresses to be made by a local spinster, and told Basilia Pumari to wear an apron and bonnet when she was serving meals, which spoiled her indigenous beauty and made her look utterly ridiculous.

At a certain point, mold began to grow around the edges of this period of bliss. Silvio noticed that sometimes Roxana would stifle a yawn behind her hand while he was talking to her or that her eyes would focus on a spot that did not correspond to his own presence. Silvio had already recounted to her ten times everything about his childhood and youth, embellishing it with the imagination of a Persian storyteller, and during long, endless evenings he had played all the music that had been written for the violin since the Renaissance. Roxana, for her part, already knew the entire hacienda by heart. There was no nook or cranny into which she had not introduced her graceful and curious nature; she was incapable of getting lost in the garden's labyrinth, she bestowed upon every tree in the orchard a glance of recognition, every bend in the river preserved the imprint of her footsteps, and the eucalyptus trees in the forest had adopted her as their deity.

But there was still one thing Roxana did not know: the word hidden in the rose garden. Silvio had never spoken to her about it, for it was his most precious secret, and anyone who wanted to discover it had to, like he, pass through all the trials of initiation. Roxana, however, was becoming more and more distracted, her spirit seemed to be trying to escape from the bounds of the estate, so he decided to regain her attention by setting her on the trail of this riddle. One day he told her that there was something at the hacienda that she would never find. Her curiosity piqued, Roxana resumed her wanderings, searching for what was hidden. Silvio had given her no further clues, so she didn't know if it was a treasure, a sacred animal, or a tree of wisdom. Wherever she went, she seemed to turn on lights in invisible rooms, and Silvio followed somberly behind her, switching them off.

After a while of not finding anything, she began to get irritated and demanded he give her more information; when Silvio refused, she became angry and told him he was a bad man and that she no longer loved him. Silvio was deeply hurt and didn't know what to do. That was when Rosa emerged from the shadows and administered the death blow.

Rosa had managed to impose her order on the hacienda, thereby concluding the first stage of her mission. That coveted estate, more prosperous than ever, would belong to them outright when Silvio disappeared. But there were other, larger estates in the Tarma region. During her frequent trips into town, she had had plenty of occasion to find out about and even visit properties with thousands of head of livestock. To possess them, she had one incomparable tool: Roxana.

On the other side, the landowners of Tarma were sensing that the girl's presence might just be their dreamed-of opportunity to finally obtain possession of El Rosedal. Roxana had never stepped foot in Tarma, captivated as she was by the charms of the hacienda and Silvio's attentions, but news of her and her beauty had come to them through her teachers.

Thus, contrary but converging interests were simultaneously set in motion, with nuptials as their petty goal, an indication that Roxana's removal from her uncle's realm would eventually come to pass.

All of this coincided with St. Anne's Festival and Roxana's sixteenth birthday. Rosa insisted that it was time for the girl to be presented to the world, and right around the same time a delegation of landowners paid a visit to El Rosedal to request that Silvio host the festival. More than an honor, this was a mark of status, one all the gentlemen wished for, but it also meant organizing large and expensive celebrations for the participation of the entire community.

Silvio said why not, perhaps this was the way to amuse Roxana, bring back the sparkle to her eyes that was fading by the day, as well as her delight at living at El Rosedal.

So he decided to combine his niece's birthday celebration and the festival and organize one big party, and he threw himself into the preparations for an entire month as if it were the most momentous event of his life. He had the courtyard leveled and fixed, the façade painted, flowerpots placed under the arcade, the veranda decorated with lanterns, the garden paths cleaned, and the orchard cleared of fallen fruit and leaves. In addition, he hired some Chinese firework makers, a dance group from Acobamba, other musicians from Huancayo, and a team of experts in the art of *pachamanca*, who would cook an array of cows, pigs, mutton, chickens, guinea pigs, and pigeons, as well as all the regional vegetables and legumes, buried in the ground with hot stones. As for the bar, he gave the Hotel Bolívar of Tarma carte blanche to provide local and imported beverages.

The party went down in the annals of provincial history. Before noon, the guests were starting to arrive from the four corners of the world. Some came by automobile, but most rode in on richly saddled horses, furnished with harnesses and stirrups of embossed silver. The men wore their traditional dress: calfskin boots, velveteen breeches, a leather or cloth jacket, a scarf tied around the neck, a felt hat, and, slung over their shoulders, a poncho, folded in thirds, made of vicuña so finely woven that the entire garment could be pulled through a wedding ring. The women were divided into Amazonian warriors and civilians, depending on whether they were married to landowners or civil servants. In total, there were some five hundred guests, for Silvio had invited landowners from as far away as Juaja, Junín, and Chanchamayo. Out of these five hundred people, at least half were the sons of landowners. Nobody knew where so many of them had come from. Dressed just like their fathers, but in brighter colors, and almost all arriving on spirited mounts, they immediately congregated in what seemed like a noisy corral of strutting roosters, each one more handsome and magnificent than the next.

Everything went according to plan, except the moment Roxana appeared, opening up a rift of silence and astonishment in the throng.

Rosa had imagined a theatrical scenario: to carpet the staircase from the veranda and have her descend to the sounds of a Viennese waltz. Silvio thought of something better: have her appear out of the air with the help of a mechanical device or rise out of an enormous cake. But finally he gave up on such baroque inventions, trusting in the majesty of her simple presence. And, indeed, from one moment to the next, Roxana was simply present, and everything else ceased to exist.

A hushed circle gathered around her, but nobody dared take a step forward or speak. Silvio also found it difficult to make the first move, but with great effort he approached the closest lady and introduced her to his niece. The introductions continued, and the din returned. But another, more circumscribed circle formed, this one made up of young men who wanted to try out their gallantry after the introductions. Having fallen in love passionately and in unison, they would have fought it out with blows and lashes if the presence of their parents and the remnants of decorum hadn't obliged them to show a certain amount of restraint.

After the aperitifs and lunch, the dancing began. Silvio started it off by dancing with Roxana, but his duties as host forced him into the arms of women who took him farther and farther away from the hub of the activity. Out of the corner of his eye he could see that Roxana was being asked to dance by an endless line of aspiring partners, who had set their minds to giving the most brilliant performance of their lives that afternoon. And there were so many, she would never end up meeting them all! The dancing continued, interrupted by toasts, jokes, and speeches until Silvio, his attention divided among the ladies and then among the gentlemen, realized that some time had passed since Roxana had changed partners. And her dance partner was no other than Jorge Santa Lucía, a young agronomist known for the soundness of his constitution, the size of his hacienda, the pleasantness of his character, and the beauty of his sweethearts. Silvio lost sight of them in the swirl, it was growing dark, and he had to give instructions for the lanterns on the veranda to be lit, after which he returned to the courtyard with inquisitive eyes and an uneasy spirit. Roxana was still dancing with her gallant, and on her face he had never seen an expression of such entranced happiness.

He offered yet another toast, danced a number with his cousin Rosa—who coiled herself around his shoulders like a clingy scarf—instructed the fireworks to be set up, and by the time it grew dark, he felt terribly tired and sad. It was, perhaps, the alcohol, which he almost never drank, or the bustle of the festivities, or the excess of food, but the truth is that he retired to the upper floor without anybody noticing or attempting to stop him. Leaning over the banister, sunk in the shadows, he contemplated the party, his party, which was gearing up into a more and more frenetic rhythm as the hours passed. The orchestra was playing furiously, the dancing couples were kicking up the dust, the drinkers crowded around the bar, the dancers from Acobamba dressed in demon costumes were leaping and bounding with mortal daring near the arcade. And Roxana, where was she? He tried to locate her, but in vain. It wasn't she, or she, or that one over there. Where was the fountain of fire, the seashell in the dark grotto, the double apple of life?

Disheartened, he went to his bedroom, picked up his violin, played a few chords, then went out onto the veranda with his instrument. He paced from one end to the other until he stopped in front of the door that led up to the minaret. It had been years since he'd gone up there. The door was shut with an old lock that he alone knew how to open. After opening it, he laboriously climbed the rotten stairs, holding on to the frayed ropes. When he reached the tiny tiled observatory, he looked down at the rose garden and searched for the figures. He couldn't make out anything, perhaps because there was not enough light. On one side there shone a bed of white roses; on another, a bed of yellow. Where was the message? What did the message say? At that moment the fireworks began, and they lit up the sky. Red, blue, orange lights exploded, shedding more light on the rose garden than ever before. Silvio again tried to distinguish the old signs, but all he saw was confusion and disorder, a capricious arabesque of hues, lines, and corollas. There was no riddle or message in that garden, or in his life. Still, he attempted a new formulation that he improvised on the spot: the letters he once thought he had found corresponded consecutively to numbers and added together equaled his age, fifty years old, the age perhaps at which he should die. But this hypothesis didn't seem either true or false, and he received it with absolute indifference. In so doing, he felt serene, sovereign. The fireworks were over. The dance began again amid cheers, applause, and singing. It was a splendid night. Picking up his violin, he pressed it against his chin and began to play for nobody amid the uproar. For nobody. And he was certain that he had never played better.

Paris
August 29, 1976

from
FOR SMOKERS ONLY

FOR SMOKERS ONLY

THOUGH I was not a precocious smoker, at a certain point my story and the story of my cigarettes blend into one. I have no clear memory of my apprenticeship, other than the first cigarette I smoked when I was fourteen or fifteen years old. It was a blonde, a Derby, offered to me by a classmate as we were leaving school for the day. I lit it fearfully under the shade of a mulberry tree, and, after taking a few drags, I felt so ill that I spent all afternoon vomiting and vowed I would never repeat the experience.

Futile vow, like so many others that followed, for when I entered university a few years later, it became essential for me to make my entrance into the Patio de Letras with a burning cigarette in hand. A few meters before passing through the portal, I had already struck the match and lit it. At that time they were Chesterfields, whose sweetish aroma I still remember. One pack would last me two or three days, and in order to buy it I had to deprive myself of other luxuries, for at that time I lived on an allowance. When I didn't have cigarettes or the money to buy them, I'd steal them from my brother. Whenever I had the chance, I'd slip my hand into the pocket of his jacket hanging on the back of a chair and pull out a smoke. I say this without a touch of shame for he did exactly the same with me. It was a tacit agreement between us and, moreover, proof that reprehensible acts, when they are reciprocal and equivalent, create a status quo and allow for harmonious cohabitation.

When the price went up, Chesterfields vanished from my sphere and were replaced by Incas—black and Peruvian. I can still see the yellow and blue pack with its Inca profile on the front. The tobacco must not have been very good, but it was the cheapest on the market. In some grocery stores, they sold them by the half or quarter pack in tissue-paper cornets. I always carried around an empty pack to hold the cigarettes I bought loose. Even so, Incas were a luxury compared to other cigarettes I smoked at the time, when my need for tobacco increased without similar adjustment to my resources. An uncle in the military would bring me "soldier cigarettes," held together by string as if they were firecrackers; a repulsive product, they contained pieces of cork, wood splinters, hay, and a few strands of tobacco. But they didn't cost me anything and could be smoked.

I don't know if tobacco is an inherited vice. Father was a moderate smoker, and he quit smoking promptly after he realized it was causing him harm. I have no memory of him smoking, except one night—I don't know on what kind of whim, for it had been years since he had given up tobacco—he took a cigarette out of the cigarette case in the living room, cut it in half with a small pair of scissors, and lit one of the halves. After one drag he put it out, declaring it to be horrible. My uncles, on the other hand, were big smokers, and the importance of uncles in the transmission of family habits and modes of behavior is well known. My paternal uncle, George, always had a cigarette hanging from his lips and lit the next one with the one before. When he didn't have a cigarette in his mouth, he had a pipe. He died of lung cancer. My four maternal uncles were slaves to tobacco their entire lives. The eldest died of tongue cancer, the second of mouth cancer, and the third of a heart attack. The fourth was about to burst from a perforated gastric ulcer, but he recovered and is still standing, and smoking.

From one of those maternal uncles, the eldest, I retain my first and most impressive memory of a passion for tobacco. We were spending the holidays at the Tulpo hacienda in the northern Andes, eight hours on horseback from Santiago de Chuco. Due to bad weather, the muleteer who brought our weekly provisions failed to arrive, and the smokers were left without cigarettes. Uncle Paco spent two or three days pacing desperately under the arcades of the house and constantly climbing up to the mirador to scan the road from Santiago. Finally, he couldn't stand it any longer and, despite everybody's protests (to prevent him from saddling up a horse, we hid the keys to the harness room), he took off on foot toward Santiago in the middle of the night and under a fierce downpour. He appeared the following day after we had finished lunch. Fortunately, he had met up with the muleteer along the road. He entered the dining room soaked, covered in mud, frozen to the bone, but smiling, with a lit cigarette between his fingers.

When I entered law school I took an hourly job with a lawyer and therefore had the means to assure my consumption of tobacco. I sent the poor Incas to hell, sentenced them to death like the cruel conquistador that I was, and placed myself at the service of a foreign power. This was when Lucky Strikes were in vogue. That lovely white packet with its red circle was my favorite. It was not only a beautiful physical object but also a status symbol and a promise of pleasure. Thousands of those packets passed through my hands, and in their wisps of smoke are shrouded my last years of law and my first literary exercises.

It is through that red circle I must necessarily venture in order to evoke those long nights of study, when I would greet the dawn in the company of my friends on the day of an exam. Fortunately, a bottle was never wanting, having appeared who knew how, and this gave smoking its complement and studying its counterbalance. Not to mention those parentheses inside of which, forgetting all about codes and briefs, we gave free rein to our dreams of becoming writers. All of that, naturally, swathed in the perfume of our Luckys. Smoking had become woven into almost every activity of my life. I smoked not only while I was studying for an exam but also while I watched a movie, while I played chess, when I approached a beautiful woman, while I walked alone along the esplanade, when I had a problem, when

I solved it. Thus, my days were traversed by a train of cigarettes, successively lit and extinguished, each one of which had its own meaning and its own value. Each one of them was precious to me, but some of them stood out from the others due to their sacramental nature, for their presence was indispensable to the performance of a specific act: the first of the day after breakfast, the one I lit after lunch, and the one that sealed the peace and repose after waging the battle of love.

Oh, woe is me, poor miserable soul that I am! I thought that my relationship with tobacco was settled and that from then on my life would be spent in the amiable, easy, loyal, and, until then, innocuous company of Lucky. Little did I know that I was going to leave Peru and that awaiting me was a nomadic existence in which cigarettes, their absence or abundance, would mark my days with rewards and disasters.

My journey by ship to Europe was truly a dream for a tobacco connoisseur like me, not only because I could buy in duty-free ports or from bootlegging sailors at rock-bottom prices but also because new vistas provided privileged settings for the act of smoking. Real-life picture postcards, so to speak: smoking while leaning on the rail of an ocean liner watching the flying fish in the Caribbean, or smoking at night in the second-class bar while playing a fierce game of darts with a gang of mafioso passengers. It was beautiful, I have to admit. But when I arrived in Spain, things changed. The scholarship I had been awarded was miserly and, after paying for room, board, and the trolley, I had barely a single peseta left. Goodbye Lucky! I had to get used to a blonde Spanish tobacco, somewhat harsh and caustic, that was called Bisonte, bison, for good reason. Fortunately we were in Iberian lands, and Franco's pathetic Spain had arranged for life to be less difficult for needy smokers. On every street corner was an old man or an old woman who sold single cigarettes out of baskets. Around the corner from my boardinghouse stood a maimed veteran of the Civil War from whom I would buy one or several cigarettes a day, depending on my available resources. The first time

I found myself without any at all, I summoned my courage and approached him to ask for one on credit. "Thought you'd never ask. Go on, take what you want. You'll pay me when you can." I was about to kiss the poor old man. It was the only place in the world where I smoked on credit.

Writers, for the most part, have been and are great smokers. Though curiously, they haven't written as many books about the life of cigarettes as they have about gambling, drugs, or alcohol. Where's the Dostoevsky, the De Quincey, or the Malcolm Lowry of cigarettes? The first literary reference to tobacco that I know of dates back to the seventeenth century and the character in *Don Juan*, by Molière. The text starts with this sentence: "Whatever Aristotle and the rest of philosophy might say, there is nothing comparable to tobacco...He who lives without tobacco, does not deserve to live." I don't know if Molière was a smoker—although at that time tobacco was inhaled through the nose or chewed—but that sentence has always seemed deep and prophetic, worthy of adoption as a motto for smokers. The great novelists of the nineteenth century—Balzac, Dickens, Tolstoy—totally disregarded the problem of tobacco addiction, and not one of their hundreds of characters, as far as I can recall, had anything to do with cigarettes. To find a literary reference to the vice, one must wait for the twentieth century. In *The Magic Mountain*, Thomas Mann places on the lips of his hero, Hans Castorp, the following words:

> I never can understand how anybody can not smoke.... When I wake in the morning, I feel glad at the thought of being able to smoke all day, and when I eat, I look forward to smoking afterwards; I might almost say I only eat for the sake of being able to smoke...But a day without tobacco would be flat, stale, and unprofitable, as far as I am concerned. If I had to say to myself to-morrow: 'No smoke to-day'—I believe I shouldn't find the courage to get up—on my honour, I'd stop in bed.

*

This observation seems quite trenchant and suggests that Thomas Mann must have been a fierce smoker, which did not prevent him from living till the age of eighty. But the only writer who has dealt extensively with the subject of cigarettes, and with unsurpassed incisiveness and humor, is Italo Svevo, who devotes thirty masterful pages to it in his novel, *Zeno's Conscience*. After him, I see nothing worth quoting, except for one sentence from the journals of André Gide, who also died in his eighties and still smoking: "Writing for me is an act that complements the pleasure of smoking."

The maimed Spaniard who sold me cigarettes on credit was a saintly man and a heavenly figure of the sort I would never encounter again. I was soon in Paris, where things took a turn for the worse. Not at the beginning, for when I arrived I had the means to adequately maintain my addiction and even enhance it further. The well-stocked French tobacconists allowed me to explore the most refined range of blonde tobaccos from the British, German, and Dutch empires, always with the goal of finding—by applying comparative and reciprocal analyses—the perfect cigarette. As I carried out this line of investigation, however, my resources continued to dwindle, until I had no choice but to make do with ordinary French tobacco. My life turned blue, for blue was the color of packs of Gauloises and Gitanes. Moreover, they were black tobacco, so my fall was doubly ignominious. By then, smoking had permeated every scene of my life, to the extent that none—except sleeping—could take place without its participation. I had reached fanatic and demonic extremes, such as not being able to open a letter without first lighting a cigarette. I often received very important letters, which I would leave on my table for hours and hours until I had acquired the cigarettes that would allow me to tear open the envelope and read it. That letter might have even contained the check that I needed to address the problem of my lack of tobacco. But order could not be overturned: first the cigarette and then the opening of the envelope and the reading of the letter. I had, by then, settled into abject madness and was ripe for the worst concessions and turpitudes.

As it happened, the day came when I was no longer able to buy French cigarettes—and, as a result, read my letters—and was obliged to commit the vile act of selling my books. I had only about two hundred, but they were the ones I loved most, the ones I had carried around for years through countries, trains, and boardinghouses, the ones that had survived all the vicissitudes of my vagabond life. I had left umbrellas, shoes, and watches everywhere, but I had never wanted to be separated from those books. Their marked, underlined, and stained pages preserved the tracks of my literary apprenticeship and, in a certain way, my spiritual journey. It was a matter of taking the first step. One day I said to myself: "This Valéry might be worth a carton of American blondes," though I was wrong, for the *bouquiniste* who took them paid me barely enough to buy a couple of packs. Then I got rid of my Balzac, which I automatically converted into two packs of Lucky Strikes. My surrealist poets were a disappointment, good for no more than one British Players. A signed Ciro Alegría, in which I had invested an inordinate amount of hope, was accepted only because I threw in Chekov's plays. I let go of Flaubert little by little, which allowed me to keep smoking those primitive Gauloises for a whole week. But the worst humiliation was when I summoned the courage to sell the last books I had: ten copies of my own book, *Featherless Vultures*, which a good friend had bravely published in Lima. When the bookseller looked at that coarse tome in Spanish written by an unknown author, he was on the verge of lobbing it at my head. "We don't take those. Go to Gibert, they buy by the kilo." And that's what I did. I returned to my hotel with a pack of Gitanes. Sitting on my bed, I lit a cigarette and stared at my empty bookshelves. My books had literally gone up in smoke.

A few days later, I was desperate, hanging around the cafés of the

Latin Quarter in search of a cigarette. Summer, cruel summer, had begun. All my friends or acquaintances, no matter how poor, had left the city for the countryside or the beaches in the south—hitchhiking, by bicycle, in any way possible. Paris seemed to be populated by Martians. At nightfall, with not much more in my stomach than a coffee and without a smoke, I slipped into a state of paranoia. Once again I walked down Boulevard Saint-Germain, starting at the Musée de Cluny and heading toward Place de la Concorde. But instead of checking out the tourist-packed outdoor cafés, my eyes were busy sweeping the ground. Who knows! Maybe I would find a fallen bill, a coin. Or a butt. I saw some, but they were crushed and wet, or somebody was walking by at that moment and the little that remained of my dignity prevented me from picking them up. Around midnight, I found myself in Place de la Concorde, at the foot of the obelisk, whose slender outline symbolized to me nothing but a gigantic cigarette. I hesitated, wondering if I should continue my rounds of the main boulevards or return in defeat to my small hotel on Rue de la Harpe. I turned toward Rue Royal, and just outside Maxim's I saw an elegant gentleman on the sidewalk lighting a cigarette and sending the porter to get him a taxi. Without a moment's hesitation I approached him and said, in my very best French, "Would you be so kind as to offer me a cigarette?" The gentleman took a step back, horrified, as if some execrable nocturnal monster had erupted into his orderly existence, and, looking to the porter for help, he turned his back on me and disappeared into the taxi that had, by then, arrived.

The blood rushed to my head, and I feared I would collapse. Like a sleepwalker, I retraced my steps, crossed the square, the bridge, and arrived at the banks of the Seine. Leaning against the railing, I looked down into the dark waters of the river and cried copiously and silently, out of rage, out of shame, like a woman, any woman at all. The incident marked me so deeply that it led me to make an irrevocable decision: to never ever again find myself in circumstances of such indigence that I would be obliged to ask a stranger for a cigarette. Never again. From then on, I had to earn my tobacco with the sweat of my brow.

I knew I was being put to the test and that better times would come, but in the meantime I pounced like a wolf upon the first job opportunity that came my way, no matter how difficult or contemptible it was; the next day I was standing in line in front of the office of *ramassage de vieux journaux* and became a collector of newsprint.

It was the first physical labor I had ever undertaken and the most exhausting, but it was also one of the most uplifting, for it allowed me to become acquainted not only with the most hideous parts of Paris but also with the most secret ones of human nature. Each of us was assigned a tricycle and a street, and we had to pedal to our street then go building-to-building, floor-to-floor, and door-to-door asking for donations of old newspapers for "poor students," until we filled the tricycle and returned to the office, rain or shine, along flat or hilly streets. I became acquainted with luxurious neighborhoods and working-class neighborhoods; I entered palaces and garrets; I came across horrible concierges who threw me out as if I were a beggar, old women who had no newspapers but gave me a franc, bourgeoisie who slammed doors in my face, lonely people who invited me to share their meager grub, randy older maidens whose insinuations were oblique, and enlightened individuals who offered formulas for spiritual salvation.

Be that as it may, in ten or more hours of work, I would manage to collect enough paper to pay for room, board, and my daily ration of cigarettes. These were the most ethical cigarettes I ever smoked, for I acquired them by slogging my guts out, and they were also the most pathetic, for there was nothing more dangerous than lighting and enjoying a smoke while riding downhill on a tricycle filled with three hundred kilos of newspapers.

The job, unfortunately, lasted only a few months. Once again, I was on the rails, though, faithful to my goal of never again begging for cigarettes, I paid for them by working as a concierge in a run-down hotel, a porter at the train station, passing out fliers, hanging posters, and, finally, occasionally cooking at the homes of friends and acquaintances.

It was during this period that I met Panchito and was able, for a stretch, to enjoy the longest cigarettes I had ever seen in my life, thanks to the smallest friend I have ever had. Panchito was a midget and smoked Pall Malls. Maybe calling him a midget is a bit of an exaggeration, for I had the impression that the more I saw of him, the taller he grew. The fact is, I met him under rather melodramatic circumstances when he was as naked as a worm. A friend invited me to cook a meal in his studio, and when I arrived I found the door ajar and a lump under a sheet on the bed. I thought that it was my friend who had fallen asleep, and as a joke I yanked the sheets off him and shouted, "Police!" To my surprise, the person thereby unveiled was a stark naked, hairless, tiny Peruvian half-breed *cholo*, who leaped up with great agility, then stood there with his horse face and stared at me in terror. When I saw him glance at the Toledo paper knife on the nightstand, it was my turn to be afraid, for no matter how defenseless a naked man may seem, he becomes dangerous when armed with a puncheon. "I'm a friend of Carlos's!" I cried out, and not a moment too soon. The little man smiled, covered himself with a robe, and held out his hand, just as Carlos was arriving with bags of groceries. Carlos introduced him to me as an old buddy who had spent the night while looking for a hotel. In the meantime, Panchito had pulled two huge suitcases out from under the bed. One was overflowing with very fine items of clothing and the other with bottles of whisky and cartons of a cigarette brand that was unknown in France at that time: Pall Mall. When he handed me the first pack of the first king size that I'd ever seen, I realized that Panchito was considerably less small than I had presumed.

From that day on, Panchito, I, and the Pall Malls made an inseparable trio. Panchito took me on as his companion, the equivalent of giving me a job, which I undertook with professional zeal. My job was to be with him. We walked through the Latin Quarter, drank aperitifs on the terraces of cafés, ate together, played one or another game of billiards, infrequently went to the movies, but most of all we talked all day and into part of the night. He paid for everything, and when we parted, he always slipped a few bills into my hand along with, unfailingly, a pack of Pall Malls.

In spite of all the time we spent together, I didn't really know who Panchito was or what kind of work he did. I gleaned many things from my long conversations with him but not enough to attain any certainty. I knew that he had spent his impoverished childhood in Lima; that as a young man he had left Peru and traveled all over Latin America; that he loved to dress well, with a jacket, hat, and Weston shoes with very high heels (which is why the first time we went out I thought he had gone through a growth spurt); that he adored gold—his watch, pen, cuff links, lighter, ruby ring, and tie clips were all gold; that he hated officers of the law and did the unspeakable to make himself invisible every time he crossed paths with a policeman; that the wad of bills he carried in his pants pocket was apparently inexhaustible; that at midnight he would disappear into the shadows for an unknown destination, without anybody ever knowing where he was staying.

After a while, some of my friends met him, and there formed around him a retinue of starving artists who had been rescued by this enigmatic Peruvian *cholo*. Panchito loved to be surrounded by those five or six white guys from Miraflores, sons of the same Peruvian bourgeoisie that had always belittled him, whom he supplied with food, drink, and housing, as if he derived an aberrant pleasure in repaying with gifts what he had received in humiliation. He paid for Santiago's violin lessons, found a studio where Luis could paint, and he financed the publication of an unsellable volume of Pedro's poems. That's how Panchito was, among other things, a patron of the arts, but he accepted nothing in return, not even gratitude.

One of the last memories I have of him, before his final disappearance, was of an event that took place on a wintry, electric, and cruel night. It was after midnight, and Panchito, Santiago, and I were sipping our last glass of wine, the one for the road, at the counter of the Relais de l'Odeon. They had closed the bar, we were the last clients, and the waiters were piling the chairs on the tables and sweeping the floor. In the mirror above the bar we saw three motionless silhouettes on the sidewalk: three Arabs dressed in heavy black coats. Santiago told us that days before, at that same bar, an Arab had tried to grope a French woman, and he, motivated by an unwary Latin sense of justice, had defended her and come to blows with the Muslim, who was forced to flee after Santiago broke a chair over his head in the best tradition of Hollywood Westerns. Speaking of the cinema, we were now living a thriller, for according to Santiago, one of the three Arabs on the sidewalk was the one he had defeated, a man who swore vengeance as he was leaving. There he was now, in that lonely and inclement night, accompanied by two henchmen, waiting for us to leave the bar so he could carry out his vendetta. What were we to do? Santiago was tall, agile, and a good fighter, but I was a scrawny intellectual, and Panchito a short Peruvian in a hat and jacket. How to confront those three sons of Allah, possibly armed with daggers with curved blades?

"Let's walk out calmly," Panchito said. And that's what we did, and we made our way down the middle of the deserted and gloomy street toward Rue de Buci. Fifty meters on we turned and saw the three Arabs, hands in the pockets of their shaggy coats, quickening their steps as they approached us. "You two keep going," Panchito said, "I'll catch up with you shortly." Santiago and I continued along our way, then stopped to watch what was happening. We saw that Panchito, his back to us, was speaking with the three Muslims, who looked like three dark mountains looming over him. One of them was holding a knife that glinted in his hand, but far from being intimidated, Panchito kept advancing as his opponents took one step back, then another, and another, as they kept getting smaller and Panchito kept getting bigger, until finally they vanished into the darkness and disappeared. Panchito calmly returned to us, lighting one of his very long Pall Malls on the way. "Problem solved," he said, laughing. "But, what did you do?" Santiago asked him. "Nothing," Panchito said, and a short while later he added, "Touch," and pointed to his chest. Santiago and I touched his coat, and under the cloth we felt the presence of a long, hard, disconcerting object.

A few days later Panchito disappeared without warning. I waited for him for hours at Café Mabillon, where we would meet every day before lunch for our first aperitif and to initiate one of our long and erratic days. I went to see my friend Carlos, who said he had no idea where he was. "You'll hear about it in the news," he added prophetically. And I did, but years later, when I was working for a news agency, in charge of selecting and translating news from France to be sent to Latin America. From Nice there arrived a telex with the title, "Peru Special. For newspapers in Lima." The telex stated that a Peruvian criminal, Panchito, sought for years by Interpol, had been arrested in the hallways of a large hotel on the Côte d'Azur just as he was about to enter a suite. I remembered that for his mother and siblings in Lima, to whom he regularly sent money, Panchito was a distinguished engineer with an important job in Europe. After crumpling up the telex, I tossed it in the trash.

The vicissitudes of life continued to carry me from one country to another, but above all from one brand of cigarettes to another. Amsterdam and oval-shaped Murattis with fine gold filters; Antwerp and Belgas in their red pack with a yellow circle; London, where I tried to smoke a pipe, then gave up because it seemed too complicated and because I realized I was neither Sherlock Holmes, nor a sea dog, nor English ... Munich, finally, where instead of completing my doctorate in Romance philology, I graduated as an expert in Teutonic cigarettes, which, not to put too fine a point on it, I thought were mediocre and lacked style. But, if I mention Munich, it is not for the quality of its tobacco but because I committed an error of judgment, which placed me in a situation of desperate need, comparable to the worst moments of my Parisian era.

I was the beneficiary of a modest scholarship, which allowed me to buy my pack of Roth-Händles at a street kiosk every day before taking the streetcar to the university. This act, by dint of its repetitive nature, established between the elderly Frau of the kiosk and me a friendly relationship, which I assumed went beyond the formalities of a commercial exchange. After two or three months of a routine and thrifty existence, however, I spent the entirety of my scholarship on a portable turntable, for I had started to write a novel and deemed it necessary, in order to finish it properly, to have background music or a sound curtain to protect me from the noise outside. I obtained the music as well as the curtain, and I was able to make progress on my novel, but a few days later I was stranded without cigarettes and without money to buy any. Since "writing is an act that complements the pleasure of smoking," I found myself unable to write, no matter how much background music I had. The most natural thing to do seemed for me to go to my daily kiosk and plead my case, requesting that I be sold a pack of cigarettes on credit. And that is just what I did, claiming that I had forgotten my wallet and would pay the following day. I was so confident in the legitimacy of my request that I innocently stretched out my hand to receive the pack. But I had to immediately pull it back, for the Frau slammed the kiosk window shut and stood staring at me from behind the glass, not only scandalized but terrified, as well. Only at that moment did I realize the mistake I had made: to think I was in Spain when I was in Germany. That prosperous country was in reality a backward country with no imagination, incapable of creating mutually beneficial institutions based on trust and conviviality, such as the institution of buying on credit. For the Frau of the kiosk, a person who asked to pay for something tomorrow could be nothing but a scam artist, a criminal, or a madman, ready and willing to murder her if necessary.

Hence, I found myself in a terrible situation—unable to smoke and as a result unable to write—and with no solution in sight, for I knew almost nobody in Munich, on top of which a dreadful winter had just been unleashed, and the meter of snow in the streets condemned me to forced confinement. I did nothing but stare out the window at the polar landscape, throw myself on the bed like a wet rag, and read the heaviest books in the world, such as the seven volumes of Charles Du Bos's *Journal intime* and Goethe's pedagogical novels. That was when Herr Trausnecker came to my rescue.

I was living in a proletarian suburb in the apartment of a metalworker, who rented me a room with breakfast and one other meal. Once or twice a week he came to my room at night to see if I needed anything and to chat with me for a while. He was an uneducated but discerning man, and he soon realized that something was tormenting me. When I explained my problem, he immediately understood and, apologizing for not being able to lend me money, he gave me a kilo of cut tobacco, some rice paper, and a little machine to roll cigarettes.

Thanks to that little machine, I was able to subsist for the two interminable weeks I still had to wait before collecting my next month's stipend. Every morning when I got up, I rolled about thirty cigarettes and arranged them on my desk in small stacks. These were the worst and the best cigarettes of my life, the most harmful and the most propitious. The tobacco was very dry, the paper harsh, and the artisanal manufacture clumsy and wretched to look at, but what did I care? These cigarettes allowed me to ride out the weather and return to my abandoned novel with brio. The fact that I finished it is due in large part to the little machine Herr Trausnecker gave me, thereby washing away the insult I had received from the elderly Frau and reconciling me with the German people.

I amply repaid him this service, which obliges me to digress, for the incident had nothing to do with cigarettes though everything to do with fire. Frau Trausnecker entered my room one desolate day; more than an hour earlier she had put an apple tart in the oven, but the door to the kitchen was stuck, she couldn't get in to take the pastry out of the oven, and it was burning. First I tried to open the door with an improvised crowbar, then with blows, but it was impossible, and the smell of burning was getting stronger. I then remembered that the bathroom was next to the kitchen and that their respective windows were side-by-side. The only option was to pass from one room to the other through those windows. I explained my plan to Frau Trausnecker and went into the bathroom, but she came after me shrieking, tried to stop me, insisted it was too risky, there was a struggle, then I managed to lock myself in the bathroom. As she continued to lodge her protests from the other side of the door, I opened the bathtub faucet and told her not to worry, I was really just going to take a bath. Instead, I opened the window and was horrified: not only did the fourth floor of this working-class apartment build-ing give out onto a very low cement patio, but the kitchen window was much farther away than I had imagined. I could not turn back, lest I appear ridiculous and a blowhard. I climbed out the bathroom window, hung onto the ledge with both hands, and using a calculated swinging motion, I jumped onto the contiguous window ledge and entered the kitchen. Just in time, for the room was boiling hot, and the oven was spewing smoke and fire through its cracks. I opened the door and Frau Trausnecker entered, turned off the gas, cut off the electricity, removed the tart—by now a mound of smoking ashes—and threw it in the sink under a stream of cold water. The house filled with steam and the intolerable smell of burning, obliging us to open all the windows to air it out. We were soon sitting in the living room, relieved, satisfied, and happy that we had avoided a fire. But there was a sound that kept distracting us: from the bathroom came the swish of the open bathtub faucet, and at that very moment we saw a tongue of water slinking down the hallway. The bathtub was overflowing! But how could I get into the bathroom? I had locked it from the inside. I had no choice but to retrace my steps in spite of Frau Trausnecker's renewed protests. From the kitchen window I passed to the bathroom window with a suicidal leap over the abyss. My recklessness saved the Trausneckers from a fire and a flood, in that order.

On many occasions—the time has come to state this—I have struggled against my addiction to tobacco, for my abuse of it was doing me increasing harm: I always had a cough, and I suffered from acid indigestion, nausea, fatigue, loss of appetite, heart palpitations, dizzy spells, and a stomach ulcer, which contorted me in pain and forced me to regularly submit to a diet of milk and ghastly gelatins. I employed all kinds of formulas and strategies to diminish my consumption and eventually stop altogether. I'd hide packs in the most improbable places, fill my desk with candy so I'd always have something within reach to put in my mouth and suck on instead of a cigarette, buy sophisticated filters that eliminated the nicotine, take all kinds of pills supposedly designed to create an allergy to tobacco, and have needles stuck skillfully in my ears by a wise Chinese acupuncturist.

Nothing worked. I finally reached the conclusion that the only way to free myself from this yoke was not by using more or less spurious tricks but rather through an act of irrevocable willpower that would test the mettle of my character. I knew people—few, truth be told, and I never quite trusted them—who had decided from one day to the next to stop smoking, and had succeeded.

Only once did I make such a decision. I was in Huamanga, teaching at the university, which had just reopened after being closed for three centuries. That old, small, and forgotten Andean city was a delight. Comrade Gonzalo had not yet appeared on the scene, and his philosophy had not yet pointed out any shining path to follow. The students, almost all from there or the neighboring provinces, were ignorant, serious, and studious young people, convinced that a degree was all they needed to gain access to the world of prosperity. But my goal here is not to evoke my Ayacuchan experience. Let's return to cigarettes. As a bachelor without obligations and in receipt of a good salary, I could provide myself with as many Camels as I wanted, for this was the brand I had taken up, perhaps due to the affinity that exists between camels and llamas and vicuñas, who could be seen everywhere around town. One night, however, while talking and smoking with my colleagues in a café in the Plaza de Armas, I suddenly felt ill. My head was spinning, I was having difficulty breathing, and I felt stabbing pains in my chest. I returned to my hotel and lay down on the bed, trusting that rest would restore me to health. But my condition worsened: the ceiling was falling on top of me, I was vomiting bile, I actually felt as if I was dying. Then I realized that this was all because of cigarettes, that I was finally paying off the debt I had accrued during my fifteen years of immoderate smoking.

A radical decision was required. And not only to make it—to not smoke anymore—but also to consecrate it with a symbolic act that would seal its sacramental nature. I rose shakily from my bed, grabbed my pack of Camels, and threw it into the vacant lot outside my window. Never again, I told myself, never again. Liberated by this heroic act, I fell back onto my bed and instantly fell asleep.

I woke up after midnight, remembered my decision from the night

before, and felt not only morally comforted but also physically improved. So much so that I rose from bed in order to consign my re-
nunciation of tobacco to a few lines that I imagined would be, if not
immortal, at least worthy of a well-deserved longevity. In fact, I wrote
several pages, glorifying my gesture and promising me a new life
founded on austerity and discipline. As I continued to write, however,
I felt increasingly uncomfortable, my ideas became confused, I had
difficulty finding words, mounting anxiety prevented me from concentrating, and I realized that the only thing I really wanted at that
moment was to light a cigarette.

For at least an hour I struggled against this summons, turning off
the light to lie down in bed and try to sleep, getting up to play music
on my portable turntable, drinking glass after glass of fresh water,
until I could tolerate it no longer: I grabbed my coat, and decided to
go out to look for cigarettes. But I didn't even make it out of my room.
At that time of night, there was nothing open in Huamanga. I then
started to look through all the pockets of all my jackets and trousers,
all the drawers in the room, the contents of my suitcases and bags,
searching for the hypothetical forgotten cigarette, tossing everything
into the air; the more fruitless my search, the more tenacious my
longing. Suddenly, a light bulb went on in my head: I had found the
solution in the pack I had thrown out the window. Looking out, I
saw the vacant lot eight or ten meters below, barely illuminated by
the light in my room. I didn't even hesitate. I took a suicidal leap into
the void and fell onto a small pile of dirt, twisting my ankle. Then,
on hands and knees, I searched the entire lot with the flame of my
lighter. There was the pack! Sitting right there in the dirt, I lit a
cigarette, lifted my head, and blew the first puff of smoke into the
magnificent Huamanga sky.

This setback was a warning I did not know how to heed or take
advantage of. I carried on with my vagabond life through different
cities, lodgings, and occupations, leaving in every place swirls of smoke
and piles of crushed butts, until I settled once again in Paris, in a
three-room apartment, where I was able to assemble a collection of
sixty ashtrays. Not because I was an obsessive collector but to always

have on hand something into which I could throw butts or ashes. By then I had adopted Marlboros, which were no better or worse than the many I had already tried, but the name of the brand conjured a lexical game that I played assiduously. How many Spanish words could be made out of the eight letters of Marlboro? *Mar, lobo, malo, árbol, bar, loma, olmo, amor, mono, orar, bolo*, et cetera. I became unbeatable at this game and forced it upon my colleagues at the Agence France-Presse, where I worked at the time. Said agency, I should mention, was not only a news factory but also a smoking emporium. I knew of statistics that showed that journalism was the most tobacco-addicted profession. And I could confirm this because the newsrooms, at any hour of day or night, were spacious dens where dozens of men were desperately typing on their typewriters, sucking nonstop on cigars, pipes, and cigarettes of every brand, and surrounded by a thick nicotine haze, to the point that I often wondered if they were gathered there to write the news or to smoke. It was precisely during my Marlboro period and my job at the agency that I crashed. It is not my intention to establish a relationship of cause and effect between this brand of cigarettes and what happened to me. The fact is, though, one afternoon I fell into bed and started to die, to my wife's great alarm (in the meantime, apart from smoking, I had married and had a child). My longtime stomach ulcer had burst and an unstoppable hemorrhage was evacuating me from this world through the lower pathway. An ambulance with a raucous siren carried me in a coma to the hospital, and thanks to massive blood transfusions I managed to regain consciousness. This was all quite awful, and I will refrain from sharing too many details to avoid a descent into pathos. Dr. Dupont healed the ulcer with two weeks of treatment and sent me on my way with clear instructions—as well as medicines and a diet—to never smoke again.

Never smoke again! Such an innocent, that dear Dr. Dupont. He had no idea what kind of patient he was dealing with. Two months later, having returned to my job at the news agency, surrounded by hundreds of rabid smokers, I tossed into the trash a couple of empty packs of Marlboros every day. M-a-r-l-b-o-r-o. My lexical game grew richer: *broma, robar, rabo, ola, romo, borla*, et cetera. This might have been charming, but along with finding new words, I had new hemorrhages, and new ambulances carried me to the hospital, with sirens and horns, depositing me lifeless in front of the horrified eyes of Dr. Dupont. It could be said that the ambulance had become my most common form of transportation. Dr. Dupont always patched me up and returned me home, after I swore I would quit smoking and after he threatened me that the next time he would forego palliatives and put me under the knife without a second thought. His threat left me undaunted, as evidenced the third or fourth time I was hospitalized, when I realized that in order to smoke I didn't have to wait to be released: all I had to do was bribe a nurse to get her to buy me a pack. Of Marlboros, naturally: *lora, orla, ramo, ropa, paro, proa*, et cetera. I would hide it in the closet, or inside a shoe. Two or three times a day I'd pull out a cigarette, lock myself in the bathroom, take several frantic puffs, and flush the rest down the toilet.

I will say, in my own defense, that what contributed to the demise of my best intentions and therefore strengthened my vice was a fleeting but decisive vision I had in the hospital. Dr. Dupont, no matter how good a specialist he might have been, held only an intermediary rank among the gastroenterologists at the hospital. At the top sat Dr. Bismuth, who had reached his position thanks, possibly, to his prophetic last name. Dr. Bismuth dealt only with extremely important cases, but since mine was on the verge of turning into one, the good Dr. Dupont arranged for me the privilege of an appointment. He announced this to me with great solemnity, and only minutes before the scheduled meeting, an older nurse came in to see if everything was in order. Shortly thereafter the door opened and in a fraction of a second I glimpsed a tall, scrawny, gray-haired man who, in a furtive movement befitting a magician, pulled a cigarette out of his mouth, put it out under the sole of his shoe, and stuffed the butt into the pocket of his coat. I thought I was dreaming. But when the wise man approached my bed, surrounded by a retinue of interns and nurses, I saw on his yellowed mustache and long brown fingers the ignominious signs of a smoker.

What kind of compensation did I derive from cigarettes that made me submit to their rules and turned me into a zealous minion of their caprices? It was, undoubtedly, a vice, if by "vice" we understand a repetitive, progressive, and dangerous act that gives us pleasure. But upon deeper examination, I realized that pleasure had nothing to do with smoking. I'm talking here about sensory pleasure, connected to a particular sense, such as the pleasure of gluttony or lust. Perhaps for my first years as a smoker, I experienced the pleasant taste or smell of tobacco, but over time this sensation had been spoiled, and one could even say that smoking had become unpleasant, for it left a bitter taste in my mouth and made my throat burn and my stomach acidic. If there was any pleasure, I told myself, it must have been mental, such as that derived from alcohol or drugs, such as opium, cocaine, or morphine. But that wasn't it, either, for smoking did not make me euphoric, lucid, ecstatic, or give me supernatural visions, and it did not eliminate pain or fatigue. What, then, did tobacco give me, in the absence of sensory or spiritual pleasures? Perhaps more diffuse or subtle pleasures, difficult to locate, define, or measure, linked to the effects of nicotine on our organism: serenity, focus, sociability, adaptability to our environment. I could say, then, that I smoked because I needed nicotine to feel well emotionally. But if what I needed was the nicotine contained in a cigarette, why the hell did I not turn to the cigars or the pipe tobacco I had within reach when I didn't have cigarettes? And I never did, not even at my worst moments, for what I needed was that thin, long, cylindrical object wrapped in paper and containing tobacco leaves. It was the object itself that subjugated me, the cigarette itself, its form as much as its contents, the holding of it, its inclusion in the web of my movements, occupations, and daily habits.

This reflection led me to think that cigarettes, besides being a drug, were for me a habit and a ritual. Like all habits, it had become attached to my nature until it had become an integral part of that nature, whereby removing it would be the equivalent of a mutilation; and like all rituals, it was subjected to strict protocols, sanctioned by the execution of precise actions and the use of occult objects that were irreplaceable. From there I was able to reach the conclusion that smoking was a vice that lent me, in the absence of sensory pleasure, a diffuse feeling of calm and well-being, the effects of the nicotine contained in the tobacco, and that was made manifest in my social behavior through ritual actions. All of this is just fine, I told myself, coherent and even beautiful, but it didn't satisfy me, for it did not explain why I smoked when I was alone and had nothing to think about, nothing to say, nothing to write, nothing to hide, nothing to pretend, and nothing to portray. The tyranny of cigarettes had to have, therefore, deeper causes, probably subconscious. It would, however, be a big stretch for me to take refuge in Freud, not because of him but because of his fanatic and mediocre exegetes, who saw phalluses, anuses, and Oedipuses everywhere. According to some of his proselytizers, addiction to cigarettes could be explained by infantile regression, the search for the maternal nipple, or by a cultural sublimation based on the desire to suck a penis. Reading these idiocies I understood why Nabokov—with undoubted hyperbole—called Freud "the quack from Vienna."

I had no choice but to invent my own theory. An absurd and philosophical theory, which I mention here as a mere curiosity. I told myself that, according to Empedocles, the four primordial elements of nature are air, water, earth, and fire. All of these are linked to the origins of life and the survival of our species. We are in permanent contact with air, for we breathe it in, we breathe it out, we change its temperature. With water as well, for we drink it, wash with it, enjoy it when we swim or go diving. With earth also, for we walk on it, cultivate it, we shape it in our hands. But we have no direct relationship with fire. Fire is the only one of Empedocles' four elements from which we shrink, for proximity to it or contact with it brings us harm. The only way to be connected to it is through a mediator. And this mediator is the cigarette. Cigarettes allow us to be in communication with fire without being consumed by it. Fire is on one end of the cigarette, and we are on the other. And the proof of the closeness of this contact resides in the fact that the cigarette burns, but it is our mouth that blows out the smoke. Thanks to this invention, we fulfill our ancestral need to bind ourselves to the four fundamental elements of life. This relationship was sacralized by primitive peoples through a variety of religious cults, earthly or aquatic, and, as for fire, through sun cults. The sun was worshipped because it embodied fire and its attributes: light and heat. Secular and nonbelieving as we are, we can render homage to fire only with cigarettes. Cigarettes then become a substitute for the ancient solar deity, and smoking, a way of carrying on the cult. A religion, in short, however banal that may seem. Hence, giving up cigarettes is a serious and harrowing act, similar to an abjuration.

Dr. Dupont's knife was my sword of Damocles, except that it actually fell on me. This happened years later, when Marlboros and that stupid word game—*bar, lar, loma, ralo, rabo,* et cetera—had been replaced by Dunhills in their beautiful maroon pack with gold lettering. At that time I lived in Cannes, undergoing a new treatment to quit smoking after yet another stay in the hospital. Dupont had prescribed distraction, athletics, and rest, a recipe that my wife, converted into the most avid guardian of my health and eradicator of my addiction, took charge of scrupulously measuring out and monitoring. My days consisted of a morning jog, a lounge in the sun, a swim in the sea, a long siesta, a row in a rubber dinghy, and an evening bicycle ride. In between were healthy meals and activities for the spirit that tended to be low-key, such as playing solitaire, reading spy novels, and watching soap operas on television. This schedule did not leave a single crack into which I might squeeze a cigarette, especially because my wife didn't leave my side either day or night. A month later I was tanned, buff, healthy, and one could even say handsome. But deep down, way deep down, I felt dissatisfied, uneasy, at moments incredibly sad. It did me no good to perceive more fully the purity of the sea air, the aroma of the flowers, and even the taste of food, when existence itself had become, for me, insipid.

One day, I could tolerate it no longer. I convinced my wife that from then on I would go to the beach an hour before her and our son, in order to take better advantage of the benefits of that recreational and healthful life. On the way, I bought a pack of Dunhills; as it was risky to keep them on me or hide them in the house, I found an out-of-the-way corner of the beach, where I dug a hole and buried them, covering them with sand and placing an oval-shaped rock on top to mark the spot. Very early in the morning I would walk out of the house with a vigorous stride under the amazed gaze of my wife, who would watch me from the balcony and beam with pride at my athletic aptitude, never suspecting that the goal of that run was not to improve my fitness or set any record but rather to get to my hole in the sand as quickly as possible. I would dig up my pack and smoke a couple of cigarettes, slowly, focused, and even anxious, for I knew that they would be the only ones of the day. This scheme, I admit, gave me pleasure and flattered my ingenuity, but it debased me in my own eyes, for I was conscious of failing to live up to my promises and of betraying my wife's trust. Besides, my plan was not immune to unforeseen occurrences, like the morning that I arrived at my citadel and failed to find the oval stone. The worker who raked and cleaned the beach had been replaced by another, more diligent one, who didn't leave a single pebble in the sand. No matter how much I dug here and dug there, I couldn't find my pack. So I decided to buy five packs and make five holes and place five markers and thereby have five probabilities available for my passion.

A full and detailed account would go on forever. But everything must come to an end, so I intend to conclude this confession.

We now come to the most dramatic part of the story, the reappearance of Dr. Dupont, his tubes and his sermons, and above all, his foreboding knife. For better or for worse, in spite of my ailments and other problems related to my abuse of tobacco, I learned how to live with them and carry on, as they say, one puff at a time. Until I fell victim to a problem that I had never experienced before: food got stuck in my throat and I was unable to swallow. This began to happen so frequently that I went to see Dr. Dupont, though this time, and for a change, not in an ambulance. Dupont was quite alarmed, checked me into the hospital, and had me undergo new and complicated exams, and a few days later, without any clear explanation, I was on a bed being rolled toward the operating room. I awoke seven hours later, cut up like a slab of beef then sewn up like a rag doll. Tubes, catheters, and needles were sticking out of every one of my orifices. They had removed part of my duodenum, almost all of my stomach, and a big chunk of my esophagus.

I prefer not to recall the weeks I spent in the hospital, fed intravenously and then by mouth with teaspoons of baby food. Or my second operation, for it seems Dupont had forgotten to cut something, and he opened me up again along the same lines, taking advantage of the seam on my skin that he'd already sewn. But I really must say something about the establishment where they sent me to convalesce, converted as I had been into a human wreck after such crude interventions.

It was called a "Dietary and Post-Operative Rehabilitation Clinic," and was located on the outskirts of Paris in the middle of a vast and beautiful park. Its rooms were quite spacious, each equipped with its own private bathroom, terrace, television, and telephone. Those who had undergone serious operations on their digestive tracts were sent there to relearn how to eat, digest, and assimilate their food, until they had recovered lost muscle mass and weight. I spent the first few weeks unable to get out of bed. They continued to feed me liquids and puddings, and every day a strapping physical therapist would come to massage my legs and have me lift small weights with my arms and sandbags they placed on my thorax with my breath—all of which kept getting heavier. Thanks to all that, I could finally stand up and take a few steps around the room, until one day the head nurse announced that I was in good enough shape to undergo daily monitoring.

The next day, I found out the nature of the monitoring when they came to get me after breakfast. It was the first time I had left my room and my first contact with the other clinic inmates. What a horrible sight! I found myself amidst a legion of sad, exhausted, and gaunt beings wearing pajamas and slippers just like me, standing in line in front of a Roman balance. One nurse was weighing them and another was writing down the results in a thick logbook. Then they dragged themselves laboriously down the corridor and disappeared into their rooms for the rest of the day.

Horror was followed by reflection: Where the hell had I ended up? What was being hidden behind this parody of a rural retreat? During the following sessions, I thought I caught a glimpse of reality. Maybe this was not a clinic but rather the waiting room for the irremediable. This is where they sent the castoffs of science so that, among trees and flowers, they could live out their dying moments surrounded by all the trappings of a holiday. The weigh-in was simply the final test that confirmed for them that there was no longer any possibility of a miracle. The patient who gained weight was the one who—among a hundred, a thousand, or more—had hopes of getting out of that place alive.

My suspicions were confirmed when two of my neighbors along my corridor stopped showing up to be weighed, and then, overhearing a conversation between nurses, I found out that they had "gently passed away." This redoubled my anxiety, which prevented me from eating and therefore from gaining weight. The dishes they brought me, insipid and unctuous, got flushed down the toilet or wrapped in tissues and thrown in the trash. My wife and a few faithful friends visited me in the afternoons and achieved the impossible, with admirable fortitude, of not showing their alarm. Certain gestures, however, betrayed them. My wife brought me elegant silk pajamas, which I interpreted through tortured reasoning as, "If you have to die, it might as well be in Pierre Cardin pajamas." Certain friends insisted on taking pictures of me, which made me realize that they were posthumous pictures, ones I would never see in any family photo album.

I was, then, dying, or rather "gently passing away," as the nurses would say. Every day I lost a few more grams, and undergoing trial by weight increasingly tired me out. The chief of the clinic came to see me and gave orders, as a final measure, to force-feed me. They stuck a rubber tube down my nose; using a huge piston, they shot ground-up food through it into my stomach. The tube had to remain permanently in place, its visible end stuck to my forehead with a bandage. It was so horrible that two days later I pulled it out and threw it on the floor. The chief of the clinic returned to chastise me, and when I resisted its reinsertion, he left in a rage, but not before saying: "I don't give a damn. But you aren't getting out of here until you gain weight. It's wholly your responsibility."

I never saw that idiot again, but I did see some hairy, dirty, and shirtless individuals who started appearing behind the shrubbery I could see from my bed through the large windows. They were building a new pavilion behind those shrubs, and as they had already built the first floor, the workers and their work were visible from my room. Based on their olive complexions, I deduced that they hailed from hot and poor places—Andalucía, southern Portugal, North Africa. What surprised me at first was the speed and variety of their movements. They appeared and disappeared, carrying bricks, bags of cement, water barrels, construction tools, all in a constant to-ing and fro-ing that was devoid of missteps or improvisations. I imagined the effort it took and through a kind of mental exchange I grew extremely exhausted, so much so that I closed the blinds on the window. At noon, however, I opened them and saw that those men, whom I imagined would have succumbed to fatigue, were sitting in a circle on the roof, laughing, conversing, and communicating with vivid gestures. They were on their lunch break, and out of lunchboxes and plastic bags they took food that they gobbled down greedily and wine that they drank straight from the bottle. These men, apparently, were happy, and for at least one reason: they embodied the world of the healthy, whereas we were the world of the sick. Then I felt something that I have rarely felt, envy, and I told myself that fifteen or twenty years of reading and writing had done me no good at all, locked up as I was among the dying, while those simple and illiterate men were solidly rooted in life, from which they derived their most basic pleasures. And my envy increased when, upon finishing their meal, I saw them take out their packs, their pouches, and their rolling papers, and light their after-meal cigarettes.

That vision saved me. At that moment a spark was lit inside me that mobilized the entirety of my intelligence and willpower so that I could emerge from my prostration and thus from my confinement. I wanted nothing more than to be reintegrated into life, no matter how ordinary it was, without any demands or ambitions other than to be able—like those construction workers—to eat, drink, smoke, and enjoy the rewards of being a normal but healthy man. To do so it was imperative for me to pass the trial of the scales, but since it was impossible for me to eat the food in that place, I devised a plan. Every morning before being weighed, I placed several one franc coins in the pockets of my pajamas. I then added five franc coins, the biggest and heaviest ones, which I received as change from the newspaper vendor. In this way I managed to gain several hundred grams, which still wasn't sufficient or even probative. I then asked my wife to bring from home a complete set of cutlery, claiming that I would be able to eat better with them than with the clinic's awkward set. They were the solid and expensive silverware that my wife had bought at a moment of delirium, in spite of my opposition, and that now, making a detour from their destiny, had become truly valuable. As I couldn't hide them in my pockets, I stuck them into my socks, starting with a coffee spoon then advancing to a soup spoon. Within a week I had gained two kilos and even more when I sewed the fish forks into my underwear. The nurses were amazed by my recovery, which didn't correspond to my appearance. A physician came to see me, checked the record of my weight, examined me, and interrogated me, and a few days later the authorization came for me to depart. Hours before my wife picked me up in a taxi, I was dressed and standing up, looking one more time out the window at the agile, weightless, airborne, and—I would even say—angelic construction workers, who were building the second floor of that new pavilion for the terminally ill.

Needless to say, one week after I left the clinic I was able to feed myself only moderately well, but I had regained my appetite; a month later I was drinking a glass of red wine with my meals; and a little later, to celebrate my fortieth birthday, I lit my first cigarette, with my wife's acquiescence and the indulgent applause of my friends. This cigarette was followed by others, and still others, until the one I am smoking now, fifteen years later, as I force myself to draw this story to a close while sitting on the terrace of a small house on Via Tragara, contemplating at my feet the bay of Marina Piccola protected by the steep slope of Monte Solaro. Twenty centuries ago Emperor Augustus set up his summer residence here, and Tiberius lived here for ten years and built ten palaces. It's true that neither of them smoked, so they have nothing to do with the topic at hand, but the one who did smoke was Vesuvius, and with so much passion that the smoke and ashes thereof covered the vineyards and houses of the island, ushering Capri into a long period of decadence.

I light another cigarette and tell myself that it's time to end this story, the writing of which has cost me so many hours of work and so many cigarettes. My intention is not to derive either a conclusion or a moral from it. Whether it is taken as a eulogy to or a diatribe against tobacco is all the same to me. I am neither a moralist nor a demoralizer, as Flaubert liked to call himself. And speaking of which, Flaubert was a tenacious smoker, so much so that his teeth were rotten and his mustache yellow. As was Gorky, who also lived on this island. As was Hemingway, who, although he was never here, did live on an island in the Caribbean. There is a tight bond between writers and smokers, as I said at the beginning, but, might there not also be one between smokers and islands? I reject this new digression, no matter how virgin the island it would lead to. I also see with some apprehension that I have only one cigarette left, so I bid farewell to my readers and am off to town to buy a pack of tobacco.

A LITERARY TEA PARTY

ADELINDA walked over to the window while her eyes, for the thousandth time, surveyed the living room to confirm that everything was in its place—ashtrays, cigarette holder, flowers, and above all, books, though these not too ostensibly on display, as if somehow they had dropped there by accident. Pulling back the lace curtain, she peeked outside, but all she saw was the front gate and past that the empty sidewalk and the tree-lined street.

"So, you've all read *Summer Storm*?" she asked, returning to the coffee table in the middle of the room to take a cigarette.

"You still have to ask!?" Doña Rosalba said. "As far as I'm concerned, it's his best novel. The style! The sensitivity!"

"I wouldn't say it's a novel," Doña Zarela said. "For me, it's a poem. It's what I'd call a poem. In prose, if you like, but a poem."

"Here's his picture in the newspaper, along with the interview. Tell me, Auntie, is this really how he looks?"

Adelinda walked over to look at the newspaper Sofía was pointing to.

"Well, a little . . . It must be a recent picture. Truth is, I haven't seen him in years, since he was a child, except one time when he came to Lima for a few days. He has the same expression, at least."

"For forty, he doesn't look at all bad," Sofía said. "Have you seen what he says in the interview? When they ask him what he desires more than anything—"

"We know, we know," Doña Rosalba said, interrupting her. "We've all read the interview. I, for one, don't skip a single one of Alberto Fontarabia's words."

"What does he say?" Adelinda asked.

"'My greatest desire is to be forgotten.'"

"Don't you think we should put on some music?" Doña Zarela asked. "Some Vivaldi, for example? I'd say his books have something very Vivaldi-esque about them..."

"Let's wait till later for the music," Doña Rosalba said. "It would be better to figure out what to ask him. I, for one, have two or three things I'd like to know. I have them here, written down in my notebook."

"Oh, no!" Sofía protested. "No questions! Better to let him talk, so he won't feel hounded. Don't you think, Auntie?"

"Let's wait and see. We can ask him a few questions, just so long as it doesn't sound like an interrogation."

"By the way, Adelinda, why in God's name did you invite the Noriegas?" Doña Zarela asked.

"I can invite whoever I want, can't I?"

"You could have invited the Ganozas, they're more cultured. The Noriegas are unbearable, especially him. He'll start talking nonsense and probably bring that book of his he published years ago to ask him what he thinks, maybe even so he'll write something about it. Didn't Gastón publish a book?"

"Not a book, some kind of brochure-type thing, it's an epic poem, something about Tupac Amaru, I think," Adelinda said.

"I agree with Zarela," Doña Rosalba said. "I would have—poof!—made those Noriegas disappear. Gastón can sometimes be so tiresome, and she's kind of vulgar, thinks she's some kind of grande dame..."

"We're not going to start badmouthing people," said Adelinda. "Sofía, can you come with me to the kitchen? Don't any of you move. If someone comes to the door, tell me so I can let them in."

Adelinda and Sofía went into the kitchen.

"I don't know the Noriegas or the Ganozas, but those two ladies—"

"Please, Sofía, don't you start as well... Rosalba is a highly cultivated woman, she belongs to the Book Club, like me, and she never misses a lecture at the Alliance Française. And Zarela might not be the brightest bulb, but—"

"I know, I know, you've been friends since high school or whatever, but Alberto Fontarabia is going to think he walked into a museum . . . But you, what can I say? You look gorgeous . . . It's your hairdo, maybe, and that dress, too . . . Tell me, Auntie, how did you meet Fontarabia? Because he's much younger—"

"Please, check if the sandwiches have dried out. I'm going to see if the cake is ready."

"Is this what you're going to serve?"

"Herminia has gone to pick up some pastries . . . What were you saying? Oh, yes, Alberto is a lot younger, of course. I knew him when he was a little boy. When I was married to Boby, we were neighbors of the Fontarabias. Then we moved. Boby died, Alberto went to Europe, and I didn't see him for years . . . Until, during one of his visits to Lima, he gave a talk and I went to it. I finally went up to him, because he was very friendly, and he signed a book for me. To this day I remember what he wrote: 'For Adelinda, my unforgettable neighbor.'"

"The cake's done? Good, let's go back to the living room. We don't want the writer to arrive and not be greeted by his 'unforgettable neighbor.'"

"Wait. I want to ask you something. Do you think I can show him my poems?"

"Of course, Auntie, they're beautiful! So romantic. I'm sure he'll like them. Especially the ones you wrote for Boby . . ."

"But, what will Zarela and Rosalba say?"

"What do you care? Let them say whatever they want. What matters is for Fontarabia to read them."

"You're right, I'll play it by ear. Cover the sandwiches with a damp cloth. I'm going to boil some water for tea."

The minute they returned to the living room, Rosalba laid into them.

"You forgot something, Adelinda, you who always remembers everything: a camera! Zarela's right. We're not leaving here without a picture with the writer. I would never forgive myself."

"It didn't occur to me," Adelinda said. "I have a camera upstairs, but I don't think it has any film in it. I can send someone out to buy..."

"Do it, now, Adelinda..."

"He's here!" Zarela said.

A car had stopped in front of the house.

Adelinda ran to the door and opened it a crack.

"The Noriegas!"

A few minutes later a portly man sporting a thick mustache and carrying a small package in each of his hands came in followed by a small brunette wearing tight pants and a button-down shirt.

"If we're late it's Chita's fault, she spent all afternoon at the hairdresser's. You know what I've got here? *Summer Storm*! For him to sign."

"But you haven't even read it," Chita said.

"What do you mean, I haven't read it?"

"We bought it last night, after Adelinda called to tell us that Fontarabia was coming over and to invite us for tea..."

"I'm a very fast reader. After you fell asleep..."

"But you fell asleep before me, with the book in your hand."

"Same thing, I had time to skim it."

"What about the other package, Gastón, what do you have there?" Doña Rosalba asked. "No, you don't have to answer, we already know, it must be your thing about Tupac Amaru."

"Your *thing*? Did you hear that, Adelinda? Your *thing*! And Rosalba considers herself an intellectual! Well, yes, it's my *thing* and I've brought four copies. One for Fontarabia, one for the Bibliothèque nationale in Paris, another for him to give to Jean-Paul Sartre, and another, another...who's the other one for, Chita?"

"How should I know..."

"It doesn't matter, but I'm sure it will end up in good hands. Anyway, Adelinda, I hope you're not going to offer me sandwiches, pastries, and other such nonsense. You've got a good shot of something for me...What? Our author is keeping us waiting? I have some things to say to him! I am his greatest admirer, but I also have my own ideas..."

"Don't start with your own ideas, Gastón. I've heard that tape at least fifty times."

"For good reason, because you're my wife and you're there to listen to me. But these ladies haven't. They are all literary ladies, as well, beginning with our hostess."

"Gastón, please, relax, I'll give you some whisky. Stop buttering us up, and anyway, there are no literary ladies here. Save it for Fontarabia."

Adelinda poured out a shot of whisky on the rocks.

"What about you, Chita, would you like a drink, too, or will you wait for tea?"

"I never drink before seven... Oh, but I see you have Fontarabia's novel on the table. I haven't read it, either, Adelinda. Give us a summary. Please."

"How can you ask, Chita!" Doña Rosalba interjected. "As if it were possible to summarize that book. You have to read it from cover to cover. Every sentence... what am I saying? Every word, you have to savor every word."

"The part that intrigues me most is the end," Doña Zarela said. "What do you think? Was Leticia in love with Lucho or not? Everything is left so vague, so confusing..."

"I didn't find it confusing at all," Sofía said. "It's super clear that Leticia was in love with Lucho. She just never told him, she was too proud."

"But besides that, whose child was it?" Doña Zarela asked.

"What child are you talking about?" Gastón asked. "Is there a child involved?"

"The child was Lucho's, of course," Doña Rosalba said.

"No, no, it was Uncle Felipe's," Sofía said.

"You see, Chita?" said Gastón. "If you'd bought the novel when I told you to, we'd know whose child it was... I'm a real Sherlock Holmes when it comes to things like that."

"The part about the child isn't important," Adelinda said. "Or if it is, it's secondary. What's important is the atmosphere, the mood in the novel."

"But, besides that, what's the novel about?" Gastón asked. "As far as I read, there was something going on at a hacienda."

"It's a costumbrista novel—" Doña Rosalba started to say.

"Costumbrista?" Doña Zarela interrupted. "No way! That's precisely what it isn't at all is costumbrista..."

"If you want to label it, I'd say it's more psychological," Adelinda said.

"Why not social?" Doña Zarela said. "Because there's a social problem in the mix."

"For me, it's much simpler," Sofía said. "It's a love novel...about teenage love."

"Just a minute," Gastón said. "One step at a time. What I want to know—"

"You don't want to know anything," Chita said. "The only thing you want is to put in your two cents."

"Auntie! I think he's here!"

A shadow slipped past the window. Adelinda rushed over to peek out from behind the curtain.

"It's Herminia. She's back from the bakery."

"Phew!" said Gastón. "And here I was, preparing myself to confront our author! With one question, just one, but one that makes you think...Why are you making faces, Chita? You're the only person here who thinks I'm not capable of holding a conversation with an author. It doesn't matter that I run an explosives factory. I've told you a thousand times about Alfred Nobel."

"If Fontarabia is late," Doña Zarela said, "I think we should serve the tea. For me, one thing is art and another thing entirely is punctuality."

"Artists are absentminded," Sofía said. "I think it would be rude..."

"As you wish," Adelinda said. "It's all the same to me. I don't stand on ceremony, but if you think..."

"I'll have another whisky," Gastón said. "As for the rest of you, have your tea now *and* when he gets here, I don't care."

"Why don't you call his house?" Doña Zarela said. "Find out if he's left yet. It's already after six."

"We've already waited an hour, we can wait ten more minutes," Doña Rosalba said. "I'm not particularly hungry. After all, tea is just an excuse. Our real nourishment will be our conversation with Fontarabia."

"I agree," Sofía said. "It will be thrilling! Won't it, Auntie? Since you're the only one who knows him, tell us—"

"What can I say? I've already told you, other than when we were neighbors, when he was a child, I've only seen him occasionally since."

"Did he ever tell you a secret?" Doña Rosalba asked. "Something about his private life or about how he writes? I love the little details about an artist's life, what's never talked about except *en petit comité*."

"I have no interest in all that," Gastón said. "It's all the same to me if he writes lying on a sofa or hopping around on one foot. I'm interested in his ideas. What does he think, for example, about the role of the writer in our society? Now that's something we'd like to know!"

"What do you think about that?" Doña Zarela said.

"But Gastón doesn't think," Chita said. "Not about that, not about anything. Gastón just talks."

"I think it's fine for him to talk," Rosalba said. "Goodness me, Chita, everybody has the right to talk, even your husband! But if the goal is to talk, let's forget all these silly things and talk about something more elevated. Nobody has said anything, for example, about Fontarabia's style."

"The style is the man," Gastón said. "Cheers!"

"But I already said that his style is pure poetry," Doña Zarela said. "The thing is, Rosalba, you're the kind of person who doesn't listen. I read his books as if, I don't know, as if I were reading the poems of José Santos Chocano..."

"I don't believe in novelists who write poetically," Sofía said. "On the contrary, there's something a little dry in Fontarabia, I'd say almost a lack of style, though that might seem silly..."

"What about you, Chita? What do you think of Fontarabia's style?" Gastón said.

"The only thing I think is that I have an empty stomach."

"Well," Adelinda said, "I think we can serve the tea. As for Fontarabia, he'll probably prefer a drink."

"Sounds fine to me," Gastón said. "Speaking of a drink . . ."

"Wait a minute, Sofía," Rosalba said. "What you said about the lack of style is nonsense. Everybody has a style, good or bad, but they have one. And Fontarabia's is—"

"It depends on the book," Adelinda said. "It changes from book to book, depending on the subject . . . I'd rather talk about Fontarabia's *styles.*"

"No, no," Doña Zarela said. "Great writers have only one style . . ."

"But what *is* style?" Sofía asked.

"The style is the man," Gastón said.

"Adelinda, please," Chita said. "Don't pour him another drink; if you do, he's going to keep repeating that all night."

"To me," Doña Rosalba said, "style is the way you put the words together, one after the other. Some put them together well, others badly . . . There are writers who just pile them up, let's say, like potatoes in a sack. Others pick and choose, weigh them, polish them, place them carefully like, like . . ."

"Like pearls in a necklace," Gastón said. "How original!"

"Okay, you people keep talking," Adelinda said. "Sofía and I are going to get the tea. You coming, Sofía?"

When they entered the kitchen, Herminia had already laid out the pastries on a platter and placed the empty tea cups on a tray.

"Not those teaspoons! The silver ones!" Adelinda scolded. "And put the sandwiches on a plate."

"Tell me, Auntie, did you actually talk to Fontarabia?"

"What do you mean, did I talk to him?"

"I mean, when you invited him, did you talk directly to him?"

"I talked to his mother . . . But I might as well have talked to him. Alberto was taking a shower, but Doña Josefa, who's an old friend of mine, told me it was fine."

"What was fine, with whom?"

"With him, of course . . . But, what are you thinking, Sofía? That I—"

"No, but it's getting late...I'll take the cups. You bring in the platters."

"Bravo!" Chita exclaimed when she saw them. "Just in time. We were about to scratch each other's eyes out."

"You know what Chita was saying?" Doña Rosalba said. "That we're a bunch of snobs! Now, it seems, anybody who wants to read and talk about literature is a snob. Thank you, Chita. I'd rather be a snob than an ignoramus."

"Please, Rosalba," Doña Zarela said. "It's not like that. Chita was just saying...anyway...what were you saying, Chita?"

"Huh? I don't even remember."

"The thing is, Chita is incapable of reading even a telegram," Gastón said. "But she spent the whole afternoon at the hairdresser's. To impress our writer, I guess."

"Help yourselves, please," Adelinda said. "How many sugars?"

"Wait a minute," Doña Zarela said. "I'm still thinking about Fontarabia...May I criticize him? I think he can be criticized for being a little too grim. All his stories have sad endings, people always end up dead, sick, wounded, disappeared..."

"I find him highly entertaining," Gastón said. "I'd even say he was a humorous writer."

"You realize what you're saying?" Doña Rosalba protested. "Fontarabia, a comic writer? His work is so sad, it tears me apart."

"But the two things don't have to be mutually exclusive," Sofía said. "It can be sad and also humorous."

"I'd say he was a pessimist," said Doña Zarela.

"That's what I'm talking about," Gastón said. "A pessimist who doesn't take things tragically, instead, he laughs his head off at reality."

"Reality?" Sofía said. "But in Fontarabia, reality has nothing to do with it...Everything he writes is invented."

"Oh, so now it turns out that Fontarabia is a fantasy author..." Doña Zarela said, "Adelinda, you're the only one who can set us straight, you know him. Or maybe Fontarabia himself...But, is he coming or not?"

"Like I told you, call him," Doña Rosalba said. "I have to be home by eight."

"I'll do it now," Adelinda said. "I just didn't want to bother him by calling so often. Can you imagine how many people are after him! But, help yourselves, the tea is getting cold. Will you come with me, Sofía?"

They both went into the hallway that led to the kitchen. On a small table, under a wall mirror, was the telephone. Adelinda picked up the receiver, looked in the mirror to check her hair, and stood there, paralyzed.

"What's the matter, Auntie?"

"I don't remember the number...I must have it written down in my address book. But I don't know where my address book is."

"Maybe you left it upstairs. You want me to go look?"

"No, now I remember it...Oh, my hair is a mess. How disappointing! Does it look okay? It's not too young looking?"

"I already told you, Auntie, it looks marvelous. Dial the number, once and for all."

Adelinda put her finger in the dial.

"Go back to the living room, Sofía. Make sure Gastón doesn't pour himself another drink."

"Let him drink, he gets less solemn."

"It's ringing!...Maybe you should do the talking, Sofía. Here, take it! I think we forgot the napkins."

In a flash, Adelinda had disappeared down the darkening hallway, leaving Sofía with the phone in her hand, a phone from which an impatient male voice sounded. Sofía answered:

"Hello? Mr. Fontarabia?...Adelinda's niece here...Adelinda Velit...You don't know her?...Velit with a *v* as in Victor...your old neighbor...his wife...Boby's widow, I mean...Yes, she lived next door to you...For tea...Your mother...I think she took the message...She didn't tell you? I understand, Mr. Fontarabia...understood...anyway...well...thank you very much...very kind...I'll tell her...goodbye."

Sofía replaced the receiver and at that moment realized that

Adelinda had reappeared; she could see her shadow a few steps away, through the darkness.

"So?"

"I spoke with him . . ." then she immediately corrected herself. "Not with him, precisely, with someone at his house . . . with someone close to him, that is, with his mother."

"What did she say?"

"She said . . . she said that Alberto wasn't well. Lunch, yes, lunch hadn't agreed with him . . . indigestion, something bad . . . Just imagine, he's in bed . . . He can't even get up!"

An angry voice reached them from the living room.

"I'm going to tell you three or four things! . . . An explosives factory, I don't deny it, but also, culture . . . Cheers, Doña Zarela! The style is the man!"

"So, he's not coming?"

Who asked that? And why in such a worn-out voice?

"It's very dark in here, Auntie," said Sofía, turning on a lamp in the hallway.

The sudden glare lit up Adelinda, but now an Adelinda who was merely another Zarela, another old lady.

"He sends tons of kisses, his mother told me . . . He apologizes, Adelinda. He's really so sorry . . . but his indigestion, Auntie . . . he says that next time, the next time he returns from Paris . . ."

"Thank you," Adelinda said. "Thank you, Sofía, thank you. He must feel really poorly. Give me your arm, please. Let's go have our tea."

THE SOLUTION

"So, ARMANDO, let's see, what are you working on now?" The feared question had arrived. They had finished dinner and were now in the living room of their home in Barranco, drinking coffee. Through the half-open window they could see the lights of the esplanade and the winter fog creeping up the cliff face.

"Don't play dumb," Oscar insisted. "I know, writers sometimes don't like to talk about what they're working on. But we're your friends. Give us a preview."

Armando cleared his throat, looked at Berta as if to say, what a drag our friends are, but he finally lit a cigarette and decided to speak.

"I'm writing a story about infidelity. As you know, it's not a very original subject. So many things have been written about infidelity! There's *The Red and The Black*, *Madame Bovary*, *Anna Karenina*, to name just the masterpieces ... But, that's just it, I feel drawn to what lacks originality, to the ordinary, the hackneyed ... Speaking of which, I've interpreted something Claude Monet said in my own way: I don't care about the subject, the important thing is the relationship between the subject and me ... Berta, please, do you mind closing that window? The fog is pouring in!"

"Not bad for a prologue," Carlos said. "Now, let's get to the nitty-gritty."

"I'm getting there. It's about a man who suddenly begins to suspect that his wife is cheating on him. I say suddenly because in twenty or more years of marriage the idea had never crossed his mind. The man, for now let's call him Pedro or Juan, whatever you want, had always blindly trusted his wife, and since he was a liberal, modern man, he allowed her to have what is called 'her own life,' without ever asking her to account for herself."

"The ideal husband," Irma said. "You listening, Oscar?"

"In a way, yes," Armando continued. "The ideal husband...Well, as I was saying, Pedro—let's call him that—begins to suspect that his wife is cheating on him. I'm not going to go into details about the reasons for his suspicions. In any case, when this happens, his world falls apart. Not only because he had always been true to her—besides a few little flings of no consequence—but because he deeply loved his wife. Without the passion of youth, of course, but perhaps in a more abiding way, with such things as understanding, respect, tolerance, all those little attentions and concessions that are born out of routine and on which conjugal life is based."

"I don't like the part about routine," Carlos said. "Routine is the negation of love."

"That may be," Armando said, "though that sounds to me like a cliché. But let me continue. As I was saying, Pedro suspects his wife is cheating on him. But since it's only a suspicion, and is that much more distressing for being so uncertain, he decides to look for evidence, and while he's looking for evidence of this infidelity, he discovers a second infidelity, an even more serious one, for it had been going on for longer and was more passionate."

"What evidence did he find?" Oscar asked. "It's difficult to find evidence of infidelities."

"Let's say letters or pictures or eyewitness accounts from totally trustworthy people. But that's secondary, for now. What's important is that Pedro sinks even more deeply into despair, because now it's a question of two lovers: the most recent one, which he already suspected, and the older one, which he thinks he has proof of. But things don't end there. As he continues to investigate the frequency, the seriousness, the circumstances of this deception, he discovers a third lover, and while trying to find out more about this third one, a fourth one turns up—"

"You mean she's a regular Messalina," Carlos interrupted. "How many did she have, in the end?"

"For the purposes of the story, four is enough. It's the number that works. Increasing it would be possible, but it would create structural problems. Anyway, Pedro's wife has four lovers. And, moreover, they're simultaneous, which shouldn't surprise anyone because each of the four is very different—one is much younger than she, another much older, one is very refined and educated, the other rather uneducated, et cetera—so they satisfy her various carnal and spiritual appetites."

"So, what does Pedro do?" Amalia asked.

"I'm getting there. Just imagine the horrible state of anguish, of rage, of jealousy this situation puts him in. Many pages of the story will be dedicated to the analysis and description of his state of mind. But I'll spare you that. I will just say that thanks to an enormous effort of willpower and, above all, a heightened sense of decorum, he does not let his emotions show; he searches for the solution to his problem on his own, without confiding in anybody."

"That's what we want to know," Oscar said. "What the hell does he do?"

"To be fair, I don't know, either. The story isn't finished. I think Pedro lays out a list of alternatives, but I don't know which one he'll end up choosing... Please, Berta, can you get me another cup of coffee?... But he tells himself, when an obstacle appears in our lives, we have to get rid of it in order to return to the original situation. But, in this case, it's not one obstacle but four! If there were only one lover, he wouldn't hesitate to kill him..."

"Murder?" Irma asked. "Would Pedro be capable of murder?"

"Murder, yes, it would be a crime of passion. You know that the law everywhere in the world carries stipulations that soften the punishment for a crime of passion. Especially if a good lawyer can show that the perpetrator committed it in a violent rage. Let's say that Pedro is willing to run the risk of committing murder, knowing that, given the circumstances, the punishment wouldn't be that serious. But, as you see, killing one of the lovers doesn't resolve anything, for there would still be three more. And killing all four would be a serious crime, a true massacre, and would get him the death penalty. Therefore, Pedro dismisses the possibility of murder."

"Murders," Irma said.

"Precisely, murders. But then he thinks of a clever idea: to confront the lovers so they eliminate each other. Here's his idea: because there are four—now you'll see why that number works for me—I'll do a kind of elimination tournament, like in sports. Have each confront one other one, then the two winners confront each other, so at least three would be eliminated."

"That sounds like a novel," Carlos said. "How the hell does he do it? I don't think it would work, in practice."

"But that's precisely where we are, in the world of literature, that is, of probability. Everything depends on if the reader believes what is being recounted. And that's my job. Anyway, Pedro divides the lovers into One and Two and then Three and Four. Using anonymous letters or phone calls or other means, he reveals to One the existence of Two and to Three the existence of Four. In all of this he uses a carefully considered strategy, and deceit as a technique that allows him to provoke in the chosen victim not only the most atrocious jealousy but also a violent desire to annihilate his rival. I forgot to tell you that Rosa's lovers—let's call her Rosa—were all passionately in love with her, and they each believed they were the sole repositories of her love, and therefore the revelation of the existence of a competitor blindsides them as much as it did Pedro himself."

"That's possible," Carlos said. "A lover is probably more jealous of another lover than of a husband."

"In short," Armando continued, "Pedro carries out his plan so well that One kills Two and Three kills Four. So only two are left. Then he proceeds in the same way with them, so that One kills Three. And Pedro himself kills the survivor of that duel, that is, he personally commits only one murder, and since it is only one, and one of passion, he gets a light sentence. At the same time, he achieves what he had set out to do, that is, eliminate the obstacles to his love."

"That sounds ingenious," Oscar said. "But, I insist, it wouldn't work in practice. Suppose lover One doesn't manage to kill lover Two, and just wounds him. Or that lover Three, no matter how much in love he is with Rosa, is incapable of committing murder."

"You're right," Armando said, "and that's why Pedro rejects this solution. Confronting the lovers in order for them to eliminate each other isn't feasible, not in reality or in literature."

"So what does he do?" Berta asked.

"Well, I don't know myself... I told you the story isn't finished. That's why I'm telling it to you. Can you think of anything?"

"Yes," Berta said. "Divorce. There's nothing simpler!"

"I already thought of that. But what would divorce solve? It would create a useless scandal, especially in a city like this one, which in many ways is very provincial. No, divorce would leave untouched the problem of the existence of the lovers and Pedro's suffering. And it wouldn't sate his desire for revenge. Divorce would not be a good solution. I'm thinking of another one: Pedro throws Rosa out of the house after shoving her betrayal in her face. He brutally throws her into the street, with or without all her belongings. It would be a virile and morally justified solution."

"That's just what I think," Oscar said. "A real man's solution. You betrayed me? Here, take that! Now, you're on your own!"

"But it's not that simple," Armando continued, "and I don't think Pedro would choose that solution, either. The main reason is that he couldn't bear to throw his wife out because what he wants most is to keep her. To throw her out would make her even more dependent on her lovers, would shove her into their arms, and push her even further away from him. No, throwing her out of the house, even if it were possible, wouldn't solve anything. Pedro is thinking that the most sensible thing would be the opposite."

"What do you mean, the opposite?" Irma asked.

"For him to leave, disappear, without a trace. Just leave a note, or nothing at all. His wife would understand the reasons for his disappearance. Leave and start a new life in another country, a different life, a different job, other friends, another woman, without ever telling her anything. This might work even if we assume that Pedro and

Rosa have children, though it would be better if they didn't, they would complicate the story too much. But Pedro would leave, even abandoning his supposed children, for romantic passion is stronger than paternal passion."

"Okay, so Pedro leaves. Then what?" Berta asked.

"Pedro doesn't leave, Berta, he doesn't. Because leaving isn't a good solution, either. What would he gain with that? Nothing. On the contrary, he'd lose everything. It would be a good solution if Rosa depended on him economically, at least she'd have that reason to mourn his absence, but I forgot to tell you that she has her own fortune (rich parents, family assets, whatever), so she could do very well without him. Besides, Pedro isn't so young anymore, and it would be difficult for him to start a new life in a new country. Obviously, his departure would only benefit his wife, who would finally be rid of Pedro, she would expand her relationships with her lovers and start up with others if she wished. But the main reason is that Pedro, even if he did manage to settle down in a new and faraway city and prosper, as they say, 'make a new life,' would always be tormented by the memory of his unfaithful wife and the pleasure she would still be deriving from her relationships with her lovers."

"That's true," Amalia said. "The idea of disappearing is stupid."

"But the idea of him taking flight has a variation," Armando continued. "A variation that attracts me. Let's say that Pedro doesn't disappear without a trace but rather that he simply moves to another house after a calm discussion with his wife and an amicable separation. What might happen then? Something that seems possible, at least theoretically. But it will require a fair amount of explanation. With your permission? I think that lovers are rarely superior to husbands, not only intellectually or morally or as human beings, but even sexually. What happens is that the relationship between a man and wife gets contaminated, corrupted, and degraded by daily life. Hundreds of problems of married life contribute to this and are sources of constant disagreements, from how the children are raised— if there are any—to the bills that need to be paid, the furniture that needs to be bought, what to have for dinner..."

"The guests to invite or invitations to accept," Oscar added.

"Exactly. Those problems don't exist in the relationship between the woman and her lover, for their relationship exists only on the erotic level. The woman and her lover meet only to make love, to the exclusion of all other concerns. The husband and wife, on the other hand, bring home and constantly confront all the burdens of their shared life, which prevents or makes difficult a romantic connection. That's why I say that if the husband left, the barriers between him and his wife would disappear, which would make room for a pleasant relationship. What I mean is that an amicable separation would have, for Pedro, the advantage of burdening the lovers with the daily problems, along with everything else that is disruptive and destructive to romantic passion. Pedro, by distancing himself from his wife, would actually draw closer to her when her lovers take on the role of the husband, and he, that of the lover. By living more closely with her lovers, thanks to Pedro's departure, and by seeing him only occasionally, the situation would be reversed and from then on the lovers would get the thorns and the husband the roses. That is, the Rosa."

"All of that sounds very eloquent and well expressed," Oscar said. "Reverse the roles through a strategic retreat. Not bad! What do you all think? In my opinion, it's the best option."

"But it's not," Armando said, "and believe me it bothers me that it's not. The author, no matter how cold and detached he may be, always has his preferences. Oh, how marvelous it would be if things could turn out like that! To keep being the husband but at the same time be the lover. But there are one or several problems with this solution. The main one, in any case, is that Rosa is probably sick of Pedro and can't stand him either from close up or far away, as a husband or as a lover. Everything related to him is saturated with the dregs of their shared life, which means that even if they don't live together, all she'll have to do is see him for the phantoms of their domestic experience to haunt her. The husband carries with him the burden of his marital past, which will always prevent him from getting close to his wife as a stranger would."

"It's true," Carlos said. "I see Pedro running out of options . . ."

"No, there are still a few other possibilities. Simply, to not do anything, accept the situation and carry on his life with Rosa as if nothing had happened. This solution seems to me to be intelligent and also elegant. It would show understanding, realism, a sense of what's expedient, even a certain nobility, a certain wisdom. That is, Pedro would accept wearing on his head a pair, or rather, four pairs, of magnificent horns and would resign himself to joining Cuckolds Incorporated, which is, as you know, an infinitely large organization."

"Huh!" Carlos said. "I disagree with that. Of course, it shows a certain elevated spirit, and absence of prejudice, as you say, but I think it would lack dignity, it would be humiliating. I, for one, couldn't tolerate it."

"I couldn't, either," Oscar said. "Pay attention, Amalia. Just in case, just so you know."

"Oh, what husbands we have!" Amalia said. "True phallocrats."

"But this alternative has its advantages," Armando insisted. "The main one is that by accepting the situation, Pedro would keep his wife by his side. A wife who cheats on him, it's true, and who physically and spiritually belongs to others, but in the end she's there, within reach, and he might sporadically receive some random gesture of affection from her. He would have neither her body nor her soul, but at least he would have her presence. And this seems to me to be a marvelous proof of love, on his part. A proof that deserves a tip of our hats."

"A hat that wouldn't fit on Pedro's highly decorated head," said Oscar. "No, obviously I don't like this business about accepting the situation. To go along with it, in this case, is to diminish himself as a man, as a husband."

"That may well be," Armando said, "but I still think that it would be a thoughtful solution and one that requires a certain largesse of spirit. Perhaps it's better to be unhappy next to a woman you love than happy away from her . . . But ultimately, we have to admit that it is not the best option."

"He can't kill the lovers," Carlos said. "He can't throw her out of the house or disappear, or get a divorce, or accept the situation. What's left to him? You have to admit that your character is in a terrible mess."

"There is still one more option," Armando said, "straightforward and clean: suicide."

Irma, Amalia, and Berta voiced their protest in unison.

"Oh, no!" Irma said. "No suicides! Poor Pedro! The truth is, I like him. And you, Berta? You have some influence over Armando, convince him not to kill him."

"I don't think he'll kill him," Berta said. "It would turn the story into a vulgar melodrama. Anyway, Pedro is too intelligent to commit suicide."

"I don't know if he's intelligent or not," Oscar said. "After all, that's just your assumption. But the situation is so complicated that maybe it would be best for him to shoot himself. What do you think, Armando?"

"Shoot?" Armando repeated. "Yes, shoot . . . But what would that resolve? Nothing. No, I don't think suicide is the answer. And not because it would be too melodramatic, as Berta says. I love melodrama and I think our lives are made out of one melodrama after another. The thing is that this solution would be just as bad as disappearing without a trace. And with the aggravating factor that it would be a disappearance without any possibility of return. If Pedro leaves home there's always the hope that he can return, and even for a reconciliation. But not if he commits suicide!"

"That's true," Carlos said. "I always prefer to have my return ticket in my pocket. But it's not really an absurd solution. If Pedro commits suicide, he is erased from the world, and he also erases Rosa, her lovers, that is, all his problems. Which is one way of solving it."

"There's something in what you say," Armando said, "and I'm going to consider this hypothesis. Though there's a big difference between solving a problem and avoiding it. And anyway, who knows! Maybe Pedro's suffering is so great that it will pursue him beyond the grave!"

"To a large extent, your character is screwed," Oscar said, yawning. "I see you haven't found a solution for your story. But our story is that it's after midnight and we have to go to work tomorrow. And we do have a solution: to leave now."

"Wait," Armando said. "I forgot one other possibility…"

"There's another one?" Berta asked.

"And one of the most important ones. In fact, I should have mentioned it first. It's also possible that Pedro will reach the conclusion that Rosa is not cheating on him, that all the evidence he has gathered is false. You all know, when it comes to something like this, the only proof is flagrante delicto. All the rest—letters, pictures, witnesses—can be disqualified. There could be a mistake in the interpretation, they could be apocryphal or falsified documents, malevolent witnesses, circumstances that lend themselves to baseless accusations. And the truth is, Pedro doesn't have absolute proof."

"That's it!" Oscar said. "You should have started with that. You've had us puzzling over a problem that in reality never existed. Shall we go, Irma?"

"Can I offer you a cognac, some mint tea?" Berta asked.

"Thanks," Carlos said. "Armando's story has been enormously entertaining, but Oscar's right, it's late. In any case, Armando, I hope that by the time we meet again you will have finished your story and you can read it to us."

"Oh!" Armando said. "The stories that interest us most are usually those that we can never finish … But this time I'll make an effort to finish it. And with a good solution."

"Berta, can you get our things?" Amalia said.

"I'll get them," Armando said. "Arrange with Berta for our next get-together."

Armando walked toward the back while Berta and the two couples said goodbye. Where will we have dinner next? At Oscar's? At Carlos's? In two weeks? In a month? A sharp, urgent sound came from the back of the house. They froze.

"Sounded like a gunshot," Oscar said.

Berta was the first to rush down the hallway, just when Armando reappeared carrying a purse, a scarf, and a coat. He was pale.

"Interesting!" he said. "This is the kind of coincidence that is very disconcerting. Looking for a pill in my nightstand I knocked my gun, and I don't know how, but it fired. It shot through the table and bounced off the wall."

"You really gave us a fright," Oscar said. "That's how accidents happen. That's why I never have guns around. Be a little more careful next time."

"Bah!" Armando said. "No need to exaggerate. After all, nothing happened. I'll walk you out the door."

The esplanade was sunk in fog. Armando waited until the cars had driven off, and when he returned to the house, he bolted the door and returned to the living room. Berta was carrying the dirty ashtrays to the kitchen.

"The maid will straighten out tomorrow. I'm too tired now."

"I, on the other hand, am not tired at all. The conversation gave me some new ideas. I'm going to work on my story for a while. You didn't say what you thought . . ."

"Please, Armando, I'm telling you I'm tired. We'll talk about it tomorrow."

Berta walked away, and Armando went to his office.

He was looking at his manuscript for a long time, striking out, adding, correcting. Finally, he turned off the light and went to the bedroom. Berta was sleeping on her side, her bedside light still on. Armando observed her blond hair spread out on the pillow, her profile, her delicate neck, the shape of her body under the quilt. Opening the drawer of the nightstand, he pulled out his gun and, stretching out his arm, he shot her in the neck.

NUIT CAPRENSE CIRIUS ILLUMINATA

As always, Fabricio arrived in Capri in the middle of September, to the small house he had rented for years on the Via Tragara. In his opinion, it was the best time of year to holiday on the island. In the meantime, his wife and son, who had spent July and August there, had returned to Paris, leaving the small house wholly at his disposal, and for a few weeks he would be able to enjoy the precious boon of solitude, tranquility, and freedom. By then, the middle of September, the flow of summer holidaymakers had ebbed, above all the children and young people, who not only jammed up and disrupted the alleyways of Capri with their games and their dalliances but were also a physical reminder to Fabricio of the burden of his own years. Also, as summer waned, it was a bit cooler, there were fewer mosquitoes, and the day often dawned with clouds or drizzle, a preview of Capri's dark, secret, wintry face.

Also, as usual, the little house was impeccably clean, orderly, and well-stocked. His wife always made sure to leave it set up for his immediate use: the refrigerator and pantry filled with enough provisions for fifteen days, the bathroom equipped with all necessary washing and medical supplies, his seasonal wardrobe washed and ironed in the closet, and the bar with his usual liquor and sodas—though this time Fabricio found, in delicate deference to his particular preferences, three bottles of an excellent Bordeaux, Chateau Pavie 1965.

Finally, as usual, Mina, the housekeeper who worked for them during their holidays, appeared in the afternoon to see if he needed anything and to remind him that, as in previous years, she would

come every morning a little before noon—except on the weekend—
to tidy up and prepare him something to eat.

Hence, Fabricio could devote himself entirely to what had become,
in the last fifteen years, his own Capri holiday. By virtue of repetition,
this had been purged of everything incidental and had acquired a
simplicity that contained a certain dose of tedium. For the first few
years, it's true, he would descend happily every day to the beach of
the Faraglioni, climb Mount Solaro, visit the ruins of Tiberius's villa,
patronize bars and restaurants, and wander through the labyrinth of
alleyways out of simple curiosity or with the vague hope of a romantic encounter that would liven up his solitary state on the island.
With the years, however, he abandoned these efforts and whims, and
spent most of his time in seclusion in his small house on Via Tragara,
lying in the sun on the small *terraza*, reading, listening to music, or
at times attempting to write something without any illusions, merely
to satisfy an old literary vocation that had foundered during the
twenty years he had spent working in Paris for an international organization. His only outings were around noon to buy *Le Figaro* and
Corriere della Sera, which he leafed through while drinking an *aranciata* at the café on the Piazzetta, and in the evenings to have an
aperitif at one of the many bars along the Via Camerelle, before
dining at home on leftovers from the lunch that Mina had prepared.
All of this was flat, petty, and lacking in fantasy—Fabricio was the
first to admit it—but at least it gave him the satisfaction of avoiding
any surprises or difficulties, all thanks to the good governance of
routine.

One morning, while sitting at the Gran Caffè de la Piazzetta and,
as usual, leafing through the newspaper, a woman walked by and
caught his eye. In fact, there were many women who caught his eye
during his mornings of *aranciatas*, with their elegance, their beauty,
or their sensuality, but he only ever registered their passage before
burrowing back down into his reading. But this woman made his
heart beat very fast. Something about her—her profile, the expression
on her face, the way she walked—felt familiar, something he had

already seen at one time in his life, but his memory was hazy. Then, suddenly, a detail he had seen and then recalled once she was gone, a mole at the corner of her lips, enlightened him. "*C'est elle, mon dieu,*" he said to himself in French, without knowing why. The woman had already crossed the Piazzetta on her way to Via Camerelle. Fabricio called over the waiter, paid his bill, and rushed out of the café.

It was Saturday, when small groups of Neapolitans take the *aliscafo* to Capri for the day, and the small streets were packed. Fabricio made his way through the crowds, stretching out his neck from time to time to see if he could catch a glimpse of the fleeting figure. According to his calculations, she was probably about two hundred meters ahead of him. From her passage through the Piazzetta, he remembered her chestnut hair tied with a ribbon at her neck, a beige summer dress, and a blue purse hanging off her shoulder. For a moment he thought he glimpsed her among the pedestrians turning onto Via Tragara, and he walked faster, but foot traffic stopped to let pass an electric cart loaded down with suitcases and then he bumped into an orderly but inopportune group of Japanese tourists, who blocked his way so they could listen obediently to the guide's explanations. Finally, Via Tragara—his street—cleared, and Fabricio could continue his search, which seemed more like a pursuit as he passed holidaymakers taken aback by his hurried and anxious expression, as he flew past his own house without even a glance, until he reached the belvedere, at the end of the street, without finding the woman he had glimpsed.

The belvedere had an iron railing and a magnificent view of the Faraglioni. There were only two ways to go from there: down the very long staircase that zigzagged to the beach or along the narrow Pizzolungo footpath that winds around the island and returns to the center of Capri after passing through the Matromania Grotto. Fabricio was confused, not knowing which path to take. Finally, remembering the woman's summer dress and her blue bag—perhaps a beach bag—he started down the stairs. He arrived in a sweat at the rocky beach, where only some twenty beachgoers were lying in the sun in their lounge chairs next to the small huts used as dressing rooms. He had made the wrong choice: she wasn't there. Now he had no choice but to climb back up—frustrated, out of breath—the thousand steps of that infernal hill that would take him back to the belvedere. Once again, Yolanda had slipped out of his arms.

Yolanda.

Madrid, twenty years earlier. Fabricio had been awarded a scholarship to do postgraduate work in international law after completing his studies at the university in Lima. One afternoon, while smoking a cigarette at the door of his boardinghouse, he saw two women walk by with linked arms and engaged in an animated conversation. One of them—why her? what was so special about her? what distinguished her from so many others?—instantly attracted him, and much against his wont, for he wasn't one to approach women on the street, he started to follow them. With no training or experience, he had no idea what to do next. But fate came to his rescue. A little before reaching Argüelles, the woman he was attracted to tripped on a cobblestone, twisted her foot, and ended up on her knees, clutching her ankle. Fabricio rushed to her side and grabbed her arm.

"Are you hurt? May I?"

The woman allowed him to help her up, then turned on him a beaming, spontaneous smile, as if he were an old friend.

"It's nothing, thank you . . . It's Milagros's fault, she was talking all kinds of nonsense."

That was all it took; contact was made. Fabricio accompanied them on their walk through Parque del Oeste. They were classmates and had just that year finished high school. They must have been between sixteen and seventeen years old. Milagros was more inquisitive, more gregarious, but she was rather homely: dirty blond hair, small blue eyes, a long nose, buzzard-like, that kind of thing. Yolanda, on the other hand, had an understated beauty without a touch of stridency: a delicate oval face framed by thick chestnut locks, almond-colored eyes, full lips ornamented by a mole in the left corner (an identical mole, Fabricio noted, to that of a cousin he visited frequently throughout his childhood), but above all, indecisive features,

features with great mobility, which allowed her to alternatively express the most natural joviality and the most impenetrable reserve.

For four or five days Fabricio ventured out with the two friends. They seemed delighted to spend time with this South American man, some ten years older than they, discreet and well-educated, who didn't court them openly and was always willing to invite them to the movies, or to cafés, without ever counting his duros. But Fabricio was growing increasingly uncomfortable with the situation, for Milagros's presence prevented him from establishing a more intimate relationship with Yolanda. And even more so when he noticed, through glances and half-spoken words, her interest, one could even say, her attraction to him. Finally, one afternoon, while they were saying goodbye, Fabricio broke the established formula of: "We'll get together tomorrow," and replaced it with, "Yolanda, I'll be waiting for you to go dancing at Pasapoga tomorrow." That "Yolanda," antecedent to the "you," which replaced the "we," was followed by a brief silence. Yolanda broke it with an "of course," while Milagros held out her arms as if she were dancing a waltz, pretending not to have heard.

From then on, Fabricio and Yolanda met alone almost every afternoon and between them there developed, rather than a friendship, a true love affair. In addition to the cafés and the movies, they took walks through Parque del Retiro, through the old Madrid of Franco's Spain, with its sirens, its censored press, its war casualties selling single cigarettes out of baskets on the streets. Yolanda was still a minor, and she was the daughter of an army colonel, so Fabricio, no matter how tempted he was, never dared go beyond caresses or furtive kisses in parks and movie houses. Once, however, when they found themselves near his residence, Fabricio suggested she see his room, and Yolanda accepted with the greatest of ease. For a long time they talked in his small room, where the only window opened onto a dark interior courtyard, then suddenly, without knowing how, they were lying on the bed, wrapped around each other. Fabricio was fully aware of all the risks he was taking, but his desire was so strong that he didn't hesitate to take off her blouse and bra, in spite of Yolanda's resistance. The sight of those virgin breasts, those erect nipples surrounded by their pink aureoles, reminded him immediately of his cousin Leticia, with whom he was in love as a teenager, of the time he saw her naked, half her body sunk in the water tank at the hacienda, breasts he could never touch, a scene that years later would come to his mind when in Paris he read Apollinaire's line: *Je rougirais le bout de tes jolis seins roses.* Fabricio was stunned for an instant, then fell upon those delicious breasts with the voracity of a hungry child. Yolanda, breathless, stopped him, stood up, and started getting dressed.

"Not now," she said. "Not now, please. There will be a next time."

There was no next time. Fabricio received news that he had been awarded a different scholarship to continue his studies in Paris, and it was imperative for him to be there at the beginning of September. It was the middle of August. During those final two weeks they went out repeatedly, but rarely alone, for Milagros resurfaced and accompanied them on their outings without there being any way—and Yolanda didn't make much effort—to get rid of her. At the beginning of September, Fabricio left Madrid. Yolanda and Milagros went to see him off at the Estación del Norte. They agreed to write to each other. As a precaution (the colonel father), they agreed that Fabricio should send his letters to Milagros's address.

It was a consistent and warm correspondence. They both wrote about their daily lives, recalled their best moments in Madrid, made plans for the future—plans that did not exclude an eventual marriage. In the middle of December, Fabricio finished the first stage of his training and announced to Yolanda that he would travel to Madrid for Christmas so they could spend a few days together. They agreed to meet at seven in the evening of December 23 at La Cachimba Café.

Fabricio would never forget that meeting. It was raining, and Yolanda was wearing a beige raincoat and an unexpectedly bright green beret, from which her chestnut hair escaped in billows. Fabricio had rented a room in an elegant and discreet inn near the Plaza Mayor. That night in the café, they only talked, their hands intertwined on the table, but they made plans to see each other the following day, on Christmas Eve. They were to meet on a street corner in the Vallecas neighborhood, where Milagros's grandparents lived, for Milagros was spending Christmas Eve with her family, and Yolanda would go by there after having dinner with hers. It was, in reality, an excuse, agreed among the three of them, so that Yolanda and Fabricio could be alone at midnight.

They arranged to meet in Vallecas at eleven. Fabricio was dressed by nine and was impatiently pacing around his comfortable room at the inn, examining every detail of the space where he would greet Christmas with Yolanda: the gift he had brought her from Paris (a Christian Dior scarf), the bottle of champagne in its bucket of ice, a plate with snacks, the bouquet of red roses in the vase. His heart kept beating rapidly, and he smoked one cigarette after another. At ten thirty he went out and caught a taxi to the spot in Vallecas where they were supposed to meet.

He never imagined that Christmas would be so boisterously celebrated in the streets in that working-class neighborhood. The sidewalks were teeming with people who talked and greeted each other from the doors of their houses, young men in groups were singing as they strolled by, and bands roamed the streets and played tambourines. Fabricio found the corner where they were supposed to meet and waited. He was five minutes early. At the appointed time he heard somebody call his name and, when he turned to look, he saw Milagros rather than Yolanda. She grabbed him by the arm and, without uttering a word, pulled him through the crowd.

"I have to tell you something," she said finally. "From Yolanda. She says not to try to see her, not to look for her, not to write to her, ever again."

Fabricio stopped, in shock. For a moment he thought he was going to collapse. His expression of disbelief, surprise, and defeat must have been such that Milagros put her arms around him.

"I'm sorry," she whispered in his ear, "so sorry for the bad news. That's just the way things are. Yolanda didn't give me any explanation. I'm just telling you what she told me."

They pulled apart, but remained holding hands. Fabricio looked into Milagros's tiny blue eyes, waiting for something more, a reason, a ray of hope. All he saw was pity, and at the same time something more ambiguous, secretive, which he could not, at that moment, decipher.

He let go of Milagros's hand and walked away without a word, walked away through the jubilant streets of Vallecas, slicing through the feverish throng, through the deafening music, set upon by gangs of young men urging him to drink from red wineskins. Finally he found a taxi. In half an hour he was at his inn. It was already midnight. The other residents were celebrating Christmas in the dining room, and they invited him to join their revels. But Fabricio continued along his way, driven by one fixed idea: to leave as soon as possible, to get far away from the center of the pain. A night train was leaving for Paris at one in the morning. He threw his things into his suitcase and, leaving behind his gift and the bottle of champagne, took a taxi to the Estación del Norte; an hour later he was on his way to Paris.

He never saw Yolanda again or heard any news from her. From Paris, after a few days of reflection and suffering, he wrote her several letters, begging for an explanation, letters he always sent to Milagros's house (Yolanda never gave him her address), but he never received an answer. The years passed, he had new loves and new affairs, he got married, his old Madrid romance remained buried in his memory until there was nothing left of it, except in disturbing dreams from which he always awoke with the disappointment of unfulfilled pleasure. Yolanda no longer existed. Not until that morning when he saw her walk through the Piazzetta de Capri and followed her desperately until he lost all trace of her at the beach of the Faraglioni.

After that failed search, exhausted by the climb back up to the belvedere (one thousand steps, according to the tourist brochures), Fabricio lay down on the living room sofa and chain smoked, disheartened, as evening fell. He didn't even feel like going through his routine of taking a bit of sun on his adorable little *terraza*, where he could enjoy the splendid view of Marina Piccola and Monte Solaro. Only after nightfall did he get up and uncork one of the still untouched bottles of Chateau Pavie 1965. With his third glass, his optimism was returning, and he decided he would scour Capri from top to bottom and inside out in his search for his lost vision. He walked along well-known streets and ventured into undiscovered alleyways; he entered bars, restaurants, and shops (in some bars he took the opportunity to have a glass of sherry), ventured into hidden courtyards and peered into the lighted windows of *pensiones*. For moments he had the impression he was striding through an invented, mythological city, where he crossed paths with Dianas and Aphrodites in miniskirts, with the robust bastard sons of Zeus dressed by Cerruti, but also with monsters risen from Lake Avernus, wrinkled and potbellied tourists who came to breathe their last summer, or local valetudinarians, who could barely drag themselves up the steep Via Sopramonte, weighed down as they were by the burden of death. Late at night, he was drunk, exhausted, confused, and defeated. He stumbled home along Via Tragara, stopped for a moment to contemplate a brick archway that he seemed to be seeing for the first time—and he had walked by there so many times!—and when he arrived he had just enough energy to reach his bed and fall asleep, without getting undressed.

In the morning he woke up exhausted but possessed with an idea that had taken root while he slept: in order to find someone, he didn't need to race through the streets of Capri but should instead settle into a café on the Piazzetta. This was the neurological center of town, the obligatory place through which all the inhabitants necessarily passed at some moment of their day. By noon he was already sitting on the terrace of the Gran Caffè sipping a Negroni. It was Sunday and the five small streets that converged on the Piazzetta were packed with dense throngs of holidaymakers and casual tourists, who mingled there then dispersed down the evacuation routes. Fabricio once again verified that at this time of year most of the holidaymakers were senior citizens, and this thought, as it applied to himself, caused sharp unease, even though he considered that at the age of fifty he still hadn't earned the distinctions required to belong to that club.

At three in the afternoon, Fabricio gave up. He had a horrible headache, not only from the Negronis he had drunk but from the attention he had paid to every woman who walked by (some of them startled him when he noticed that they shared some particular with his model). Resigned, he told himself that the previous day he had been the victim of a mistaken perception or an hallucination. All he could do now was forget the incident and resume his calm if tedious island sojourn. He called over the waiter, and just as he was paying, a woman walked hastily across the Piazzetta. At first he didn't recognize her, for she was wearing blue jeans (he had never seen Yolanda in pants), tight blue jeans that clung to her very youthful body, and a straw hat with a blue ribbon. But just as she was exiting his field of vision, he saw the mole. Without picking up his change, he stood up and took off after her, for she had already turned down Via le Botteghe. It was one of the narrowest and busiest streets in Capri because of all the small shops selling clothing and handicrafts, and all the bars and grocery stores. Fabricio feared losing her again among the throng, but at last he saw her standing in front of the window of a pharmacy. He stopped behind her, his heart pounding.

"Yolanda," he whispered, and immediately the woman turned around.

She stood there staring at him for a long time without showing any sign of recognition. Fabricio noticed that she was younger than he had expected, and he wondered once again if he had not been the victim of confusion.

"Yolanda Gálvez, or am I mistaken?"

And a few second later, that cold, suspicious face opened into a luminous smile (the same one, Fabricio discovered, that had caught him off guard twenty years before when he helped her get to her feet on the Paseo de Argüelles).

"But I can't ... I can't believe it ... Fabricio? What are you doing here?"

"The same question I can ask you."

"Let me ... let me recover ... I never thought ..."

Fabricio took her hand.

"Let's go have a drink. We have so much to talk about."

Yolanda looked at her watch.

"I can't now. I'm in a rush. I have to get back to the hotel to wait for a call from Naples, from my husband, and then I'm going to Anacapri. I just stepped out for a minute because I needed to buy something at the pharmacy...some nail scissors. I always forget something when I travel. But let me look at you for a moment. No, you haven't changed. Maybe...I don't know, something in the eyes. But, you stink! Have you been drinking?"

"Yolanda, please, let's go have a coffee, you're not going to stand me up, after so many years."

"Wait for me for a minute. I'll buy what I need and then you can come with me to my hotel. We'll talk along the way."

Yolanda entered the pharmacy and came out smiling a few minutes later.

"Let's go," she said, taking his arm. "I'm at the Hotel Quisisana. But hurry. I don't have much time."

Fabricio let himself be carried along while Yolanda told him all about how she had accompanied her husband to an international cardiology conference in Naples and had taken the opportunity to hop over to Capri for the weekend. It was the first time she'd been on the island. She loved it. The day before she'd gone down to the beach of the Faraglioni—

"I followed you there," Fabricio interrupted her. "I followed you to the end of Via Tragara. But when I got to the beach, you weren't anywhere."

Yolanda looked at him incredulously. They had reached the door to the hotel.

"I'm going to Anacapri this afternoon with some of the other wives of the cardiologists. But I'm free after six."

"I was waiting for you to say that!" Fabricio sighed. "Come to the house for dinner, a small house I rent on Via Tragara. Number 115. Remember: 115 Via Tragara."

"I'll be there at seven," Yolanda said, and, brushing her lips across his cheek, she disappeared behind the door of the hotel.

Fabricio returned elated, almost at a run, to prepare the stage for the unexpected reencounter. As he walked under the small archway on the Via Tragara, he stopped, without knowing why, and looked closely at the fine brick structure and the bright red bougainvillea crowning it. At home, he had to tidy things up, for it was Sunday and Mina wouldn't be coming. Then he returned to Via le Botteghe to do the required shopping: Parma ham, melon, Capri raviolis, cheeses, ice cream, and champagne. His only problem was figuring out where they would eat: on the jasmine-perfumed patio, on the small terrace shaded by palm trees and lined with flower pots overflowing with geraniums and greenery, or in the living room, which had the advantage of being next to the kitchen. He opted for the small terrace, for the splendid day promised a warm and clear night.

A little before seven everything was ready, and Fabricio was smoking on the terrace, sipping a glass of sherry and watching the sun set behind Monte Solaro. How many times, during his previous holidays, had he sat right there, looking at the same spectacle, but then he wasn't waiting for anybody! Due to random good luck, his gray and monotonous life in Capri had been turned on its head.

A small gray cloud appeared behind Monte Solaro, followed by another larger one. The sirocco began to blow. At seven, high dark clouds sped faster and faster across the sky. Fabricio, who had already experienced some of those terrible island storms that drenched the streets and shut the natives away in their homes, was wondering if the weather was going to play a lousy trick on him when the doorbell rang. He ran to the gate and upon opening it he found Yolanda wearing a very low-cut gray dress, and with no relationship to it, a green beret from which her abundant chestnut hair escaped in billows.

"Madrid, 1953," Fabricio muttered, as if to himself.

"Indeed," Yolanda said. "But, come on, let me in and offer me something, I'm exhausted."

They had only just sat down on the small terrace with their respective glasses of champagne—Yolanda was recounting to him in detail her exhausting excursion to Anacapri—when there was a flash behind Monte Solaro and an instant later came the first roll of thunder. A gust of wind shook the palm trees, and heavy rain began to fall. They dashed into the living room, glasses in hand. Yolanda pulled off her beret then cheerfully began to examine the room's décor. Fabricio, for his part, didn't take his eyes off her, still unable to calm his emotions, asking himself how she, Yolanda, could be there, with her youthful figure, her schoolgirl charm, her luminous smile, but also her brusque and impenetrable reserve . . . And he recalled that painful moment of their failed encounter in the Vallecas neighborhood.

Yolanda opened her mouth as if to make a comment, but Fabricio interrupted her.

"I never understood, Yolanda, I never understood why that night in Vallecas, that Christmas Eve, when I'd come from Paris specifically to see you, you didn't show up, and instead you sent Milagros to say . . ."

Another peal of thunder, this time even stronger, deafened them. The walls of the house shook and the lights flickered.

"I'm surprised to hear you say that," Yolanda said. "You're the one who didn't show up."

This time the boom was closer and suddenly the lights went out.

"Don't be afraid," Fabricio said. "These blackouts last only a short while. I'll get some candles."

His prudent wife always had a package of candles stashed away somewhere. Fabricio stood up and tripped over the furniture as he dug into his pockets for his lighter so he could see through the darkness, but then he remembered that he had left it on the terrace and went out through the living room to face the storm. He flicked it on when he returned: Yolanda's place was empty.

"But . . . but, where the hell have you gone?" he exclaimed, lifting his hand that was holding the lighter to check the room. Nobody responded. Fabricio was confused, entered the kitchen, and was about to look for her in the bedroom when he heard some noise from the bathroom, and in an instant, Yolanda appeared.

"What?" Fabricio asked. "How did you get there?"

"I can see in the dark," Yolanda said, smiling.

"Sit down and don't move, please. I'm going to look for some candles.

Fortunately, he found the package in one of the cupboards in the kitchen. Since there weren't any candlesticks, he put them in empty bottles and on saucers and distributed them around the living room.

"I'm not afraid of the dark but it would have been sad to be with you and not be able to see you," Fabricio said. "Anyway, dinner is going to be a disaster. How am I going to heat up the raviolis? And the ice cream is going to melt!"

"Do you care?" Yolanda said and, after a short silence, she added, "*Nuit caprense cirius illuminata.*"

"What did you say?"

"I don't know. Something that just popped into my head. But relax, you're a bundle of nerves. Come on, let's make a toast."

"You're right," Fabricio said, sitting next to Yolanda and picking up his champagne glass. "*Chin-chin!*"

They clinked glasses and drank down their champagne.

"But back to what we were saying," Fabricio said. "Christmas Eve in Vallecas, one of the blackest nights of my life. What happened? You said I didn't show up, but I swear to you I was there, I met Milagros, and she told me that—"

"I know, she probably told you that I hadn't shown up for dinner at her grandparents. It was all a lie. It took me a long time to realize it. Milagros was jealous, envious, she couldn't stand that I—"

"Damn harpy!" Fabricio exclaimed, pouring himself another glass of champagne. "I'd wring her neck in an instant!"

"I was at her grandparents' house, and I asked her to go meet you. We agreed that she would come get me when you arrived, and I'd find some excuse to leave so I could be with you. But she returned and told me that you hadn't shown up. It seemed very odd to me, I didn't believe her, and on my way home I called your inn. They told me that you'd left at midnight, gone back to Paris."

Fabricio sat for a minute, thinking.

"You mean, because of that harpy, my life, our life, perhaps . . ."

"Some people are like that. And it wasn't the only time. A year after you left I met a very intelligent Colombian poet, and she played the same trick on me again. Since then, I haven't seen her. They assigned my father to Barcelona, we moved, and that was the last I saw of her."

"Let's return to the present," Fabricio said. "The fact is, we're here, together again, or near each other, to be more exact, in spite of her manipulations... I'm so happy, Yolanda, let me pour you another glass of champagne... But the lights, when will they go on again? At least we can eat the Parma ham and the melon. Come on, tell me more about yourself as I prepare something to eat."

The kitchen was next to the living room, connected by a window without glass, whose wood sill doubled as a bar. While Fabricio busied himself in the kitchen, Yolanda sipped her champagne and spoke intermittently.

"Well, in Barcelona I studied literature at the university. Then I met Miguel, my husband, who's about ten years older than me, like you—and now I see that he does have something of you, something secretive, I don't know. He'd finished medical school, and we got married... have you ever heard of Miguel Sender? He's the top cardiologist in Spain, well, one of the top, I don't want you to think I'm pretentious, and then..."

Fabricio had stopped what he was doing to observe Yolanda through the window. He saw her in profile, sitting on the sofa and talking about her life, and in the uncertain light of the candle he saw her as almost ghostly, her voice like a recitation from another world, to the point that he asked himself if she was there or if this was a new hallucination.

"When was the accident?" he asked unexpectedly.

"What accident?" Yolanda asked.

"That scar on your temple, I can just barely see it under your hair."

"Oh, a car accident we had on the way to Valencia. It was nothing. But, as I was saying, Miguel is an important cardiologist. Just so you know. If you ever have any heart problems, don't hesitate to be in touch."

"Unfortunately," Fabricio said, "the problems I have with my heart aren't treatable by a cardiologist."

"That's a platitude," Yolanda said. "I knew you'd say something like that."

Fabricio came into the living room carrying a tray with the ham, the melon, and some cutlery.

"I have no pretensions of being original. Shall we keep drinking champagne or should I open a bottle of Bordeaux?"

"I don't care. But come on, I'm the only one doing the talking here. Now it's your turn. You're an important lawyer, I presume."

"No, no, much worse than that! I'm an international bureaucrat. I've been working for UNESCO for almost twenty years. I manage a department that deals with ... But why talk about that? Let's just say I form commissions that produce reports that are sent to other commissions that write other reports and so on and so forth ..."

There was another peal of thunder, and the walls shook so strongly that the candles almost went out, while outside, on the patio and the terrace, the rain was coming down more heavily.

"The storm is saying goodbye," Fabricio said. "I know these. In five minutes ..."

Suddenly he stopped. He noticed that Yolanda had not taken a bite and was sitting there absentmindedly, looking into the void. In the candlelight, her chestnut hair seemed to shimmer, releasing sparks as if it were a faggot of burning hay. And next to her lips, that mole.

"It's curious," Fabricio said, "did I ever tell you? When I was fifteen I fell in love with my cousin, who had a mole exactly in the same place you have one. It was a crazy love, stupid, but I could never even kiss her. What's up? Are you listening to me?"

"Yes," said Yolanda, startled. "Your cousin Leticia, the mole ... and then?"

"And then nothing," Fabricio mumbled. He had the impression that at some point the thread connecting him and Yolanda had broken and he immediately felt profoundly despondent. He took a sip of wine and placed his head between his hands.

"Come here," he heard Yolanda say.

As he lifted his head he saw her lying on the sofa, her arms stretched out and her palms open to the ceiling.

"Come, Fabricio, come ... Don't make that face of a scolded child. Forget about your cousin and her mole. Am I not here now?"

Fabricio went to her and took her hands. This touch was enough to feel a rush of warm vitality throughout his body, one that expelled his despondency and filled him with passion. Yolanda was breathing deeply, her eyes half closed, and with each inhalation her chest swelled, overflowing the neckline of her dress. Her chest, that chest he contemplated in that rooming house on Argüellos so many years before in all its youthful splendor, that chest like a double herald that opened the gates of the virginal palace, but that he could only just barely graze . . .

"Come Fabricio," Yolanda repeated. "Remember what you said to me in your room? *Je rougirais le bout de tes jolis seins roses.*"

Immediately Fabricio slid Yolanda's dress off her shoulders to reveal her breasts, the same as then: white, round, firm, with their pink aureoles and erect nipples. But a strange thought passed through his head.

"I didn't say that, I swear I didn't. How could I have? I didn't know French and I hadn't yet read Apollinaire."

"Are you sure? Wait. Maybe, maybe . . . maybe it was that Columbian poet I mentioned. He used to read me poems. We were—"

"To hell with your Columbian poet!" Fabricio shouted, and, unable to control himself, he fell on Yolanda's chest. Silence reigned outside. The rain had ceased to pound on the rooftop, the patio, and the palm trees on the terrace. The candles sputtered and went out in their improvised candlesticks. "*La seconde chance*," Fabricio thought, biting Yolanda's lips with fury.

He woke at dawn, naked and shivering on the sofa in the living room. The lights were on, the electricity at some point having returned. But Yolanda wasn't there. He looked for her in vain throughout the house, but found not a single trace of her—no object, no message. The table was a mess—the empty bottles of Bordeaux—but the dishes were clean and stacked in the drying rack next to the kitchen sink. Wrapping a towel around himself, he went out onto the terrace in the hope that . . . But all he saw was the small table and the empty chairs and a glimmer behind Monte Tuoro and a blue sky that was getting lighter and lighter, announcing a splendid day.

Returning to the living room, he tried to recall in order the events of that senseless night. At some moment, he had lost consciousness. He remembered his clothes strewn on the floor, the sound of a bottle opening, a candle going out. And then fatigue, shadows, oblivion, and sleep. He took a few more turns wrapped in the towel, and suddenly had thoughts about the emperor Tiberius, who, twenty centuries before, must have wandered at dawn through the corridors of his palace wrapped in his tunic after a diabolical night, looking for himself among the rubble of his memories. But his legs buckled from tiredness and, without the strength to interrogate himself further, he collapsed on the sofa and fell back asleep.

He awoke refreshed and lucid late in the morning. On other occasions, other holidays, he would have remained loyal to his routine and made coffee and toast, then gone out to take some sun on the terrace, waiting for noon to go to the Piazzetta to buy the newspapers and leaf through them at the Gran Caffè, while drinking his *aranciata*. But now that was impossible. His routine had been blown to pieces. It was urgent for him to see Yolanda again. He was still infused with her scent, surrounded by her invisible presence. He remembered that at some point she told him that on Monday at noon she was returning to Naples to meet her husband and return to Barcelona. Immediately he got dressed and rushed to Hotel Quisisana. That chance, belated meeting could not have been a dream or the product of his imagination. He went straight to the reception desk and when the clerk asked him whom he was looking for, Fabricio hesitated.

"Yolanda Gálvez," he said, finally.

The clerk looked at the register.

"There's nobody here by that name."

Fabricio figured she must have registered under her married name and for a moment he racked his brains to remember her husband's name.

"Yolanda Sender," he said, finally.

The clerk looked again in the register.

"There's no Sender here."

"I came here with her yesterday," Fabricio insisted. "I left her at the door to the hotel. She had an excursion to Anacapri in the afternoon."

"I'm telling you, she's not registered. Many people come into the hotel who aren't staying here."

"And the women with her? The wives of the doctors? There's a conference of cardiologists in Naples. Please check."

The clerk turned to a colleague.

"Do you know of a cardiology conference in Naples?"

"No conferences that I know of. As far as I know, they start in October."

Fabricio left, confused and discouraged, and started on his way home. The Negroni, the champagne, the Bordeaux he'd drunk the day before, had they unhinged him to such a degree that he imagined everything that had happened? He rejected that idea, but another occurred to him. Yolanda had been in Capri, he had no doubt, but not at Hotel Quisisana. She simply pretended to be staying there because it was the most expensive and elegant hotel on the island, and she had wanted to impress him. Maybe she had stayed in a modest *pensione* on Via Sopramonte and maybe even her famous cardiologist husband had been a fabrication.

He was on Via Tragara, the long street he walked down every summer and that always produced in him an inexplicable emotion, evoked not only by the beauty of its mansions—many of which had been converted into hotels—and the magnificent view of the Tyrrhenian Sea. When he reached the brick archway, he stopped. And his memory glowed: yes, that simple archway, crowned with bright red bougainvillea, was the one he had seen as a child in an album of postcards and prints at home. His father loved the picture of that archway, which he'd found in an old tourism magazine, so much that he decided to build one the same but smaller over a path in the garden. The work began, but his father took ill right in the middle of it; he died shortly thereafter, and the archway was left unfinished forever. But the real one was there, the one he had never been able to pass under at home. And under that archway, what could not be had come to life, and that's why—now he understood—every time he passed under it he felt something like a breath of springtime excitement, as if he had returned to the most beautiful days of his childhood. Passing under the arch was a way of returning to the past to relive what had taken place or remake what had not.

Exalted by this discovery, which was also a foreboding, Fabricio kept walking, ever more quickly, looking nervously in his pocket for his keys, eager to arrive home as soon as possible. He stopped for a moment at the gate, then trembled when he saw that the door to the living room was ajar and heard the sound of footsteps from inside. He pushed open the gate and quickly walked across the patio, just when the door to the living room opened and Mina, his housekeeper, appeared, a bag of garbage in hand. Mina! He had forgotten that she came just before noon to do the cleaning.

"Everything in order, *Signore* Fabricio. *Domani* at eleven, as usual. *Bon giorno.*"

Fabricio leaned against the doorway of the living room, once again disappointed. Finally, he took a step inside just as Mina called to him from the gate.

"I found something under the sofa, *Signore* Fabricio. I left it on the *tavola. Arrivederci.*"

When he entered the living room, Fabricio saw on the coffee table an object that glowed among the magazines and the tile ashtrays: the green beret. He took it in his hands, squeezed it, breathed in its scent, Yolanda's scent, and another scent, much more subtle, that seemed to come from much farther away. A small piece of paper fell out of it. Picking it up, he read:

"*Tu as rougi le bout de mes jolis seins roses.*"

And below, a scribbled initial that could have been a *Y* or an *L*.

Capri
September 17, 1993

from
TALES OF SANTA CRUZ

MUSIC, MAESTRO BERENSON, AND YOURS TRULY

FATHER cultivated in us from an early age an appreciation for classical music; he played Bach fugues, Mozart sonatas, and Chopin nocturnes on his old wind-up Victrola with a steel needle, and hummed arias from Italian operas in his weak but melodious tenor voice. But Father died quite young, taking to his grave his love of music and putting an end to our musical education, which would have faded away and possibly been extinguished altogether had it not been for Teodorito and, above all, the appearance in Lima of Maestro Hans Marius Berenson.

Teodorito was my classmate and notorious not only for his short stature but for the slow and long-winded way he told every story, no matter how simple, such that by his second or third digression his audience had already vanished. Teodorito, however, had a secret characteristic: he was an ardent aficionado of highly select music. I discovered this one afternoon as we were leaving school, a little apart from the rest, and I overheard him whistling Liszt's "Liebestraum" with the brio of a goldfinch and the virtuosity of a soloist.

This discovery was enough to make him my best friend and, from that day forward, I visited him two or three times a week at his house on Avenida Pardo, where an elderly and childless aunt and uncle—Teodorito was an orphan—gave him lodgings in a large room in the backyard. There Teodorito had erected a temple devoted to music: a Victrola like mine, though larger and more modern; shelves filled with dozens of record albums; portraits and busts of his favorite composers; and an open dance floor, for at moments of particular enthusiasm Teodorito could not resist the temptation to corporeally expressed his musical delight.

Thanks to Teodorito, my affinity for music was reborn and strengthened, and I could go on forever if I started to describe the endless nights I spent in his temple listening to symphonies—heroic, pathetic, Italian, fantastic, and new world—as well as sonatas, overtures, fugues, suites, and concertos. At home, on my own, I spent more long hours with my ear glued to Radio Selecta and writing down in a notebook the names of the pieces I listened to. Thus, upon finishing high school, I was able to consider myself if not an erudite scholar of music, at least a young and enthusiastic aficionado. Unfortunately, however, my knowledge of this art suffered from one serious deficiency: it was purely bookish knowledge, so to speak, for I had never attended a public concert nor listened to a live symphony orchestra. Never, until the appearance of the maestro.

How in the world did Hans Marius Berenson end up in Lima? Through a series of circumstances in which *Führer* Adolf Hitler played a principal role. Berenson was a young, brilliant, and polymorphous instrumentalist in the Vienna Symphony Orchestra of the nineteen-thirties under the direction of the celebrated Bruno Walter. Though he began his career as a cellist, he continued as a violinist, then became first violinist, until he was promoted to assistant music director. Everything indicated that one day he would replace the elderly Bruno at the helm of this prestigious orchestra. But clouds were gathering over Europe, Nazi Germany annexed Austria, the Second World War broke out, and Bruno Walter and his disciple, both Jews, were suddenly forced to leave Austria or risk losing their lives as well as their jobs. Berenson spent some time in Paris, then London, then emigrated to the United States, where he spent a few years and had difficulty finding work, this due to fierce competition and the best positions having already been filled by other European musicians who had arrived before him. Through a friend, he heard that Peru's symphony orchestra was being reorganized and was in need of a competent music director. Hence, he decided to play the South American card and landed one day in Lima with his wife, his violin, and a trunk full of sheet music.

It was Teodorito who informed me of the appearance of this "genius of the baton," as he called him, and the compelling need to go hear him. After only a few months in Lima, according to Teodorito, he had managed to make the national symphony orchestra sound as sublime as a rose. It was summer and Sunday concerts were held in the open air, in the outdoor amphitheater of the Campo de Marte.

One Sunday I decided to accompany him. I was excited and terrified. I wondered what it would be like to see an orchestra as well as listen to it, if the direct and visual experience of the music would enhance or detract from my pleasure, which until then had been purely auditory. The experience was decisive. Although at first it was unnerving to have to associate melodies I knew so well with a hundred-odd gentlemen in tuxedos laboriously playing their instruments, in the end I understood that the two things were inseparable and that my entire knowledge of music had been, until that day, wholly phantasmagoric. To all this one must add the presence of Hans Marius Berenson, his fragile and elegant silhouette, and his winged baton, which seemed to weave and unweave the chords with infallible accuracy. My devotion reached its zenith when the orchestra attacked Beethoven's Fifth, the centerpiece of the program. I had listened to this symphony hundreds of times and knew it almost by heart, but when that fourfold stampede of chords announced its opening, I leapt out of my seat as if "the blow of fate" had resounded within me. I listened to the entire piece in a state of ecstasy, and when it ended to thundering applause I was unable to budge, and Teodorito had to pull me by the arm to remind me that we had to leave quickly if we wanted to reach the bus stop before the rest of the audience. I obeyed him like a zombie, staggering over the grass of the Campo de Marte, making my way through the thousands of spectators who continued to applaud, watching Teodorito run to the bus stop with his back to the stage, though, in homage to the orchestra, leaping into the air every few minutes and making a hundred-and-eighty-degree turn in the air and clapping his hands before his feet touched the ground, only to regain his original position and continue along his way.

From that moment on I became an avid devotee of the National Symphony Orchestra and Berenson, and I came to swell the ranks of Lima's not-very-numerous but highly select crowd of music lovers. After the summer season was over, the concerts started up again in the Teatro Municipal, and not a week went by when either alone or with Teodorito I didn't climb, panting, the five flights of stairs that led to the gallery, the theater section that, according to the cognoscenti, offered the best acoustics as well as the cheapest tickets in the house. The gallery was always full of a mostly young and well-versed crowd, and a festive air reigned in the aisles. There were students from the conservatory, one or another composer, painters, aspiring philosophers, poets, journalists, and a few beautiful or emancipated or sophisticated girls who embodied for me the full flowering of artistic intelligence. It was the audience in the gallery that clapped most heartily, whistled loudest when appropriate, and whose clamorous *bravos* summoned the orchestra's encores.

But my musical passion did not end there. When I began studying law, I had no choice but to walk past the Teatro Municipal to reach the building where my classes were held. As I was always in a hurry, I barely had time to glimpse out of the corner of my eye the posters announcing the next weekly concert and to hear a few muffled chords of the orchestra rehearsals. One morning, I could no longer resist the temptation and snuck in through the artists' entrance. For the first time, I could attend a concert rehearsal from backstage, and see, from just a few feet away, Berenson, in shirtsleeves, trenchant and sweating, as he executed the perfect performance piece by piece and after thousands of interruptions and repetitions, like a writer who achieves the long dreamed-of page after infinite corrections. My admiration for the maestro grew, and from then on, most mornings that I walked past the Teatro Municipal, I would blow off my law classes and allow myself to get sucked in through the artists' entrance. My musical education flourished while my law studies floundered. By the end of the year I could recognize with closed eyes the sound of a violin as opposed to that of a viola and could distinguish the slightest wrong note from one of the trumpets, but I failed to pass my exams in family and civil law.

This was not the only effect my musical passion had on my life. It also had consequences in my family circle and in particular on my older sister's destiny. Mercedes was eighteen years old and had a throng of suitors. After giving several the boot, she retained two and was unable to decide between them, for they both conformed to the same type rather than each being an individual. Both were cadets at the military academy, both were young, handsome, well-built, sons of well-known families of the Miraflores bourgeoisie, equally dogged in their courting and assiduous in their visits. In addition, they came together to see her, both taking advantage of their weekend leave. My brother and I had no preference and couldn't have cared less about her final choice. Hernán was perhaps better-looking, but Genaro was more intelligent. Until, that is, we found out that Genaro loved classical music and that his family had a noteworthy record collection. Genaro, also aware of our passion for music, immediately understood the advantage he could thereby wield over Hernán, and from then on, a Saturday did not pass in which he failed to bring us a record from his house. For the most part they were operas sung by Enrico Caruso, Beniamino Gigli, and Amelita Galli-Curci, rare recordings worthy of a collector and that delighted my brother, who disdained symphonic music and preferred bel canto. As Genaro's record collection diminished, our affection for him increased. And this affection turned into open complicity and underhanded combat against his rival. Not only did we disparage Hernán's qualities and glorify Genaro's within the intimacy of the family circle, but because Mercedes remained undecided we employed the lowest of means, such as failing to pass along phone messages from Hernán, or even worse, inventing romances he was carrying on in other neighborhoods of Miraflores, employing vague and unverifiable allusions, such as "I think I saw him . . ." "Someone said . . ." et cetera. Mercedes, who was jealous and possessive, was easily deceived, and without Hernán ever understanding why, she sent him packing for good. Two years later she married Genaro.

Teodorito and I could not, as it were, marry Maestro Berenson, despite adoring him quite as much as my sister did Genaro, but we continued to pay our respects by attending his concerts at the Teatro Municipal. Other conductors passed through Lima, such as Erich Kleiber or Fritz Busch, but we continued to prefer the nervous, fragile, and elegant Hans Marius Berenson and his flying baton, which—through its finesse and intelligence—seemed like one more musical instrument.

At last, one night, we decided to wait for him after a concert, approach him, and confess to him our great admiration. Stationed at the main doors, we watched as the audience dispersed and some members of the orchestra departed. We then realized that other musicians were leaving through the artists' entrance around the corner. This worried us, so we decided that Teodorito would watch the main door and I the other one. At last Teodorito came running to announce that the maestro had left alone and was walking toward Jirón de la Unión, the main pedestrian street. We turned to follow him and when we got there, we saw him heading toward the Plaza San Martín. We followed, about twenty steps behind, uncertain how and when to approach him. At moments we would lose sight of him among the other pedestrians, then we'd pick up our pace. We watched him pause hesitantly at the Plaza San Martín. We thought he might be trying to decide whether to take a taxi or the express bus back to Miraflores. But suddenly he turned resolutely toward the Romano. A few minutes later we entered and saw him in that noisy, bustling establishment, leaning on the bar and drinking a beer. We had no choice but to go up to him, and that is just what we did. When Teodorito began with "Maestro Berenson, we—" the maestro seemed quite taken aback and inspected us with clear and penetrating eyes. From close up we saw his smooth, rosy skin, which made him look younger, but there was a certain weariness in his expression, something anxious and old. When Teodorito finished his halting speech, the maestro very courteously thanked him for his words of appreciation, then quickly finished off his beer, and with a brusque "good night," he got up and walked out, leaving us quite frustrated.

In spite of this, Teodorito and I remained loyal to the concerts of the symphony orchestra, and every week we climbed the five flights of stairs in the Teatro Municipal to fiercely applaud our Viennese idol. New and brilliant musicians brought by Berenson—in particular an oboist and a flautist—had joined the orchestra, and the group reached masterful heights of sonority. The celebrated Hermann Scherchen, who came to Lima to conduct a few concerts, said in an interview that our symphony orchestra was the best in South America, due specifically to the excellence of its current music director.

This praise filled us with renewed pride, and Teodorito and I again considered the possibility of approaching the maestro. We finally did so under quite unusual circumstances. It was October and in celebration of Lima's patron saint, El Señor de los Milagros, the Lord of Miracles, lively street fairs and bazaars were held in various neighborhoods. As a result, and because we felt like living it up, we decided to forgo, for the first time, that night's concert in order to enjoy the fair on Avenida Tacna. We wandered past the kiosks, pitching pennies, participating in drawings, eating grilled chicken hearts, and drinking various fermented corn brews, including *cachina* and *chicha de jora*. A little before midnight we remembered that the orchestra was holding its weekly concert just a few steps away, and, imbued with courage from the alcohol, we made our way toward the Teatro Municipal to await the maestro. The doors were closed and the hall was in total darkness. The concert had ended half an hour before. Far from deflated, we made off toward the Jirón de la Unión, the Plaza San Martín, and the Romano, with a remote hope of finding him. At that late hour, the bar was filled with euphoric denizens of the night, who seemed to stagger and drift toward the irreparable. Then we spotted him in the crowd. He was leaning on the bar, like the first time, but now he was accompanied by two of his musicians, the oboist and the violist, who had left their instrument cases leaning against the wall behind the bar. From the doorway we watched him converse, laugh, and offer toasts. The presence of his colleagues had dampened our spirits. Luckily, they both soon offered him their hands, picked up their cases, and departed, leaving the maestro alone in the crowd in front of his glass of beer. That was the moment to approach him. He may have recognized us, though there was no way for us to know, but this time his small, keen, and shining eyes seemed friendlier as they looked us over. Teodorito took the opportunity to launch into his old routine about our passion for music and our admiration for him. The maestro received these declarations with modesty and offered to buy us a drink. We ordered pisco martinis and a short time later we were engaged in an animated conversation. He asked us what we did, and when he found out we were not students at the National Conservatory of Music but rather anonymous habitués of his concerts, his interest in us seemed to grow.

He invited us to a second round, and he ordered another beer, accompanied, I noticed, by a shot of pisco, which he drank by taking small sips of each in turn. He spoke for a long time about his musical training, his life in Vienna before the war, while I, as I was starting in on my third martini, began to sink into a dense fog, from the depths of which I required an enormous effort to understand what the maestro was saying and remain aware of where I was. At one particular moment the noise and lights of the bar were left behind, and we found ourselves on the street—the maestro, myself, and a Teodorito whom I barely perceived as a tiny scrap of ectoplasm. Berenson waved his arm, probably trying to hail a taxi. When one stopped, he shook our hands goodbye, then, when he found out we lived in Miraflores, offered to give us a ride. We sat down in the backseat, and just as the car took off I felt my head spin, and a cold sweat drenched my forehead. The fact is, I was totally drunk. My situation got worse as we continued along Avenida Arequipa, watching the swiftly moving parade of cars and trees. When we were halfway there, I could no longer contain myself, and I began to vomit. *What a fiasco!* I thought, *what a terrible impression I am making on Maestro Berenson!* The driver blew up, shouting and insulting me, threatening to throw me out of the car, and just when I thought the maestro would come to my rescue and take a stand against that madman's suggestions, I heard him tell the driver to stop in the middle of the block, where he opened the door and practically threw me out of the taxi, saying things I couldn't make out but which seemed to be expressions of intense disgust. I ended up sprawled on the dark and lonely sidewalk, drowning in a sea of my own vomit, feeling as if I were dying of nausea, shame, and humiliation.

I woke up at noon in the house of an uncle who lived near where I had fallen, a place I reached thanks to some unknown instinct. I vowed never to repeat that mixture of *cachina*, *chicha*, and martinis (a vow I kept but mocked by indulging in other equally mortal mixtures). Only in the evening could I make it to Teodorito's house to discuss with him the not-so-glorious moments of the previous night. Teodorito was in his musical temple, listening to the overture to *The Mastersingers of Nuremberg* at full volume. When he saw me he turned off the music. He looked pale, agitated, on the verge of exploding. I thought he was going to scold me harshly for my behavior the night before, accuse me of grinding our eventual friendship with the maestro into the dust forever, but I was wrong, for he lit a cigarette and took a long pause, then began one of his slow and long-winded stories, this one about the continuation of his ride with the maestro in the taxi along Avenida Arequipa. He told me about how the driver kept grumbling, about some birds chirping in the trees along the way (which evoked for me a trip I had taken as a child to an Andean village), about Maestro Berenson's silence punctuated by short sighs, about the sleepiness that overwhelmed him, and finally about a strange sensation, something like a weight on his leg, something slithery and warm on his thigh, finally a hand, the maestro's hand caressing him, more and more deliberately, moving up toward his belly...

"I had to get out!" he shouted with rage. "I told the driver to stop before he got to the park in Miraflores. The old man got out, too, I don't know what he was saying, but I took off running along Pardo to my house."

He said "the old man," not the maestro. That in itself was sufficient.

Our disappointment was deep but did not prevent us from continuing to attend the concerts at the Teatro Municipal. But we listened to them now without the same passion, perhaps making greater demands, believing at moments we had discovered some minor error in the performance. Once in a while we'd walk by the Romano after a concert and occasionally we spotted the maestro at the end of the bar, with a glass of beer and a shot of pisco, alone or conversing with some occasional and young drinker. Rumors then began to circulate that Berenson had been implicated in a nocturnal scandal, the details of which never became clear, and that some members of the orchestra were questioning the maestro's competence. This last item was doubtful, for toward the end of the year he conducted some memorable concerts when Claudio Arrau and Yehudi Menuhin passed through Lima, and both musicians lavished high praise on the orchestra and its music director.

Some time later Teodorito got married and, to complement my studies, I took a job with a law firm. This not only created distance between us but also diminished our devotion to the concerts. We went rarely, until we didn't go at all. I then began to make preparations for my trip to Paris, and Teodorito was awaiting his first child. Shortly before I left Peru I heard that the maestro had triumphed with a moving performance of Tchaikovsky's Symphony *Pathétique* just days before his wife left him to return to Vienna.

I spent many years in Europe, where my passion for music grew, diversified, became more refined, until finally, though it didn't die altogether, it achieved a moderate level of serenity, roughly halfway between obligation and boredom. Such is probably the fate of all passions. After hearing the grand philharmonic orchestras of Paris, Vienna, London, and Berlin, I stopped attending concerts altogether and returned to my youthful preference for recordings, which I listened to calmly and distractedly at home. I managed to acquire a valuable record collection—my brother-in-law Genaro would have paled with envy—which accompanied me like a sonorous decor during my exercise of other passions, such as love and writing. Once in a while as I listened, there passed through my mind the memory of the maestro, with his strengths and his defects, memories I welcomed with gratitude and indulgence.

At the beginning of the seventies I returned to Lima after an absence of ten or more years. The city, the country, had been transformed, whether for good or ill is another question. For a few weeks

I revisited my youthful haunts, looking for signs, traces of happy or unhappy eras, and found only the ashes of some or the flickering flame of others. A few months later I decided to breathe the air of the provinces. My brother-in-law Genaro, who was by then a major, was stationed in Cuzco. He lived in a large villa on the outskirts of the city, where he loved to host family and friends. One day, out of the blue, I decided to pay him a visit and boarded an airplane. I arrived in the imperial city at noon, but as soon as the bus from the airport dropped me in the Plaza de Armas, I felt so sick from the altitude that rather than go straight to my brother-in-law's house, I took a room in the first hotel I came across and fell asleep as if I were one of the blessed.

I woke up in the evening and immediately called Genaro to let him know I had arrived.

"Come right away," he insisted. "There's a concert tonight at our house. Berenson will conduct Beethoven."

"Berenson?"

"Didn't you know? He's been living and working here for a long time. He's the mainstay of our musical Tuesdays."

No, I didn't know, as I also didn't know there was a philharmonic orchestra in Cuzco. Without delay I got dressed, called a taxi, and left for Genaro's house. It was a colonial mansion, a bit run-down but stately nonetheless, right on the boundary between the city and the countryside. Several automobiles were parked out in front. Genaro led me into the drawing room, where he introduced me to about thirty guests—the music lovers of Cuzco—an eclectic crowd, which included the subprefect, two military officers, a priest, and several society ladies. Everybody was very excited, holding glasses and cigarettes and being served by my sister, Mercedes.

"And the maestro?" I asked.

"He's coming now. He's getting ready."

A few seconds later he appeared through a side door, baton in hand, wearing the striped pants and black jacket I remember seeing him in when he conducted those unforgettable concerts in Lima. But his garments were shiny and worn, as worn as his own figure, which looked pale, bowed, and abbreviated. Genaro handed him a glass of beer, introduced me to him—he had no idea I knew him—and the gathering continued apace while I, looking from side to side, tried to figure out where the orchestra was and where the concert would be held. In these villas there was always a chapel or a courtyard reserved for such events. A moment later Genaro asked for silence, the guests took their seats, and the maestro took his place in the front of the room, under an archway leading into an enclosed patio behind which one could see an empty cloister. In the meantime Genaro went to a corner where—only then did I notice—there was a modern stereo set. He inserted a cassette and turned on the player. In a second there burst forth the powerful opening of Beethoven's Fifth, at the same time as Berenson's baton swept through the air to accompany the fourfold groan of chords with energetic and inspired movements.

During the entire first movement I stood dumbfounded, not moving my eyes from the maestro, who from time to time stopped to pick up his glass of beer, which was standing on a table within reach. His eyes avoided the audience and wandered over the night sky, God knows contemplating what celestial visions, and on his thin lips, between his sparse beard and moustache, there floated a foolish grin. As the spectacle continued, it became more and more intolerable to me. Even so, during certain passages, the maestro's movements were convincing, and for moments I had the illusion of being in the presence of the great Hans Marius Berenson of my youth, the first time I saw him conducting that same symphony in the Campo de Marte in front of a perfectly tuned orchestra. But it was only an illusion. I was in the presence of a puppet, defiling his ancient glories in order to earn a few drinks, a little human warmth, and a bit of affability in a city where there was no orchestra at all, only one or another chamber ensemble with whom he might play the violin at weddings and funerals to make ends meet.

"The blows of fate," I said to myself as the horns picked up the initial motif. "Poor Maestro Berenson!" But I found comfort in the thought that only those who have known splendor have the right to decadence.

OTHER NEW YORK REVIEW CLASSICS

For a complete list of titles, visit www.nyrb.com or write to:
Catalog Requests, NYRB, 435 Hudson Street, New York, NY 10014

* *Also available as an electronic book.*

LOUIS GUILLOUX Blood Dark*

OAKLEY HALL Warlock

PATRICK HAMILTON The Slaves of Solitude*

PETER HANDKE Slow Homecoming

THORKILD HANSEN Arabia Felix: The Danish Expedition of 1761–1767*

ELIZABETH HARDWICK The Collected Essays of Elizabeth Hardwick*

ELIZABETH HARDWICK Seduction and Betrayal*

ELIZABETH HARDWICK Sleepless Nights*

L.P. HARTLEY The Go-Between*

NATHANIEL HAWTHORNE Twenty Days with Julian & Little Bunny by Papa

ALFRED HAYES My Face for the World to See*

PAUL HAZARD The Crisis of the European Mind: 1680–1715*

ALICE HERDAN-ZUCKMAYER The Farm in the Green Mountains*

WOLFGANG HERRNDORF Sand*

GILBERT HIGHET Poets in a Landscape

RUSSELL HOBAN Turtle Diary*

JANET HOBHOUSE The Furies

YOEL HOFFMANN The Sound of the One Hand: 281 Zen Koans with Answers*

HUGO VON HOFMANNSTHAL The Lord Chandos Letter*

JAMES HOGG The Private Memoirs and Confessions of a Justified Sinner

RICHARD HOLMES Shelley: The Pursuit*

ALISTAIR HORNE A Savage War of Peace: Algeria 1954–1962*

GEOFFREY HOUSEHOLD Rogue Male*

WILLIAM DEAN HOWELLS Indian Summer

BOHUMIL HRABAL Dancing Lessons for the Advanced in Age*

DOROTHY B. HUGHES The Expendable Man*

DOROTHY B. HUGHES In a Lonely Place*

RICHARD HUGHES A High Wind in Jamaica*

RICHARD HUGHES The Fox in the Attic (The Human Predicament, Vol. 1)*

RICHARD HUGHES The Wooden Shepherdess (The Human Predicament, Vol. 2)*

INTIZAR HUSAIN Basti*

MAUDE HUTCHINS Victorine

YASUSHI INOUE Tun-huang*

DARIUS JAMES Negrophobia: An Urban Parable

HENRY JAMES The New York Stories of Henry James*

HENRY JAMES The Other House

TOVE JANSSON Fair Play *

TOVE JANSSON The Summer Book*

TOVE JANSSON The Woman Who Borrowed Memories: Selected Stories*

RANDALL JARRELL (EDITOR) Randall Jarrell's Book of Stories

UWE JOHNSON Anniversaries*

DAVID JONES In Parenthesis

JOSEPH JOUBERT The Notebooks of Joseph Joubert; translated by Paul Auster

KABIR Songs of Kabir; translated by Arvind Krishna Mehrotra*

FRIGYES KARINTHY A Journey Round My Skull

ERICH KÄSTNER Going to the Dogs: The Story of a Moralist*

HELEN KELLER The World I Live In

YASHAR KEMAL Memed, My Hawk

WALTER KEMPOWSKI All for Nothing

MURRAY KEMPTON Part of Our Time: Some Ruins and Monuments of the Thirties*

RAYMOND KENNEDY Ride a Cockhorse*

DAVID KIDD Peking Story*

ROBERT KIRK The Secret Commonwealth of Elves, Fauns, and Fairies